I0554553

Issue 7
February 2018

Heart's Kiss

Contents

Lezli Robyn & Tina Smith, Editors

Shahid Mahmud, Publisher

Published by Arc Manor/Heart's Nest Press
P.O. Box 10339
Rockville, MD 20849-0339

Heart's Kiss is published in February, April, June, August, October and December.

www.HeartsKiss.com

Please refer to our website for submission requirements.

All material is either copyright © 2018 by Arc Manor LLC, Rockville, MD, or copyright © by the respective authors as indicated within the magazine. All rights reserved.

This magazine (or any portion of it) may not be copied or reproduced, in whole or in part, by any means, electronic, mechanical or otherwise, without written permission from the publisher, except by a reviewer who may quote brief passages in a review.

Available by subscription (www.HeartsKiss.com) or through your favorite online store (Amazon.com, BN.com, etc.).

ISBN: 978-1-61242-402-6

Advertising in the magazine is available. Quarter page (half column), $95 per issue. Half page (full column, vertical or two half columns, horizontal) $165 per issue. Full page (two full columns) $295 per issue. Back Cover (full color) $495 per issue. All interior advertising is in black and white.

Please write to advert@HeartsKiss.com.

FOREIGN LANGUAGE RIGHTS: Please refer all inquiries pertaining to foreign language rights to Shahid Mahmud, Arc Manor, P.O. Box 10339, Rockville, MD 20849-0339. Tel: 1-240-645-2214. Fax 1-310-388-8440. Email admin@ArcManor.com.

EDITOR'S NOTE

by Tina Smith

Things are a bit different around here. Lezli Robyn and I sort of took over this magazine. Maybe not sort of—we actually did! Denise Little did an amazing job bringing in her years of insight and expertise to get this venture off the ground in its first year. She is sadly moving on and Lezli and I have big shoes to fill.

With change comes opportunity. And through our brainstorming we decided to go BIG. We talked about the kind of romance fiction we'd like to see. We wanted to skirt the edges of the genre and syphon out the essence of the best part of it. We wanted to explore the boundaries of relationships and delve deep into what it means to get that first tingle of interest to falling into lust and love.

We wanted to see risk in the genre. The same kinds of risks indie writers are taking with their romance. The publishing industry once believed that there was a dead zone of writing about students in college. They wanted to see those heroines out and about in the working world—but then the New Adult movement came along and proved that old belief had shifted. Right now there are no-man's lands of romance; character set ups we don't normally see. Older couples? We wanted that (and we have a perfect story for you in this very issue by Andrea Dale!). I remember the first time I read a romance novel focusing on a couple older than me. It was a Jennifer Crusie book and there was a passing comment that the main characters were in their forties or fifties. I double checked it. Every book I read up until then—literally every one—had made a point of having the characters in their twenties or thirties. I really loved the change.

I'd been talking to a friend about our ideas to expand the magazine to be as inclusive as possible, yet still appeal to fans of the genre, and she said "So, not like your grandma's romance?" and I couldn't quite agree. Because what if grandma is a kick ass, cool lady and she had a blackbelt and grandpa drove a motorcycle and they both fought off a drug cartel, and in the process they of course fall (or re-fall) madly in love. Or maybe grandpa is not her love interest. Maybe it's another grandma?

Our beloved genre has been a leader in reinventing love—over and over. Times are changing, and fans want the next amazing love story. Sure, we want familiar, but we want familiar (falling in love) mixed with something exciting, new, and fresh.

My interests are eclectic, and I read in every subgenre of romance. I'm ecstatic the selection in romance is broadening as well as deepening—more explorations of where relationships can go and the ever-changing conflicts in today's world. Our magazine hopes to change with it and look forward.

We fell in love with each story in this issue for their own unique reasons. (Of course you'll love them all. How dare you not!) Our hope is that readers will find new ideas and corners of romance they didn't expect. We want to discuss topics that are timely in our genre. Romance is beaten down every day by those who've never picked up a proper romance. But as fans know, our genre offers the very best. And we've found just a sliver of examples of what's out there.

From fabulous fan favorites and seasoned authors like Jayne Anne Krantz, to new undiscovered talents—we believe we've curated a great selection. We have a wonderful dark historical with romantic elements taking place just after World War One from newcomer Meghan Ewald, a fun paranormal from bestseller Leslye Penelope and the first part of yet another paranormal, our serialization, from award winning and bestselling author Anna J. Stewart. You'll also find a fun sweet contemporary retelling of The Princess Frog from Melinda Curtis (also a bestselling writer) and our first same-sex story by Petronella Glover. Romance flash (stories written in less than a thousand words) is a particular challenge, but our in-house writer Alia Mahmud has seemed to master the skill with a very sweet gender-bending meet-cute.

Along with our fiction selections we have articles on timely topics. Julie Pitzel is starting a re-occurring column called You Read *That?*. The Column will overview various concepts and tropes in romance in a fun, insightful way; this issue she will discuss covers. Also a wonderful interview with Jayne Anne

Krantz about her newest release, an opinion piece on the #MeToo movement and how consent is sexy in romance, a romantic tour of *Outlander* filming locations, and recommended reads.

You provide the cozy blanket and hot tea, we provide the entertainment. We hope you come for the stories and stay for the romance.

The author of a string of New York Times *bestsellers, Jayne Ann Krentz uses three different pen names for each of her three "worlds". As Jayne Ann Krentz (her married name) she writes contemporary romantic-suspense. She uses Amanda Quick for her novels of historical romantic-suspense. Jayne Castle (her birth name) is reserved these days for her stories of futuristic/paranormal romantic-suspense. In addition to her fiction writing, she is the editor of, and a contributor to, a non-fiction essay collection,* Dangerous Men and Adventurous Women: Romance Writers on the Appeal of the Romance, *published by the University of Pennsylvania Press. She earned a B.A. in History from the University of California at Santa Cruz and went on to obtain a Masters degree in Library Science from San Jose State University in California. Before she began writing full time she worked as a librarian in both academic and corporate libraries. She is married and lives with her husband, Frank, in Seattle, Washington.*

HEART'S KISS INTERVIEWS JAYNE ANN KRENTZ

by Lezli Robyn

It was my absolute pleasure to conduct a phone interview with the delightful Jayne, just prior to Christmas. She was warm and welcoming and shone an insightful light onto the wonderful genre that is romance, while also giving her readers a window into her personal experience as a writer.

Lezli Robyn: Hello, Jayne! Is that you?

Jayne Ann Krentz: This is me! Hi, Lezli!

LR: Nice to meet you!

JAK: Nice to meet you!

LR: Can you understand my Australian accent? We should get that out of the way first!

JAK: I just came back from Australia! I'm good with that! *laughs*

LR: I saw that on your website. It's like you were practicing to talk to me!

JAK: Yeah! *laughs* I guess it was all in the stars. It was fabulous and Australia was definitely one of the big highlights.

LR: Ohhh, that's lovely! I will always love my country. I have a bittersweet reaction about leaving it.

JAK: Well, do you know what I felt over there? Granted, I was there on a tour where I only stopped in four different cities, but at each of those cities I was meeting up with local readers and writers—so it felt like I was meeting like-minded people. And I had the time to talk; it was more than just a casual visit. Everybody was so warm and so welcoming and there was a kind of cheerful optimism about everything. I don't know if it was the crowd I was with or just the nature of the country, but it was very refreshing.

LR: We are usually an optimistic people….

Thank you for letting us call you today. I really appreciate it. I read your Except from *Promise Not To Tell* and it is a great teaser.

JAK: Thank you!

LR: You have written a lot of books over the years. When did you realize "Oh, I am a writer!"? Were you writing for years before you sold, or did you make a career choice change?

JAK: Well, this was so long ago that it was before you could actually self publish. It just was not an option. In those days there was really only one track to getting published and that was New York. And at the time Harlequin was based in Toronto, so it took me six years to sell my first book. Once that happened things opened up for me fast, but these days an aspiring author can start building their audience online first.

LR: How did you decide you wanted to write?

JAK: What happened was I was a lifelong reader. Somewhere in my twenties—I was out of college, I was working—I entered that phase of life where I had more time to read again; I got drawn back to fiction. I discovered romance, which hadn't really existed in the form we would recognize today. It was just starting to burst into the big time, in terms of publishing in New York. I was enjoying reading the books, and it wasn't that I thought I could do them better, but there came a time when I wanted to tell the story *my* way.

LR: Yes. I understand that urge.

JAK: If that hits, you are a writer. If it's doesn't hit, you are a reader. *laughs* You're kind of stuck, because if you are rewriting the story, or retelling the dialog in your head, at some point you just *need* to write it down on paper, or get it into a computer. I think if that urge does not happen, you lucked out—more power to you. But if it does hit it almost becomes a compulsion until you have written your own fiction.

LR: So, then the next question begs to be asked… Why romance?

JAK: I attribute that to the fact that I grew up on Nancy drew, Robert A. Heinlein—early Heinlein—and Andre Norton. Somehow those three jelled into my first book that I wrote and could not sell, which is what we call now a futuristic romance. There was absolutely no market for it back then but I realized if I pulled out the futuristic elements, there was the main market.

LR: Contemporary romance.

JAK: Yes, exactly. So, I attribute my formative reading to the fact that I wound up—there was no escaping it—a romantic suspense author.

LR: Andre Norton was one of the authors I read as a child, so I see what you mean. I was forever imagining new scenarios in my head and daydreaming while listening to music at night.

JAK: I think that is the key. You tell the stories first in your head—you tell them to yourself. And to this day I *still* tell those stories to myself, first. And then I just hope that the readers can get into the fantasy with me.

LR: It also sounds like the most organic, authentic approach too.

JAK: Like I said, I think writers get power from telling stories to themselves. You try to write for another audience, and it's another weaker form of writing.

LR: Yes, I agree that you have to consider what the market wants, but you also have to be telling *your* story, as opposed to trying to manufacture something specifically to fit a specific market.

JAK: Which leads me to another point for aspiring writers. It's not that you have to write intuitively and indefinitely—a lot of writers can—but if you run into trouble in the market, and sooner or later you *will* run into trouble in the market, it really pays to know your core story. That throws people at times because a lot of people going into writing think, like I did, that the core of the story is the landscape you paint it on. Like a futuristic landscape, paranormal landscape or a historical landscape. And that just is *not* your core story. Your core story is composed of the themes, the kind of conflict, the kind of emotional interactions, and the kind of relationships that compel you again and again and again. I think it is useful for aspiring writers to know the core of your story does not have to belong to any one landscape. You have options, if the book doesn't sell in one sub-genre market.

LR: Yes, I focus on the human story I try to tell, and then pick the landscape that best suits the emotional impact I am trying to create, so the landscape is my last consideration. I can see what you mean when you say that it is possible to change the landscape if it is not the focus of the book.

JAK: Yes, and I actually had to do that at one point in my career. I have been around long enough that I have managed to kill a couple of fiction careers—and had to resurrect them. And that is how I found my Amanda Quick career. Early on I had to kill my career because of the futuristic romances. They didn't sell, so I stepped back and realized that what I was really telling in those futuristic romances was a romantic suspense built around an arranged marriage or a marriage of convenience. That's a well-known historical romance trope, so that is how I got my Amanda Quick name.

LR: So that beautifully leads me into my next question about multiple pseudonyms. I now know why you created your Amanda Quick name, but you seem to have *three* main author names, and several more listed on your bibliography page. What led to picking those names?

JAK: Trust me, it was not my career path plan. *laughs* There was *no* plan. One new name I stumbled into was simply because I got into a contractual bind. Early on it was pretty common, in the old days, to tie the author to the publishing house. So at one point, during the stage of my career when I did not think I needed an agent, I managed to sign my own name away for a few years. I had also killed off another name because there was so much baggage, in regards to futuristic romance novels; no one wanted to touch me because of poor sales. So when I was able to legally use those names again, I had already started using a third.

I'd always said that I would eventually settle with the one name. The plan—such as it was—was I would study which would sell the best. No one was more amazed than me to find out that *all* of them took off.

LR: Would you say your pseudonyms are separated by genre, then?

JAK: Well, they are separated by genre *landscapes*. Historicals are under my Amanda Quick name. The Jayne Ann Krentz name is for my contemporaries. And I save Jayne Castle—which happens to be my birth name—for my futuristic romances.

LR: That is a very romantic name.

JAK: Yes. And that is the one that I signed away. *laughs* But I have got it back now.

In the past authors worked so alone in terms of the business angle, they believed everything their publisher told them because they had absolutely no way to verify it.

LR: The internet has helped inform the writers of today.

JAK: Yes, and you should also attend one of the Romance Writers of America conventions. You will learn more in four days than I learned in six years.

LR: Do you find one pseudonym easier to write than the others?

JAK: No. I enjoy the different kinds of thought processes for each of my pseudonyms, because coming out of one landscape and going into another is refreshing to me. I do not find one process easier than the others....

Actually, I have never quite thought about this before. When I first moved Amanda Quick into the 1930's era I spent an extra couple of months to get myself up to speed on the research. So I guess the *beginning* of a historical series needs more work getting familiar with the world, but that is a one-time research event, then the process kicks into a normal rhythm for future books in the series. I now keep my eye out for 1930's items or info automatically, as I know I will be writing another book in that series.

LR: Which of your books do you think was the one that "made" your career? Was it because of an award, recognition, or sales?

JAK: The first Amanda quick book. It surprised everybody by doing so well. That was *Scandal*. It was also my first historical romance to come out and I really landed firmly with both my feet in that subgenre. I had written a lot of contemporary romance novels by then, too, so I knew what I was doing by then as a writer, but the publisher also gave it a *great* cover. They didn't give it a bodice ripper cover. Seriously, it was classy.

LR: I do not think that publishers had thought it all the way through with the bodice ripper generation of covers. It was *women* reading these books. Why would they want to see other women with their clothes getting torn off in a manner that was clearly for the male gaze? Also, what was the fascination with Fabio?

JAK: Well, the story with Fabio was what the publishers thought his image would sell books, but most women read them *in spite* of the cover, not *because*

of the cover. But even earlier covers—the heaving bosom covers—gave us such bad press. The legend was that they were used back in the days when the wholesale market was everything. You *had* to get your books into drugs stores, grocery stores—everywhere. And in those days the truck drivers were all men, so the argument was that the cover wasn't for the reader, the cover was for the truck driver to entice him to load it up into the truck, and make sure that the books made it into their stores. We do not know if that really is true or not, but that was the story I got from people who had been in publishing for a long time. All the publishers cared about was getting the books onto the shelves.

LR: And of course, now with Amazon, ebook availability, and online stores in general, you can market books directly to women from a distance, which means more covers, book design and blurbs that are female-centric.

JAK: The whole industry has changed, and it did not necessarily improve the numbers. God bless them, the wholesale markets used to be huge.

LR: I see you were the editor and contributor for *Dangerous Men and Adventurous Women: Romance Writers on the Appeal of the Romance*. So how did that come about?

JAK: I can't believe that book is still in print. It was published in the 1990s!

LR: That is an impressive amount of time to still be in print!

JAK: Well, I do know that at the time that we did the book the editor at the University of Pennsylvania Press said academic books are different—they survive for generations or decades. I didn't believe her, but I grasped the message that if the book was useful in terms of academic research, it hangs around. Apparently, it is still useful.

LR: What is it that makes this book "useful" to students and readers alike?

JAK: Every so often I will take the book down and flick through it. The essays were written by me and eighteen of my friends, and everyone had the same title, which was "What do you think the appeal of romance is?" We each took on one sub-topic and wrote on that. We wound up with nineteen very different essays, but they all come together to make the same point, which is this: women's fiction empowers women, because ultimately the heroine *always* wins.

In what other genre is that the case? Romance was the only genre—there might be others one day—in which you could guarantee the hero was always the woman. It would be *her* story.

LR: That is such an empowering message about the romance genre, and another reason we should be proud of our authors. Is there anything about yourself that you think your readers don't know but is intrinsic to you?

JAK: I think if my readers and I meet, if they respond to my books, we probably have a lot in common, then we usually become friends right off the bat. I also think they will already know all the central stuff about me because my sense of humor, world views, and sense of right and wrong are infused into my books.

LR: I find it fascinating that some authors write very differently to their personal views.

JAK: Well, I certainly write bad guys, but I always think the essence of the storytelling is through the hero and heroine's point of view.

LR: Indeed. Which brings us to our last question…. What did you want to tell your readers about your new book?

JAK: *Promise Not to Tell* is the second book in a romantic suspense trilogy set in Seattle, involving three foster sons who were saved from a cult. Each of them will have their own story; I am writing the third book now. *laughs* It is kind of an in-joke with my readers. I have started a fair number of connected storylines in the past and I have had to drop them for one reason or another. I just want to assure them that this one is getting written. This trilogy *will* be finished! So, to those who know me, don't worry, there is a third book coming!

LR: *laughs* Okay, I will make sure that statement (declaration?) makes the interview!

JAK: Okay! *laughs* Sometimes—you know how it goes—it sounded great at the time, then all of a sudden the market changes, the publishers change, or you change....

LR: Exactly! Such is the nature of the publishing business.

I thank you so very much for your time, Jayne; I know it's precious. We need to make sure you finish your third book!

JAK: *laughs* It was my pleasure! Stay in touch!

Copyright © 2018 by Lezli Robyn.

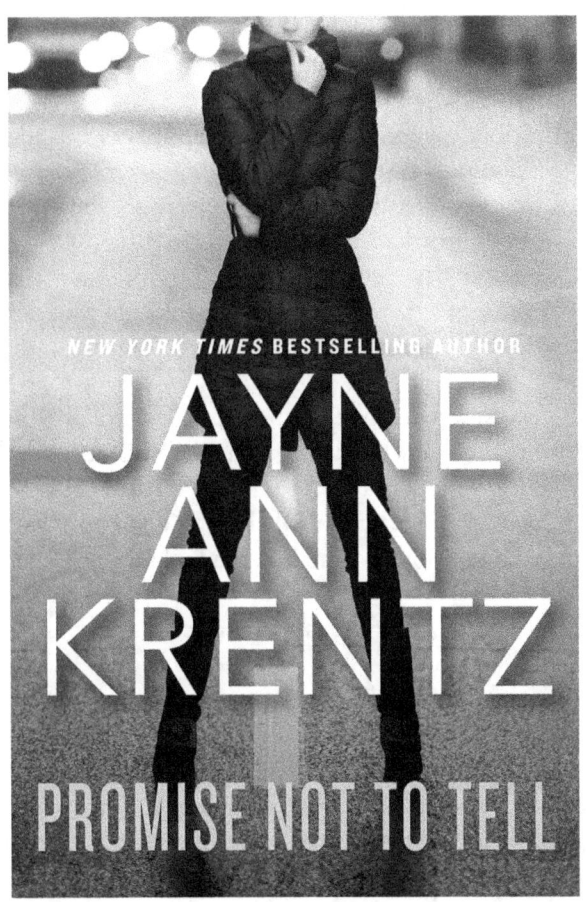

NEW YORK TIMES BESTSELLING AUTHOR

JAYNE ANN KRENTZ

PROMISE NOT TO TELL

EXCERPT FROM
PROMISE NOT TO TELL

by Jayne Ann Krentz

Most men wouldn't know how to handle a woman like Virginia Troy. Sure, some would be damned interested at first, maybe even see her as a challenge. But he figured that, in the end, the average guy would run for the hills.

A short time ago, when she had walked into the room, she had taken a moment to size up everything in sight, including him. He had been relieved when he and the expensive new furniture appeared to have passed inspection.

Although his name was on the door, technically speaking he was the office manager, receptionist, researcher and general gofer. Max and Cabot were the licensed investigators in the firm. Both had complained mightily about the stiff rent on the newly leased office space as well as the money spent on furnishing the place, but Anson had refused to lower his newfound standards of interior design.

Before embarking on his career in office management, he had never paid any attention to the art of interior design. But after hiring a decorator and immersing himself in the finer points of the field, he had become convinced that the premises of the firm had to send the right message to potential clients. That meant leasing space in an upscale building and investing in quality furniture.

The result, however, was that Cutler, Sutter & Salinas now had to start making some serious money.

Virginia crossed her legs and gripped the arms of the chair. Anson knew that she was ready to tell him why she had come looking for him.

"I own a gallery in Pioneer Square," she said. "One of the artists who occasionally exhibits her work with me died a few days ago. The authorities have ruled the death a suicide."

"But you don't believe it," Anson said.

"I'm not sure what to believe. That's why I'd like to hire you to investigate the circumstances."

The door opened before Anson could ask any more questions. Cabot walked into the room carrying two cups of coffee—one balanced on top of the other—and a small paper sack emblazoned with the logo of a nearby bakery. He was slightly turned away from the desk because he was using the toe of his low boot to close the door. He did not immediately notice Virginia.

"The Coffee Goddess said to tell you she's got a new tattoo that she might be willing to show you if you'll let her surprise you with one of her own custom lattes," he said. "Evidently she's tired of you ordering regular coffee instead of one of her specialties. Says you need to be more adventurous."

Anson felt himself flushing. He cleared his throat but before he could warn Cabot that there was a client in the room, the client spoke.

"Some things are best appreciated in their purest, most essential forms," Virginia said.

Cabot turned very quickly to confront her. Anson stifled a sigh. *Confront* was the operative word when it came to Cabot. Not that he was *confrontational* in the sense that he was always looking for a fight. If anything, he usually came across as unnaturally aloof and unemotional. It took a lot to make him lose his temper and, on the rare occasions when that happened, you didn't want to be standing in his vicinity.

The issue was that he regarded anything or anyone new, unknown or outside his normal routine, as a potential problem at best and, at worst, a threat until proven otherwise. The result was that he *confronted* situations and people until he could decide what to do about them.

He also had a bad habit of being attracted to women who thought they needed a man to rescue them. Unfortunately, that type of woman was attracted to him—but never for long. Anson had observed that needy women were happy enough to use Cabot for as long as he was useful, but sooner or later they found themselves dealing with the whole man, not just the rescuer part. And Cabot was nothing if not complicated. His relationships, such as they were, usually ended badly.

The swift, sure way he moved to deal with Virginia said a lot about the man, Anson thought. Most people would have lost the top cup of coffee with such a sudden turn, but Cabot had excellent reflexes and an innate sense of balance. He'd had those talents from childhood and had honed them over the years. Some men ran or lifted weights to stay in shape. Cabot had a black belt in an obscure form of martial arts.

He contemplated Virginia now with a cool, calculating gaze. People often got nervous when Cabot fixed his attention on them. It was the primary reason why Anson or Max usually took on the task of dealing with new clients. Those seeking the services of an investigation agency were already uneasy when they came through the door. There was a general consensus that Cabot might scare off new business.

Virginia seemed unaffected by the infamous Cabot Stare. If anything, she appeared amused.

"Sorry," Cabot said. "Didn't know we had a visitor." He held out one of the paper cups. "Want Anson's coffee? It's straight. No sugar, no mocha, no foamy milk, no chocolate sprinkles, no caramel."

Anson winced. Some people might have assumed that Cabot was trying to make a small joke. They would have been wrong. Cabot was inclined to take things literally. He often spoke the same way. He possessed a sense of humor but you had to know him really well before you could tell when he was joking and when he wasn't.

Virginia glanced at the cup Cabot was offering and then looked at the other cup.

"Out of curiosity, what are my options?" she said.

Cabot's brows rose. "Options?"

"You've got two cups of coffee," Virginia said with an air of grave patience. "You just told me that one is straight. I am inquiring about the status of the second cup."

"That would be mine," Cabot said. "It's straight, too. Anson's the one who taught me how to drink coffee."

"I see," Virginia said. "Thank you, but I'll pass."

Cabot nodded once, as if she had just confirmed some conclusion that he had made. He placed one of the cups down on the desk in front of Anson. Every move was fluid and precise. There was no wasted motion.

"You're the fully-loaded-latte type," he said.

"Actually, no," Virginia said smoothly, "I'm not."

She did not elaborate.

Cabot's eyes tightened a little at the corners. He did not take his attention off Virginia. Anson recognized the expression and suppressed a small groan. Cabot's curiosity had been aroused. It was a fine trait in an investigator but it could also cause problems.

Posted by arrangement with Berkley, a member of Penguin Group (USA) LLC, A Penguin Random House Company.
Copyright © 2018 by Jayne Ann Krentz.

L. Penelope has been writing since she could hold a pen and loves getting lost in the worlds in her head. She is an award-winning fantasy and paranormal romance author. She lives in Maryland with her husband and their furry dependents. Sign up for new release information, updates, and giveaways on her website: http:// www.lpenelope.com.

BEFORE I GO

by L. Penelope

CHAPTER ONE

If Mom was alive, she never would have let me get on that plane. She would have yelled, cried, bribed and begged me to stay home. In that order. But she's gone, my credit card is that much closer to being maxed out, and I'm here.

Standing on one of those iconic San Francisco streets, at the top of a hill, the city ripples out around me. I've always wanted to come here. There's a buzz in the air you can sense through the pictures. I feel it now, though it might just be anger pulsing though my bloodstream.

Behind me, the automatic door clicks shut. I take a deep breath to clear my lungs of the cloying scents of death and antiseptic. Instead, I get a lungful of exhaust fumes from the ambulance idling at the curb. Do they just sit out here waiting for people to die?

Of course, that's the pot calling the kettle black. Isn't that what I'm doing?

I walk back to the Hotel Montagne. These two blocks are the only part of the city I've seen since I arrived two days ago. A well-to-do couple emerges from the building; the man holds the door for me. His wife is sleek and sparkly—diamond studs, necklace, bracelet, rings. I shrink inside the door, pulling my battered department store coat closer around me.

The gleaming lobby is a gallery of mirrors, marble and chrome, with strangely shaped furniture dotting the space. I keep my arms close to my body, so I don't sully anything with my fingerprints. I imagine a squadron of maids must lurk in the shadows, scampering out to dust and polish an object as soon

as it's been touched. This is definitely the poshest place I've ever been.

The same day I received The Phone Call, the one that upset my quiet, meandering life and turned it into this exercise in futility, a gold and purple envelope covered in glitter arrived in the mail bearing a coupon for The Montagne. A very generous coupon for a very expensive boutique hotel two thousand miles away. Once I looked it up and found the place was two blocks from the nursing home, I thought the coincidence was just too much. For better or worse, my decision was made.

Mom's voice rang in my head as I paid for a mind bogglingly expensive plane ticket for the next day. She screeched at me all the way to the airport, quieting down once I'd actually boarded. She'd always been afraid to fly. Her voice has also been silent the entire time I've been here. Maybe the silence is a punishment from beyond.

Growing up, we only ever visited roadside motels. Mom would leave a husband or a boyfriend and we'd move in for what she said would be "just a couple of days," but inevitably turned into months. As funds dwindled, the quality of the places would deteriorate. But they were usually a welcome reprieve from wherever we'd just left.

Mom would get a kick out of this place.

"Welcome back to the Montagne," the desk clerk greets me with a smile. I smile back; everyone is so friendly. It's like they don't know I don't belong here. The paltry amount I'm paying doesn't even come close to what my stay must cost. But it's nice, for once, to not feel like the rich kids are looking down their nose at me. I even go so far as to wave at the clerk.

The click of my heels echoes in the empty lobby. I'm headed to the elevators, but the idea of being cooped up in another tiny room, albeit a gorgeously decorated one, does not appeal. The clerk is young and apple-cheeked and looks like he stepped out of a J. Crew catalog.

"Hi, is the bar still open?"

"Yes, it closes at one-thirty, ma'am."

I check my phone for the time, stunned that it's so late. The nurses never enforce the visiting hours in the hospice wing, and that place is like a casino—curtains drawn tight, no clocks on the walls. Maybe they don't want to rub it in to the dying people that life is going on without them.

I thank the clerk and change direction towards the small bar. It's more muted and comfortable looking than the lobby—less chrome, more leather. It's also currently empty, no patrons and no bartender. I settle in on a barstool and take off my coat. The hotel is pretty small. I figure the bartender will be back soon.

To pass the time, I scroll through my phone looking at the pictures I took today. An old man in a bed, tubes attached to his arms. He looks so harmless. The giant hands I remember from childhood are now shrunken and shriveled, like the rest of him. I click the phone off. Nothing about that man is harmless.

The anger creeps back and I'm eager for a drink to whittle away the tension in my neck and shoulders. I turn at the sound of footsteps behind me.

"You're not the bartender." It comes out more harshly than I mean it to.

The man in the entrance looks down at himself and then back at me, cracking a half-smile. "No, I don't think I am."

He's the picture of a modern rake. Tallish with a medium build, black jacket over a white shirt, top buttons undone, grin set to mischief. Dark eyes flash as they appraise me. Lean, sexy, dangerous.

I swallow as the energy in the room changes. This man is an electrical storm; I could swear the lights short out as he enters. He sits one barstool down from me and I stifle the urge to adjust my skirt where it's ridden up, exposing a tiny sliver of thigh. Though as he assesses me, I'm not sure whether I really want to pull the skirt down or slide it up and feel the heat of his gaze sizzle over my skin. The place between my thighs hums to life, and with a mouthwatering whiff of his cologne, a furnace switches on inside me.

Can you have a hot flash at twenty-six?

"So, this bar is missing one important element," he says, scanning the empty room. My heater cranks up another notch when his gaze comes back to me along with a high voltage smile.

He gets points for not staring at my chest, which is covered in a very modest V-neck sweater. His focus stays on my face with the intensity of a spotlight. I'm caught in the beam, hoping someone else comes in to divert his attention and spare me the scrutiny.

But my skin tingles, and I may actually be starting to sweat.

I break our eye contact. Clear my throat. "Should we, um, alert the hotel staff? Perhaps the poor guy has met with foul play." I shift in my seat and re-cross my legs, tugging my skirt down in the process. Subtly swiping at my brow, I'm convinced I'm dripping like a hog, but my fingers come away dry.

"Maybe we should start a search." His eyes twinkle devilishly and he stands and leans over the bar. "He's not down there."

"Hmm," I say, swiveling on my stool, glad the focus is off me. I bend at the waist and look around. "Don't see him hiding under any tables."

He moves to the wall and peers behind the over-sized flat-screen TV mounted there. "Not here either."

I shrug. "I think we've mounted a pretty exhaustive search, don't you?"

Hands in his pockets, he saunters over and stands next to me, his thigh brushing my knees. "So, what are you having, assuming a bartender does appear?"

I try to ignore his closeness. "Tea."

"Tea?" He raises an eyebrow. "Iced or—"

"Scalding, preferably. Yes, I'm one of those people who goes into a bar and orders tea. I'm a tea-drinking teetotaler, sad to say."

"I'd ask if you were the designated driver, but..." His lips are so sexy. A day's stubble dusts his face and I struggle to focus.

"Alcoholism runs in the family. So I just stay away."

"Ah," he rocks back on his heels nodding. I could be imagining a hint of respect in his eyes. "Well, I don't think this place will lose their liquor license if I make you a cup of tea."

"You?"

With a wink, he walks behind the bar like he owns it. I open my mouth to say something, then close it when he bends down to search the shelves, allowing me to appreciate certain of his, uh, assets. He catches me staring in the mirror and I look away. He chuckles and shakes his head, returning to his task, and produces a cup and saucer.

"Decaf?" He holds up a generic teabag.

"No, give me the good stuff."

"Long night ahead?"

"Long day behind me. But..." I look out the front window to the street beyond. The nursing home isn't visible from here, thankfully. "I don't think I'll be able to sleep much tonight." I face him again and catch the tail end of a somber expression on his face before he replaces it with a smile.

"One sleepless night, coming up." His tone is light, playful, but his words set off a firestorm of images in my head.

"Are you sure you should be back there? Doesn't it take some kind of training or a certificate to operate a bar?"

"Are you doubting my tea-making abilities?" He holds a hand to his heart and feigns shock. "I guarantee this will be the best cup of," he looks at the teabag, "generic black tea you've ever had."

He produces a container of sugar packets and a little bowl of creamer.

"No, thanks—I like it black." I catch the flicker of a question on his face. "Black and hot." His eyebrows shoot up. He didn't expect me to flirt back. Hell, I didn't expect it myself. But the distraction is nice. I allow my gaze to linger on his smooth, café au lait skin and, good God, those lips.

His voice, low like the purr of an engine, penetrates my haze. "What brings you to San Francisco?"

I sit back and pull out a sugar packet, just to feel it between my fingers. "My father is dying."

The words settle like stones on the counter between us. "I haven't seen him in close to fifteen years. He wasn't…" I shift in my seat. "He wasn't what you would call father of the year."

"I always wondered who these fathers of the year guys are and where they come from. I've never met any." His eyes are warm and he leans forward, bringing his head just a tiny bit closer to mine. I don't really believe he wants to hear my life story, but he's listening intently, so I keep talking.

"A social worker from the VA tracked me down as his next of kin when he was moved to the hospice." I flip the sugar packet over and over, the granules inside sliding with a whoosh. He reaches out, covering both of my hands with one of his, stilling my movements.

His skin is warm. The veins of his hand stand out in sharp relief. Strong fingers. Long. My skin, a few shades darker than his, hums in response. Neither of us moves, locked together, even the rise and fall of our chests in sync as we breathe.

I exhale to break the spell. "I bought a plane ticket the next day. Dropped everything. Granted, it wasn't much, but still, everything, to come out here and sit by the side of a man who…"

I shake my head, sliding my hands out from under his. They feel different after his touch. Like they're no longer a part of me, but part of this other woman who meets strange men in bars and opens her heart to them. I chance a glance, expecting him to be plotting an escape. He probably came in here for some harmless flirtation, maybe a hookup, and instead he finds…me.

He pours the boiling water into my mug, then pours another for himself before rounding the bar to sit directly next to me. His legs are long and our knees touch. This tiny point of contact crackles up my body. Why is he still here?

"Where's home?" he asks.

"Cincinnati."

"The 'Natti," he smiles, as if he has some fond memory of the town. Which I highly doubt. "And what do you do there?"

I chuckle. "Isn't that the question of the hour? I'm currently, as we like to say, in-between positions."

He grins, stirring two packets of sugar into his tea. "You're keeping your options open?"

"I'm not a flake. I work hard, mostly retail, I just haven't found my—thing. My last job was selling used cars."

He stops stirring for a moment, then resumes.

"It's okay to laugh."

"No, I'm just trying to picture it." He closes his eyes and tilts his head in a move I find completely adorable.

"Can I interest you in a lovely, pre-owned sedan? It only has two-hundred fifty thousand miles on it?" I shake my head and blow on my tea before taking a tentative sip. It isn't one of the fancier brands I splurge on even though I can't really afford them, but the hot liquid feels so good going down. It enters my bloodstream, unsnarling some of the knots and loosening me all over, the way I imagine alcohol might.

I didn't realize I'd closed my eyes, but when I open them he's staring at me, raw desire etched onto his face. It takes me aback. I'd thought he was intense before, but that was only a preview. He seems caught off-guard as well and focuses on his mug, taking too big a swallow for liquid that hot.

"Best you've ever had?" he says, wincing slightly.

I chuckle. "Like you need the ego boost. But, yes, it's the best I've ever had." I say it in a mock sexy voice, aiming for playful. He stares at my mouth, then takes another gulp.

"Careful," I say, as he winces again. "You need that tongue, am I right?"

He licks his lips and the energy in the room changes on a dime. The low crackle of attraction is now supercharged. I suddenly regret my attempts at flirtation. I am so far out of my league here. If I'd had any sense, I would have packed up and left when he first walked in. I'm a farm team kind of girl, and he is definitely major league.

My track record with the majors is pretty much a disaster. I tried it once, a long time ago and still bear the scars. Worse, they still hurt. So yeah, Cinderella may get a ticket to the ball, or a coupon as the case may be, and she may even dance with the prince, but that whole happily ever after scenario doesn't happen for girls whose childhood address was the Budget Inn. Princes don't want girls with my kind of baggage. It's certainly not Louis Vuitton.

I turn to face the counter, removing my leg from contact with his. The energy simmers back down to non-lethal levels and we're just two strangers drinking tea in a bar.

"Thanks." I sip the tea for a minute, then push away from the counter and stand, determined to leave before things get out of hand again.

"You're leaving?"

"It's quarter to two. I'm pretty sure this is last call." I drain the last drops from my cup. If I don't get away now I may end up doing something I regret. The last thing I need is more scars.

I'm turning to go when he touches my shoulder. I freeze. Everything inside me crackles like a live wire.

"I never got your name," he says, maintaining the contact. When I turn to him, his gaze is potent, but there's something else behind it. Something I can't define and don't want to.

My eyes drop to his lips. A vision of how the night could go runs on a projector in my head. I tell him my name, he tells me it's pretty. I'm pretty. Would I like to come up to his room, or could he

come to mine? He has a wide selection of the finest soft drinks to tempt me with. I say yes, because, really—who wouldn't? And the night is amazing. Or not, but considering the sparks shooting from a simple touch through the polyester of my sweater, it'll be amazing.

And then, I'll start asking him questions. I won't be able to stop because I won't want him to leave, or for me to have to make the walk of shame. I'll pepper him with questions and I'll pretend they're just light, getting to know you chatter, but really I'll be gathering enough information to stalk him on Google later. I'll imagine we can start dating, a long-distance relationship from wherever he lives. Of course, I could barely afford to get here so there's no way I can handle a long-distance relationship and, geez, who said anything about a relationship anyway, wasn't this supposed to be a one night stand? He'll figure out I'm crazy. He'll figure out I have issues and realize that he's a prince, he doesn't need this shit.

I'll have memories of one night that will haunt me for years. Years of wondering, years of hoping, following his Facebook updates to find out when he changes his relationship status. When he gets married. How many kids he has. The topic of their first-grade science project.

I shiver as Trevor's face pops into my head. Specifically, the smile on his face in his wedding photo. He's looking at his wife like she's made of gold. I'd always wanted him to look at me that way. She's definitely princess material, she's even wearing a huge, poofy, princess dress.

The man in front of me is waiting for my answer. I can practically see the crown on his head. I shake my head. "Names are overrated."

His eyebrows shoot up.

"I'm not—this isn't a challenge. You seem," I rake my gaze over him searching for the right word. Incredibly sexy. Gorgeous. Orgasm inducing. "Nice." I wince for him. "But, um, my life is just too complicated for names…and things. You know?"

He takes a step closer. So close our toes are almost touching. His hand on my shoulder occupies almost all of my attention. "So, no names. Maybe we could use code names, like call signs."

"Or superheroes?"

He grins. "What's your super power?"

"Trouble," I answer immediately.

"I was thinking you looked like trouble."

"You would not be wrong. What about you? What's your super power?"

He shrugs. "Amazing tea making?"

I laugh and despite my best efforts not to, reach out to straighten his already perfect collar. "You know, I think you're dangerous to a girl's health." I get trapped in his eyes. "Danger, that's what I'll call you."

"Danger and Trouble."

I release him, pulling out of his grip and backing away. Take a mental picture of him standing there. The desire to stay is so strong, I know I'm making the right decision to leave.

"A match made in heaven if I've ever heard one," he says.

I turn and walk away.

CHAPTER TWO

My legs are leaden as I drag myself the short distance back to the hotel. Each step is agony. The bell of a streetcar chimes nearby. If I run, maybe I can catch it. Ride it to the end of the line. It must end at the ocean. I could just sit there and stare at the endless, black water. Let the lapping waves soothe the ache in my chest.

When I arrive, the Montagne's lobby is once again empty. With the hours I keep, I haven't seen many other guests. Either everyone here goes to bed early, or they're all out enjoying the nightlife.

The one guest I did meet has not been far from my mind all day.

I find myself moving towards the bar, unable to stop the forward motion of my feet. Once again no one seems to be manning the place. All the stools are empty and I pretend the disappointment I feel is something else. Exhaustion maybe. Why *would* he be here? And even if he was, it would be to pick up someone else. Someone new. After all, I blew him off.

"You're not the bartender," a voice calls out from a table at the side of the entrance. Dark eyes glint above a roguish grin. Tonight he's in a pinkish shirt with a navy jacket and pants. It's sort of corporate and sort of hip and all the way sexy.

My mouth wants to smile, but I try to stifle it, resulting in a weird mouth dance that probably makes me look like I'm having a stroke.

Was he waiting for me?

"I've already done the search," he says, standing. "Just to save time."

"How thoughtful of you."

He approaches the stool he sat at last night. Once I get a whiff of cologne, my brain scrambles. I take a step back and walk behind the bar to get some space. But the counter between us might as well not exist. Even from several feet away he crowds me. His presence takes up all the space in the room, and singes me with combustible heat.

He leans forward, his forearms on the counter. "A cup of your finest tea, barkeep."

"At your service." I bow with a flourish and turn to search for the mugs, mindful not to bend at the waist and stick my ass in his line of sight. I've never been behind a bar before, but this one has little to no organization. The shelves are a riot of bottles, glasses, stacks of paper, napkins, jars and boxes.

"Need a hand?" His voice comes from directly beside me, causing little earthquakes to rattle inside my body.

I usher him forward with a sweep of my arm. "You're the professional, after all."

"Go on, have a seat. I've got this."

I most certainly should not have a seat. I should leave, go back to my tastefully decorated room, and go to sleep. But my butt hits the stool without protest. My butt is not interested in being anywhere else at the moment.

"How did it go today?"

I take a deep breath. Whatever polite non-answer I was going to give dies on my lips under the force of his expression of sincere concern. He seems worried about me. Like he cares. It leaves me so off-kilter I tell him the truth.

"His organs are shutting down. He's signed a 'do not resuscitate' order so it won't be long."

He frowns and puts two mugs on the counter.

"Part of me is relieved—the world is better off without him. But part of me wishes I'd gotten what I came for."

"What was it you came for?"

I stare at my hands. The middle three fingers are crooked from where my father slammed them in the bedroom door after I'd tried to run away from his fist. I catch Danger looking at the misshapen digits and form them into a fist. "I was looking for a reason why. Some kind of explanation. Something that would make it make sense. Why did he hate us? Why did he hate us so much?"

My hands are shaking so I slide them into my lap. "I think I came here believing that I had to forgive him before he died. My life has been stuck in so many ways. I watched this documentary about forgiving and moving on and when I got that phone call…. I thought I had to come here and try.

"But you know what he said, while he could still talk?" Danger's eyes are on me, they haven't left my face. He's listening. The words spill from me, providing way too much information, but he's really listening. "He said I should have stayed home." I meet his eyes as my voice starts to waiver.

"He wouldn't admit to anything. Said I was crazy, that he never hit me unless I deserved it. That my mother was—" I shake my head. Shrug. "So, maybe he was right. Maybe I should have stayed home."

A steaming cup of tea slides toward me. I wrap my hands around it, relishing the sting of the heat. The stool beside me shifts as he settles into it, and I shake off the melancholy.

"But enough of that. What about you, Danger? Why are you here?"

He stares at me for a long time before a slow smile spreads across his face. He's going along with my change of subject, though I have the sense he wanted to say something else.

"I live here."

"Here as in San Francisco or here as in…"

"The Montagne."

"You can live here?"

He nods. "The top three floors are residential."

"Wow, so, why do you live in a hotel?"

He fidgets uncharacteristically, like this is a topic he's uncomfortable with. I can't imagine how expensive it must be to live in a place like this. I'm starting to feel like we're not just in two different leagues, we're playing two different sports.

"It's convenient. You pick up a phone and there's room service. Laundry and housekeeping are included. What's not to love?" His voice is light, but there's pain tucked away there in the words he's not saying.

"My room here is approximately the size of my car—it's gorgeous, I love it, but it's tiny. And normally way, way above my budget, but I got in on the special deal."

"I didn't know there was a special deal."

"Some place called Delilah's Travel Agency sent me a coupon in the mail. It was really weird—handwritten calligraphy on fancy paper—but I called and it was legit." I look around the space. "I guess it would be kind of nice to live here."

My gaze is on the ceiling when he reaches out to push a chunk of hair behind my ear. I gasp as his fingertips graze my sensitive skin. Close my eyes. The energy crackles between us like a lightning strike and I'm ready to forget about baseball, forget about royal hierarchies and years of social media stalking and just give in to the thrumming in my veins that's begging for more of his touch.

His thumb is skirting the edge of my bottom lip when a jangling sound draws our attention to the doorway. A young Asian woman in tuxedo pants, a white shirt and bow tie tears into the room like a Tasmanian devil. Her hair is in long purple dreadlocks pulled back in a ponytail and her makeup consists mostly of glitter.

"Ohmygosh! Customers! I didn't think anyone would be here so late, I just stepped out for a second to check my—Time works so differently here. Sorry, it's my first day and so I didn't realize—oh wow! You already have drinks, that's so crazy."

She whirls behind the bar, a tornado of sound with clanging bracelets and tiny bells woven into her hair.

"You're the bartender?" Danger asks.

"Yup," she nods, the movement causing a chorus of chimes.

"Do you have some ID?"

The girl pauses, her eyes growing wide before she plunges her hand into her pocket and rummages around. The slim pants couldn't hold much, but her arm disappears to the elbow before she pulls it back out, displaying a laminated ID swipe card with the logo of the hotel and a picture of her face.

He nods and sits back, though his brow is furrowed. "You can't abandon your post, you know. If you have to step out you should find someone to cover you."

I never asked him what he did, but he must manage people for a living. Although anybody who's ever had a job before should know not to just take off without telling someone.

"You guys are drinking tea, well, that's on the house, I assure you. I'll have them take it out of my check, don't worry. I'm really sorry. So where are you from? What do you do there? How do you like the hotel? Isn't it fab?"

Danger's frown deepens as he stares at the strange girl and I down the last swallow of my tea, seizing the moment of clarity. "I actually better get going. It's late." I stand and avoid looking at him.

"Thanks, come again!" The bartender says cheerily.

I walk out, trying to convince myself that I don't want him to follow me. It's ridiculous really, this attraction. What's the point of feeling so drawn to someone you can never really have? Someone who could only pile one more hurt on top of so many others?

"Trouble," he says. I keep walking to the elevator, but stop before pushing the button. I fish my key card from my purse then turn to him, not sure of what to say. We stand there like that, just staring at each other, until a Financial District type—slicked-back hair, power suit—comes up and stabs the button several times.

When the elevator dings open, we all pile in. The suit chooses the second floor. Danger gives me a look that says, *What, he couldn't take one flight of stairs?* I can't help breaking into a grin. I was thinking the same thing. When the doors shut after the suit's exit, the elevator doesn't move. We haven't picked another floor yet.

I step back and lean against the wall. Take a deep breath. He crosses his arms and leans next to me. We stand in the immobile elevator playing this strange game of chicken.

He looks like he's got all the time in the world. Doesn't touch me. Doesn't say anything, but the closeness of him in this tiny space makes the attraction from earlier seem like a mere sparkler. We have now entered the extended grand finale. 3D images are being created with the fireworks going off between us.

I shoot him a dirty look from the corner of my eye. His smile does nothing but grow wider. Damn those damn sexy lips.

I punch the button for the fourth floor. When the elevator arrives, I stomp out, not surprised when he follows. I spin around. "I'm not inviting you in."

"I didn't ask to come in. I'm just escorting to your room to make sure you get there safely."

"Is this a dangerous hotel?"

"You never know." He's smug and sure of himself, but, amazingly, not in an obnoxious way. His hands are in his pockets and he starts to *whistle*. What a bastard. Who does he think he is?

We stop at my door and I'm ready to say goodnight. Ready to banish him to the farthest reaches of space, where he can invade some other poor woman's psyche with his flashing eyes and strong hands.

He lifts my hand and brings it to his lips. "Have a good night, Trouble."

The fireworks have become a full-scale nuclear explosion. He releases my hand. Backs away.

Shit.

I hate baseball.

"Hey, Danger?"

"Yes."

"Come here."

CHAPTER THREE

I back into the room, my eyes never leaving his as he closes the door. The lights are off, but the ultra-bright street lamp spears the room through the oversized window, creating harsh shadows. My heart races so fast it makes me dizzy. I wobble when the backs of my legs hit the bed. And then he's all around me, his hands drawing my face in, his lips singeing mine with a four-alarm kiss. I seriously think I may spontaneously combust right here.

I tilt my head, drawing him deeper, pressing myself against the hardness of his body to feel the strength underneath the expensive clothes. My hands slide down and I pull him closer. He comes up for breath and, with a mischievous look, picks me up, palming my ass in his grip. My skirt slides up, legs wrap around him. I think he's going to lay me on the bed, but he turns and my back hits the wall before he attacks me with another searing kiss.

My lungs don't work and my brain has abandoned me, leaving me with only nerve endings on fire from his touch. The ache between my thighs pulses hotter and harder. He presses open mouthed kisses on the heated flesh of my neck, but I grab his head and pull him away.

"Bed. Now."

He grins and we spin around, then I'm spread across the bed and he's on top of me. I wriggle, struggling to get out of my clothes. My skirt finally comes off, revealing plain cotton panties, but at least I brought my good bra with me. He's only halfway out of his shirt when he stops, and I think something's wrong.

"What?" The panties can't be *that* bad.

"Nothing. You're gorgeous." His stare is appreciative, but it's like he's not even looking at me, he's looking into me. It's a little too much, so I grab his belt and start to pull. He brushes my hands away and makes quick work of slipping out of his clothes.

Black boxer briefs highlight how happy he is to see me. And this man's chest belongs on the cover of a fitness magazine. I run a hand over the planes of sculpted muscle. Just for tonight I've been called up to the majors. I hope I don't embarrass myself.

Needing to taste him, I close the distance between us. I moan as my lips and tongue run over his skin. He hisses when I scrape his nipple with my teeth. I bite down a little and he jerks, tries to push me away, but I don't move. I palm his erection through his underwear, just starting to get the feel of it when he tosses me down with lightning quickness and shifts the lace of my bra cups out of the way to lave my breasts with his tongue.

This position puts him right where I want him, his cock rubbing against my drenched panties, the blunt head stoking my fires. Proving himself a pro, he undoes my bra clasp, one-handed. My back arches at the unfettered contact as he kneads and licks his way across my chest. He flicks my nipple, then rolls it between his fingers and I feel close. The pent-up attraction is ready to overflow.

"Condom," I breathe into his ear and he rises and sheaths himself while I get rid of the panties. I rise to my hands and knees and turn to look at him over my shoulder. I'm burning so much for him that any position will do as long as he's inside me immediately.

He slides his hands over my ass, squeezing each cheek before flipping me onto my back again. He kisses the questioning look off my face.

"I want to look at you. I want to see what you like. I want to see your face when I make you come." He rubs the head of his dick against me once then slides all the way home, spreading and filling me, turning the fire into an inferno.

Painstakingly slow strokes have me thrashing around, begging him to go faster, harder, turning me crazy. I literally see the moment his control breaks and he slams into me, burying himself all the way inside as our pelvises smack together.

I shiver as sensation consumes me, turn my head away as his powerful strokes turn me into jelly. He caresses my face gently, turning my head even as his body pummels into me. "Look at me," he insists.

My eyes flutter open then closed. I struggle to meet his eyes.

He kisses me again, deeply, eyes open, and a fire hose of emotion blasts me. The intensity of eyes-open sex is beyond what I can even process. I can't believe I've never done this before. My gaze glides down to where our bodies meet, him pistoning inside me, the friction and slide pushing me over the edge.

It occurs to me that he's a stranger, but he doesn't feel like one, wringing every last drop of pleasure from my body. Something about looking into his eyes while he comes—you can't hide anything in that moment. You're not in control and whatever mask you're wearing slips away. What I see in that moment is all sincerity. There's no mask—it's a revelation I don't have time to ponder because then my own orgasm crashes into me, lifting my back off the bed with its strength. I can't help but close my eyes as it stretches on and on.

When it's over I lay there shaking, embarrassed as tears pool in my eyes. I can't be one of those women who cries after sex. Especially not after a *one night stand*. I turn away as he slides out of me and throws away the condom. In a second, he's back, wrapping his arms around me. Pulling me into his chest, accepting my random outburst of emotion.

I don't cry, I don't let myself, but I do take a moment to bask in the fantasy. How could this man, who doesn't know me, offer something so intimate? He's not yet on his way out the door, which is in itself surprising. Settling into his warmth, inhaling the clean scent of his sweat, I let myself imagine for a moment that life could be like this. That I could spend nights held safe in the arms of a man who loves me.

The thought shatters my daze. I shoot out of the bed on unsteady feet. Where the hell had that come from? He's looking at me like I'm freaking out, maybe because I am freaking out. I run to the bathroom and lock myself inside.

CHAPTER FOUR

I run the water in the sink for a long time, giving him a chance to make his exit. The shower is tempting, but I hate bathing at night. I'll need the water in the morning to help me wake up, and after all of this activity, I'll also need the hot steam to sooth my aching muscles.

After what I feel is approximately half an eternity, I wrap myself in the hotel robe and go back into the room. The fact that he's still here shouldn't surprise me. But it's not comforting, it's annoying and presumptuous. He should know how this goes down.

He has the nerve to grin at me when he hops up, still naked as the day he was born. His body crowds me in the tiny space between the bed and the dresser, but he doesn't touch me, just enters the bathroom. While he's in there, I fold his clothes into a neat pile and place them on his side of the bed. Just so he gets the message.

When he comes out he picks up the pile, sets in on the dresser and climbs back into bed, pulling up the covers. My look would turn him to ice if he were a normal human being. But he's steadily ignoring me. I'm just about to give him a piece of my mind when the phone rings.

It's almost two a.m. and my stomach clenches. He's sitting nearest the phone and picks it up, holding it out to me. His eyes are on me, but I think my face may have turned to stone.

I press the phone to my ear. "Hello?"

"Hello, Ms. Abernath?"

I swallow. "Yes."

"This is Bayside Nursing Facility. I'm sorry to tell you that your father has passed away. The time of death was one fourteen a.m."

The room is quiet and the phone's receiver is loud. Danger can hear every word. He wraps an arm around me. I don't feel anything but cold.

"Thank you for letting me know."

"If you'd like to come in tomorrow to make arrangements—"

"No, I—I won't be making any arrangements. The social worker will handle whatever has to be done. Thank you. Good night."

"But Miss—"

I hand him the phone to hang up. He pulls me into the broadness of his chest and wraps both arms around me.

"I'm sorry."

"Don't be. I'm not. He was a miserable man. Don't waste any tears for him, I won't."

"I'm sorry for your loss." The way he enunciates each word, it's like he gets it. Like he understands that I didn't lose my father tonight. I lost him years ago. With every crack of the belt or blow from his fist, little by little I became fatherless. The scars I bear, both the ones that can be seen and traced with fingers and the ones deep inside are aching. But not because of tonight. Because of all the nights.

He strokes my hair and I melt into him.

"Tell me something," I say, wanting just a little more time inside the bubble of this fantasy. "Not your name, just something about you. Something you can't find on an internet search."

His hands stroke my shoulder for a moment. He kisses it, absently. It's a long time before he answers.

"I watched my mother die. She swallowed a bottle of painkillers right in front of me. She made me promise not to call for help."

I pull back and look at him. Here is the mask, for the first time. I can tell the difference between the him I've seen up until now and this—this is the face he wears for the world. I slide a hand behind his neck and pull his forehead down to meet mine.

"I kept the promise," he whispers. "Sat with her for hours. My father walked in and found us. He's hated me ever since. But she needed to go. He drove her crazy and she had to go. I couldn't save her."

"How old were you?"

"Thirteen."

"I'm sorry." I pull him into my arms. "I'm so sorry."

"He's well-respected—a self-made man, on the boards of charities, pictures with heads of state. And he's one of the worst men I know.... But everyone looks at me, hears my last name, and they see him." He tightens his grip on me. "I can't be anything like him."

He breathes into my neck and I shift my head. Our kiss is slow and from the heart. I taste tears and am not sure if they're mine or his. We soothe each other, hold each other, and my heart breaks for him.

I pull back and bite my lip. "You're something else, Danger. Do you know that?" I stroke his face, peering into dark eyes.

"Please tell me your name?" he asks.

My laugh is filled with tears and I shake my head. "I'm a mess. You do understand that? Not a cute scatterbrained mess, a real mess. Daddy issues, right? More baggage than you want to deal with. I promise you."

"You don't have a monopoly on baggage—"

"But it's different for guys. And men like you have options. I can tell you're one of the good ones. You don't have to settle for someone like me. You shouldn't."

"Settle? You're not settling. Why would you think that? Is it because of your father?"

I shake my head. "I just know." The look on his face tells me he needs more. I sigh and sit back.

"I had this boyfriend in high school. Trevor. He was the golden boy: popular, athletic, gorgeous. The world at his fingertips type—like you.

"My mom was a mess. She'd gotten remarried to another alcoholic, so home was a mess too and Trevor was like an island of calm in a torrential storm. I thought…. Well, I wasn't ready, you know? I just, I wanted more time before we had sex. But I guess he thought dating a girl from where I'm from meant a guaranteed score. When I wouldn't, he told me he couldn't deal with someone with so much baggage. All my issues were just too much for any guy with options. And then he left. He ended up marrying a cheerleader and has three kids."

I shrug. "At the end of the day you can't escape where you come from. My mom could never land anyone decent. Just once, I thought maybe I could break the mold. Fall a little further from the tree, but…I don't get to keep you. And pretty soon, you won't want to keep me."

"Shouldn't I be able to decide?"

I hold his eyes so he can see who I am. "I Am. A. Mess," I say slowly, so he understands.

"I don't exactly have *my* shit together. I don't even have an apartment."

"Yeah, you live in a hotel with rooms that cost more per night than one month of my rent. That's the definition of having your shit together."

He picks up a lock of my hair between two fingers. "You gonna try and kick me out again?"

"I'm leaving tomorrow." I check the clock. "Today, really. Turning back into a pumpkin. Wouldn't it be easier to go now than in the morning?"

He releases my hair to run his fingers across my scalp. I close my eyes involuntarily as the sensation ripples through me. He kisses the shell of my ear.

"I can't go yet. If you kick me out now, I'll just camp outside your door like a stray puppy." He pushes the fabric of my robe down to kiss my shoulder. "There may be howling involved. I could wake the other guests. Do you want that on your conscience?"

I tilt my head to give him better access. He presses kisses to my neck, quickening my pulse. My breath hitches, becomes erratic as his hands slide down to my waist, shucking off the robe in the process.

"That certainly would be inconsiderate," I say, breathless.

"Let me stay the night, if only for the sake of everyone else. Think of it as community service." He pulls me into him, spreading my legs and reaching down to stroke the wetness there once, then twice, charging me up and leaving me ready to ignite.

"When you put it like that, how can I refuse?"

CHAPTER FIVE

I wake up surrounded in warmth, inhaling a lush, enticing aroma. The smell of man. I snuggle closer, still half-asleep, when a large hand palms my behind. Desire ripples through me and I shift, my movements tinged with soreness. Wincing open one eye, I'm greeted with his face, inches from my own.

He is so beautiful in sleep. He looks younger—that mischievous quality he often has about him is absent. Just a sleeping man, calm and kind. I move to roll out of bed, but he tightens his grip, unconsciously.

I can't believe I let him stay. Can't believe I told him about Trevor. Admitted to all of it. Though I didn't tell him about the internet stalking, or how, even now, I wish I had Trevor's life. What if I had said yes instead of no when he'd try to cajole me into bed? Would my life be charmed now? Or would he have still discarded me with the rest of the trash? And why do I still care?

Danger's lashes brush his cheek and a swell of emotion fills me to bursting. Last night was a fantasy. It doesn't even matter that in the harsh light of day he's even more beautiful than he was before. He's still a bubble about to burst.

As if he can read my thoughts, he opens his eyes.

"Good morning," I say and shift, trying to slide out of the bed. Once again his arms trap me back to his side. He kisses my neck and nestles in. I laugh and swat at him. "Time to get up, sleepyhead."

He groans in protest and refuses to release his grip on me. Finally, I worm my way out of his arms and go to the bathroom. When I come out, he's sprawled out across the entire bed grinning at me.

"What?"

"Nothing," he says.

"You look awfully pleased with yourself." I sit down beside him and he pulls me to him. "What if I am?"

He continues looking at me significantly.

"What?"

"I'm waiting for you to say it."

"Say what?"

He just waggles his eyebrows in response. I rack my brain to figure out what he means, before a lightbulb clicks. "Best I've ever had?"

"Ahh!" he says, falling back on to the bed. "I knew it."

I turn to fully face him, growing serious. "Yeah, you are."

He sobers as well and reaches out to grab my hands. "I know you have your rules and everything but—"

I shake my head, pulling out of his grasp. "It was perfect. The perfect night. Now that the sun's up, I don't want to ruin it. Isn't it enough to be able to look back and have this one unspoiled thing to take with you? I guarantee if we try for more it will blow up in our faces."

I think he'll protest, try to make his case. I steel myself against his arguments, hoping he can just understand where I'm coming from. To my surprise, he nods and gets up. Puts his clothes back on. For a moment, I regret the covering of that gorgeous body.

He stands, fully dressed, looking at me through the mirror. I want to look away, but I can't. I owe him at least this much—to see him. His intensity is set to full blast, but his face is unreadable. He picks up a pen and scribbles on the hotel stationery, then seals it in the envelope.

"This is me." He holds up the envelope. "If you ever want to know who I am, want to get in contact, it's in here. Your choice."

A sharp longing pierces me as I look at the paper held in his long fingers.

"I need you to know that I do want more. I don't believe you're as much of a mess as you think you are. What I see is a beautiful, intelligent, strong woman who's been through some shit, and come out the other side. Not everybody does."

He places the envelope in the side pocket of my suitcase, then turns back to me.

"And for what it's worth, your high school boyfriend was a dick. And your dad. You don't have to believe anything either of them said. They weren't right. If you've had bad relationships, if you've chosen the wrong guys, that doesn't mean you don't deserve someone better. You absolutely do. Don't sell yourself short anymore."

He takes a step towards me, cupping my face in his hands before kissing me, hard and meaningfully, imprinting himself onto me. My eyes close involuntarily.

"You can't fix me," I whisper.

"I don't think you're broken."

I open my eyes when the door clicks shut.

I am alone again.

CHAPTER SIX

An hour later, my return flight is booked and I'm ready to leave for the airport. I've already called my father's social worker—he'll be given a military burial in one of the available veteran's cemeteries. No way am I spending another dime on him.

There was judgment in her voice when I talked to her, but she only knew a dying old man. Letting go of any further responsibility for him feels good, not cold or callous. If there could have been reconciliation or forgiveness I would have been open to it. But there wasn't. I don't forgive him. And I'm okay with that.

A knock at the door startles me. My gaze lands on the envelope peeking out of my suitcase. I'd contemplated doing a dozen things with it: chucking it out the window, except the windows don't open; burning it, but I don't have any matches; flushing it down the toilet, but I don't want to create a clog. And, of course, opening it. Some part of me desperately wants to open it, to stay and spend another night in his arms. Over and over, I shake off the feeling, repeating to myself why it's better this way. I almost believe it.

I pad to the door and open it to find the bartender from last night, the odd girl with the bright purple hair.

Today she's in a bellhop's uniform, complete with pillbox hat. A nametag on her jacket reads, "Delilah."

"Good morning," she says.

"Aren't you the bartender?"

"Yeah, that didn't work out so well. I think bell-hopping is more my thing."

"But, I didn't call for a bellhop."

"Oh, you didn't?" She frowns. "So, you're not checking out?" Hope lights her face, like for some reason she wants me to stay. Maybe the work of being a bellhop doesn't appeal to her any more than bartending.

"No, I am checking out. But I only have one bag, I can get it."

"Oh, no, I insist," she says, barging into the room and over to the suitcase.

"Everything all zipped up?" she asks, running her hands across the green and pink floral fabric of my hideous discount bag. Her fingers brush the corner of the envelope, pushing it deeper into the pocket and zipping it up. She swings it off the luggage stand and carries it into the hall.

"I'll go ahead and take this down for you. It'll be waiting at the front desk."

And with that she's gone.

Standing alone in the room, I exhale, feeling like I just survived some kind of freak storm interrupting a quiet, sunny day. I do a final check of the room, stopping just short of sniffing the pillow he used.

Then I sniff it anyway. Try to memorize his scent. Grab my purse and head out.

For once, the lobby is teeming with activity. A family reunion, all wearing matching fluorescent t-shirts reading "The Hollisters—Building Our Legacy, Y'all," is checking out. They all have southern accents, and I bob and weave through huge teased bouffants and cowboy hats to get to the front desk.

"Sorry, sugah," a large woman says as she rolls a gold-trimmed suitcase over my foot.

The young man behind the front desk looks harried, but smiles warmly at me.

"Hi, the bellhop just brought my bag down, I'm checking out of 409."

"409," he repeats, clicking on the computer.

"Are you all short staffed?"

He grimaces. "A flu hit a bunch of the staff this week. Sorry if there was anything about your stay that was unsatisfactory."

"Oh no, my stay was delightful. I would definitely recommend the Montagne to anyone I know who could afford it."

The young man passes me my receipt and scans the bags behind the counter.

"What does your bag look like again?"

I look around. "You can't miss it—bright green. Looks like flower vomit."

The man frowns. "Let me check the back," he says and disappears behind a door marked STAFF.

A few minutes later he reappears with an older man in tow.

"I'm sorry, ma'am, who did you say brought your bag down?"

"The bellhop. She was young, Asian, bright purple dreadlocks."

Both of their faces remain blank and a sinking feeling hits me. "Not ringing any bells?"

The manager looks at the desk clerk, then back at me. "No one by that description works on the staff of the Montagne."

"She was working the bar last night. She had an ID badge."

The manager kneads the bridge of his nose. "Jake, call the police, please." To me he says, "I'm so sorry ma'am, it seems you've been the victim of a theft."

I need to be at the airport in an hour. I've already paid a fortune for the tickets and can't afford a flight change fee. Fortunately, the cops come quickly. I give them my statement and a description of the woman. Then I'm headed back through the swamp of Hollisters to hail a cab.

I hadn't packed much for the trip. I wore the same skirt or slacks every day, dressing up in a vain attempt to present an air of respectability to my father. There were no valuables and the suitcase itself was no great loss, though it was new. The hotel promised to pay for the value of my belongings, but it won't be much.

I miss a step when it hits me that I had one priceless, irreplaceable item in that bag. I falter, trying to decide whether to go back to the front desk and ask them about all of their permanent residents. Will they tell me the identity of the gorgeous man with the sparkling, mischievous eyes?

The doorman waves me forward, holding a cab at the curb. I look back, through the sea of people. There's a man at the counter who could be him. Dark hair. Brown skin. Tall. I strain my neck to see.

Someone on the street honks, and I shake my head. Maybe this is a sign. I'm not supposed to know him. Contact him. Want him. Isn't this just what I wanted?

I climb into the cab. The door shuts, sealing me in. I look back as we pull away.

It's for the best.

It has to be.

CHAPTER SEVEN

From across an immaculate desk, Delilah's supervisor, Neenah, stares her down. Delilah taps a glittering nail on her thigh, looking anywhere but her boss's iron gaze.

"Explain this to me again," Neenah says. "What am I looking at?"

Delilah takes a deep breath, a habit gleaned from living around humans for so long. Breathing usually helps her fit in better.

"He's logging in to the database to search the guest registry. But he always stops himself. Tells himself that if she'd wanted to contact him she would have."

"And how many times a day does he do this?"

Delilah sighs, another unnecessary action. "Several."

Neenah sets the tablet down gingerly, the live feed still playing. She straightens it into perfect alignment with the edge of the desk. "And how long has it been?"

Delilah looks at her bare wrist and tilts her head, counting. "Approximately 2 months, 3 weeks and 4 days. Time works differently over there, you have to realize."

Neenah shakes her head, causing the ruby-red hair she's chosen for her human body to briefly shift back into her natural smoke-like form. When meeting with her subordinates, she usually matches the form they hold, though staying human is tricky without a great deal of practice—especially when strong emotions come into play.

For a second, she flickers into a murky haze, then comes back full force. "This is unacceptable. Why didn't you predict that she'd leave without her bag?"

Delilah picks at the polish on her nails and shrugs. "It was a miscalculation."

"And where is the suitcase in question?"

"Tech support is on it. They'll have it put back together really soon."

"How many dimensions did it end up in?"

"Only a few hundred."

Neenah blinks. Too slowly to really pass for human, but she's never spent any time in the human realm. Delilah wants to fidget in her seat, but stays still under the scrutiny.

"Your first assignment is hanging by a thread, Delilah. Your future in the Guild is in jeopardy if you don't fix this now."

"It could have happened to anyone."

"*Most* of our liaisons understand how trans-dimensional transportation works. And it didn't happen to anyone—it happened to you." Neenah stares her down. "Fix. This. Now!" Her voice reverberates through the office as she de-manifests into a plume of smoke.

CHAPTER EIGHT

The coffee shop is nearly empty after the lunch rush. I crack my back and sit up from my laptop; take a moment to calm the jitters that always happen after I press send. I'd tweaked my resume for the millionth time and it's now on its way to yet another job prospect. I feel really good about this one. For starters, they have an office in San Francisco.

Closing the many tabs I have open in my browser, I stop at the one I can never bring myself to get rid of. The Montagne's website.

It's glossy and slick, just like the place itself. I've stared at the photo of the bar more times than I care to think about. I can picture just where he stood when he made me that first tea. Where I sat when he ran his fingertips across my face, moving my hair and emblazoning himself across my soul.

After a week back home, I called the hotel and tried to find him. But just as I thought, they don't give out personal information about their guests or permanent residents. It was a dead end, and short of hopping on a plane and sitting in the lobby until he appeared, I don't have any other way to figure out who he is. Once I get a job and can pay down my credit card, I can go back.

There's no guarantee that he'll be happy to see me or that he'll even be there, but the hope spreads out before me like something I can grasp. The hope is new.

I pack up my computer and wave goodbye to my favorite barista. Yes, I splurged on coffee today, and I don't even feel bad about it. I just have this feeling that everything is turning around. It's gorgeous out; I pause on the sidewalk just to feel the sun warm my face. There's this idea that's been forming inside me that things can be different. It's grabbed hold of that pessimist inside me and put her in a strangle hold. I don't know exactly where it came from, but sometimes it makes me giddy.

I think it's called happiness.

I don't really have any reason to be happy, but I am. Maybe it's the hope.

I make it only a block towards my apartment, when I hear someone calling my name. The familiar deep voice causes me to turn around slowly.

"It *is* you."

He hasn't changed a bit. Still cocky and self-assured, still just as handsome as I remember. Trevor stands before me, grinning widely.

"Hi," I say, a little in shock.

His perfect teeth sparkle with an almost feral quality.

"You're back in town," I say.

"Yeah, I'm here visiting my mom. She just had knee surgery, so I'm helping out." He lifts his pharmacy bag as proof.

I smile. Perfect son. Almost perfect boyfriend. But not quite.

The harsh light of day exposes bags under Trevor's eyes. He wears a polo shirt and khakis, the blandest clothes known to man. I shade my eyes from the sun's glare as I look up at him.

"How's your family? The wife? Kids?"

He looks down, the smile faltering a bit. "We're, um, we got separated a few months ago."

"Oh, I'm sorry to hear that," I say, really meaning it.

He shrugs, looking off down the street. "Yeah, well, it happens." He seems very blasé about the loss of his family. I mean, I wouldn't expect him to be crying in the street, but still, some emotion would be nice. "You know, we should go out some time. Catch up."

I freeze, not sure what I'm hearing. Is he asking me out? Is this really happening?

"Um, I haven't really kept in touch with many people from high school, but a bunch of folks are still in town. Maybe we could get a group together one night," I say. After years of longing, suddenly the thought of being alone with Trevor leaves me cold.

"No, I mean you and me." His hand snakes out to touch my arm before I can stop it. "You look really good. You haven't changed a bit."

His palm is cool and dry. Sort of reptilian.

"You and me?" I repeat, incredulous.

"Yeah," he shoots me with his biggest caliber grin. "We used to have fun together."

If by fun he means I used to let him stick his tongue down my throat and pry his hand out of my panties, then sure, I guess that was fun for him.

"You're right, I haven't changed. I still have the same baggage I did back then. Don't you remember, I had too many *issues* to deal with? You didn't have time for it then. Why would you now?"

His grin falls away. "Did I say that?"

I have to catch my mouth from falling open. "Yes, you did."

"Well, that was a long time ago." His eyes run appreciatively down my body not once, but twice. They get stuck on my breasts with each lap. This morning, when I put on the sundress and strappy sandals, I felt good. That hope had wormed its way into my mind again and I wanted to look nice, just because. But his eyes on me make me want to find a sweater and cover up.

Suddenly, I remember why I didn't want to sleep with him in the first place. It hadn't felt right. He hadn't been right. All these years I thought I'd missed out on someone wonderful. A perfect guy with a perfect life.

But Trevor isn't a prince. He never was.

I pick his hand off my arm and take a step back. "Sorry, I'm busy." I turn and walk off, swaying with every step just so he'll know what he's missing.

Everything that Danger told me suddenly clicks into place. I'd let Trevor's words hold so much power over me all these years. I thought he was the pinnacle, that it couldn't get any better than him. I've never been so happy to be wrong.

I round the corner to my apartment, still feeling on top of the world. Lost in thought, I notice someone standing outside the apartment doors, but don't really look at them until I bump into a pink and green floral suitcase sitting on the stoop.

"Ooh, I'm sorry. You know I had one just like—"

My jaw drops as mischievous eyes crinkle, grinning at me. He's in grey slacks and a black dress shirt, rolled up at the sleeves, the top two buttons undone. Sexier than ever, if that's even possible.

I swallow. We stand there for a few moments drinking in the sight of one another.

"Hi," I say.

"Hi."

"You brought my suitcase."

"The hotel apologizes profusely for losing it."

"The hotel? They make you work for room and board?"

He shrugs. "It's my hotel."

I blink. "*Your* hotel."

"I own it."

"Oh." Of course he does.

He stuffs his hands in his pockets and jingles his keys. I've never seen him nervous before.

"I—I'm not trying to invade your privacy, I just thought you might need this back," he motions towards the bag.

"Where was it?" I ask, still dazed.

He shakes his head. "Just showed up one day, out of the blue. Sitting in the lobby. It was covered in glitter. Not sure what that was about." He takes a step towards me. "A hand delivery just felt like the right thing to do."

"A hand delivery?" I quirk an eyebrow. "Sounds like a good thing to do with your hands."

He's caught off guard by that, but then his face morphs into that dangerous one, the one that got me hooked that first night.

"Well, since you came all this way," I say, "I'm guessing you want a tip."

His eyes never leave my lips as I close the distance between us and rise, pressing my mouth against his.

Nothing has changed—not the heat, not the intensity, not the driving desire that makes me forget for a moment that we are standing out in plain view, blocking the doors to my building.

The door opens. I don't know if someone's coming out or going in. All I can sense is him around me, and I can't wait to get him inside of me again.

I pull away, breathless, panting, looking at my reflection in his eyes.

"So," he says, tightening his hold on me. "Can I finally tell you my name?"

"Later," I say. "I don't think I can hear anything you have to say while you're wearing this many clothes."

EPILOGUE

The door to the apartment building across the street shuts. Delilah rolls up her window and picks up her tablet, tapping out a message to send back to the office.

Within seconds, Neenah has sent her reply.

GOOD WORK. YOUR NEXT ASSIGNMENT IS IN SANTA ROSA, CALIFORNIA. I HOPE YOU LIKE ROCK MUSIC.

Delilah punches in the coordinates on her slightly modified GPS system. Her vintage, purple Volkswagen Beetle roars to life and disappears in a waft of smoky, leaving behind the sound of bells.

Copyright © 2018 by L. Penelope.

Melinda Curtis is an award-winning, USA Today bestselling author of over 40 romance titles. She writes sweet romance for Harlequin, sweet romantic comedy, and fun, sexy sports romances. Sign up for her book release newsletter and download two free reads.

YOU GOTTA KISS A LOTTA FROGS

by Melinda Curtis

ONCE UPON A TIME

Do you believe in fairytales and fairy godmothers?

You should.

If you come to the farmer's market in Brody Falls, you'll see an old woman sitting at a card table. She dresses in red. Magical apple red.

In winter, she wears a woolen red cape. In warmer months, a red scarf flutters around her silver hair like silken butterflies. Her purse is a large red satchel with a crocheted rose hanging on the side (red, of course).

Unlike other vendors, the woman in red offers no fresh produce or handmade goods. She hangs no professionally made banner and puts out no painted sandwich-signs. She sits behind a simple card table with a piece of pink notebook paper taped to the edge. Her sign has two simple words on it: *Love Advice.*

Young or old, no one in Brody Falls can remember a farmer's market without her. Ignore her invitation if you like. She'll remain a mystery. Those who've sat on her folding chair won't discuss what's been said.

They don't call her odd.

They don't call her old.

They simply call her their Fairy Godmother....

CHAPTER ONE

"You've gotta kiss a lotta frogs."

"Haven't I kissed enough already?" Julia Mackenberry slumped in a folding chair at the Love Advice table at the farmer's market in Brody Falls. She was on a mission—find her Prince Charming before her eggs died an untimely death. She rubbed her throbbing temples. "I mean…you should have seen my date last night. Tall and handsome, yeah. But death-lily white."

Did she want to have a child with a vampire?

Yes, chorused her soon to be sacrificed eggs.

"Let me check your frog-o-meter." The old woman's plump fingers gripped Julia's hand. Her thumb and forefinger pressed the flesh between Julia's thumb and forefinger—hard, like an acupuncturist who'd forgotten their needles.

"Ow," Julia yelped.

Suck it up, the eggs shouted, because they knew the Love Lady had helped Missy Lancaster find a man (a wealthy realtor), landed Belinda Higgans a stockbroker husband (owned an island in the Caribbean), and shown Ana Zapata the way to bump into a sexy soccer star (that concussion in the park was totally worth it).

Mama ain't just getting you a daddy, Julia told the eggs. *She's getting you a sugar daddy!*

"No." The Love Lady removed her calloused, vice-like grip from Julia. Her voice had a happy, high-pitched quality that contradicted her bad news. She sounded like Glinda the Good, but she looked like an ancient Red Riding Hood. "You have many more frogs to kiss."

The good news was: the old woman's pressure point treatment had relieved Julia's throbbing temples.

The bad news was: Julia was no closer to finding true love than she'd been three months ago when she'd been told her female equipment had to go. Given her mother and her sister had both battled cancer, Julia had been tested recently for mutated BRCA1. The result? She was a mutant (and she didn't even have X-Men powers), being 50% more likely to contract breast and ovarian cancer than the average woman. Julia wanted a baby before all her lady parts were removed.

The old woman tightened the knot on the red scarf covering her gray curls and nodded at Julia with both her chins. "You're looking for love for all the wrong reasons."

She must have talked to Julia's mother. "I'm thirty," Julia said firmly.

The eggs applauded.

The Love Lady grinned, a spectacle of color given she wore two slashes of rosy blush and a couple of coats of apple red lipstick. "Your eggs must be ancient."

Julia gasped. The eggs gasped. Even the passerby in the crowd seemed to gasp. (Okay, maybe that was a kid choking on a corndog for a moment.)

"Never fear." The Love Lady patted Julia's hand. "I have something that will speed up the process."

"Now you're talking."

The old woman held up a red notebook the size of an address book. "You must follow this to the letter."

Now, Julia was no spring chicken when it came to the promise of love. She'd tried online dating, singles nights, business networking, fortune tellers, matchmakers, and wedding crashing. "What do the letters spell?" The ones she had to follow.

"L-O-V-E."

Sold! the eggs chimed.

"Okay. Why not?" Julia reached for the book. Maybe it had a list of eligible men in Brody Falls. That was better than the love potion perfume she'd purchased last week. The scent had given the produce man an allergic reaction. And she had yet to get the stench out of her 1950s vintage sundress.

The old woman pulled the book just out of reach. "That will be fifty dollars."

"Fifty? I only have forty in my purse." That was the Love Lady's usual fee.

"That's too bad." The Love Lady tucked the book back in her red satchel. "The book is ten dollars extra."

"Wait." This was like waving a cinnamon bun, fresh out of the oven, under Julia's nose and then taking it away. "Would you accept forty in cash and a ten dollar gift card to Consignment Couture?" The shop Julia owned.

A slow smile spread across the old woman's face. "Your wish is granted."

"What's that you're reading?" Paula asked Julia two days later, pausing while dusting a display of rhinestone-studded heels at Consignment Couture. "Another love advice book?"

"Yep." Julia leaned on the counter and flipped a page. The work day was coming to a close and those letters the Love Lady promised hadn't materialized (not so much as an L, much less an O or V or E).

"What does this one recommend?" Paula was sixty-five, and dressed like she came from the Mad Men secretarial pool. Julia could make a fortune selling Paula's wardrobe. Today's vintage ensemble was a white dress with large red roses, scoop-necked and belted. "Are you to do yoga? Dancing lessons? Teeth whitening?"

Julia flipped to the beginning. "Lesson #1: Greet every man with a continental kiss. Coming and going."

"Smoochy air kisses?" Paula flitted over to a display of specialty bras that hadn't seen a customer since prom season ended, and spaced the hangars evenly to showcase each colorful, satin cup.

Julia nodded. "Lesson #2: Put your house in order by hiring Jacks of all trades." She'd already called in an electrician and a plumber. The electrician was married and disqualified from her list. The plumber's butt crack made it impossible to put him on her list. But there you have it. She'd kissed two more frogs. "Lesson #3—"

"Hello." A tall man filled the doorway. His maroon T-shirt said he was from Green Gardening, which she'd called for a bid on landscaping in front of the shop and in back. His eyes gave away he was shy and single. Those sky blue orbs shied away from a display of revealing prom dresses, bounced off the rack of bullet bras, and landed gratefully on Julia.

She'd meant to laugh when their eyes met, but the laughter died in her throat. His eyes were a soft blue, his hair a soft brown, his left hand ringless. And it didn't look as if butt-cracks would be an issue.

The eggs sighed.

"Lesson #1," Paula sing-songed as she joined Julia behind the counter.

"Of course. Where are my manners?" Was that a French accent coming out of her mouth? Julia tiptoe ran to the man in her man-meeting high heels and air kissed his woodsy smelling cheeks. "I'm Julia."

"Hank." He stared at her as if she'd tried to sell him parachute pants from the retro rack. "I've seen your front—"

"*Indeed,*" Paula intoned in a raised brow kind of voice.

"—Can you show me your back?"

"I love a man who doesn't waste time," three-times divorced Paula murmured. "My current husband proposed to me the night we met."

The eggs applauded in admiration.

"We'd like to hold fashion shows out here." With a don't-scare-him-away scowl toward Paula, Julia led Hank to the back sun-baked terrace. The small garden behind the shop was an overgrown jungle. There was a flagstone patio (fighting cracks of their own), a fountain with a frog centerpiece (and frogs living in the sludgy water), vines crawling around the fountain, and hip-high weeds in what had once been flower beds. "Let's start with the fountain. I hate the frog. His tongue is out and he's about to eat a dragonfly." Belatedly, Julia realized the logo for Green Gardening on his chest was a leaping frog.

As if on cue, a frog surfaced in the murky green water and croaked.

"Had this place long?" Hank touched a vine trailer blowing in the weak breeze, and then snapped off the tops of several blades of wild grass.

"I bought Consignment Couture a few months ago." Back when she'd thought she had all the time in the world for her happily-ever-after. "I've been making changes inside and haven't had a chance to work outside."

"The weeds are taunting you." His voice. It filled the overgrown space and made it seem not so much a lost cause.

"It's not personal," Julia said.

A frog croaked his disagreement. Hank raised an eyebrow. Even the eggs were quiet.

Julia's gaze drifted to the fountain. "They aren't taunting. They've just had time to sprawl." While Julia focused on making her social life not non-existent.

He brushed his hand through the tops of the high grass. Something moved at his feet and slithered onto the flagstone.

"Snake!" Julia did a modified version of the potty dance, backward and in heels.

Hank hunkered down by the slithering thing, picked it up and brought its face too close to his. "Common garden snake. Eats mice. And frogs." He put the snake back in the grass.

"Wait, wait, wait!" Julia rushed up to him, clinging to a nicely muscled bicep. "Aren't you going to take it away?"

"You haven't hired me." Hank named an astronomical figure the electrician would've blushed at.

"That's highway robbery." That would eat into her in vitro budget.

Julia wasn't totally naïve. No one was going to fall in love with her and agree to father her baby in the next three months. She'd settle for strong liking and a sperm donation without any strings.

"Snakes. Vines. Frogs." Hank shrugged. "Untrippable patios. Special lighting."

Julia countered with a figure a thousand dollars less.

Hank dropped his jaw nearly to his chest and stared at her over the top of his mirrored sunglasses. "This job requires two pairs of hands for five days. I've got a pair." He paused, staring at her in the same assessing way he'd done the snake. "The only way you're getting a discount is if you provide the extra pair of hands."

"My hands? In that snake infested patch?" Oh, no. Oh, no-no-no.

Hopeless, the eggs murmured.

"Yes, your hands," Hank said. "Yes, in your snake infested weed patch."

Julia hated snakes. She hated frogs. She hated weeding.

But there was the potential income from fashion shows, and the fact that he was bartering. She thrust out her hand. "Deal."

He was eyebrows-to-heaven surprised. It took him a moment to name a start date. She double-air kissed him, and then those dark brows inched higher toward the fringe of brown hair on his forehead.

After he left, Paula shook her head. "You don't strike me as the weeding type."

She wasn't. "Lesson #3: Accept all offers involving bartering."

"That'll make you very busy."

"That's the idea."

CHAPTER TWO

She'd kissed him.

In theory.

Four times.

Meant nothing.

But still…She'd kissed him.

It'd been a long, long, exponentially long time since a woman had kissed Hank, especially a beauty with long blonde hair and bright blue eyes.

Hank Green had to get out and date more. Although he had too many problems to think about dating.

There were weeds for one, at too many clients' homes. And a tree that needed trimming over at the courthouse. And lawns. Lots and lots of lawns. But he always made time in his growing gardening business to speak with potential clients.

Potential clients weren't usually as pretty as Julia. She had all her teeth, which was more than Mr. Dartmouth could say. And she had eye-catching curves, which was more than Miss Olive could say. And she had spunk, which was more than the glazed-eyed public servants at city hall could say.

And she'd kissed him.

He'd had a tooth filled before he stopped at Consignment Couture. Half his face was numb, so he'd tried not to talk too much and drool all over himself. He'd probably come across as a half-wit, especially when she'd dismissed the beautiful fountain for having a frog's tongue. In his experience, frogs were good luck for business. Hank was going to make sure she fell in love with that frog before the project was over.

He pulled into the driveway of Brody Falls Daycare.

"Daddy! Daddy!" Kimmy ran to Hank as soon as he entered. She wrapped her arms around his legs and squeezed, angling her pixie features up to him. "What's for dinner? Did you run out of gas today? My shoes make farting noises."

"Kim." Miss Clark's severe tone cut through his four-year old's excited ramble. "Your outside voice is for outside."

"She always says that," Kimmy whispered, grabbing Hank's hand in her smaller one and tugging him to the door.

The late summer afternoon heat hit them like dragon's breath, hot and muggy.

Kimmy skipped next to him. "I bit my tongue at lunch today. Gideon said if I stick my head underwater, I could hear goldfish talk." Kimmy's little hands fanned out from her ears like moving fish gills. "It would be cool to go underwater and talk to sharks, even with my sore tongue." Kimmy lowered her hands and her voice. "Don't eat me, Mr. Shark, or I'll bop you in the nose." She giggled.

And so it went, non-stop (Kimmy would make a good comedienne if she could learn to pause for the *ba-da-bum*). All the way home. All the way through dinner. All the way through PJs and brushing teeth. Kimmy was the most exhausting part of Hank's day. And the most satisfying. She'd talk like a runaway train. And then once those teeth were brushed and she was tucked into bed, it was time for a story. She hardly ever made it to page two before falling asleep.

And then, while he was reading her Where the Wild Things Are and feeling like life couldn't get any better, Kimmy asked, "When is Mommy coming home?"

"Are you kidding me?" Hank pushed a wheelbarrow through the side gate of Consignment Couture the following Monday to find his extra pair of hands totally ill-equipped to help him.

Julia sat in a white plastic chair, her head thrown back to catch the sun's rays, leaving her long blonde hair flowing behind her. She wore gray plaid shorts and a black tank top that clung to every curve and slope of her body. When she saw him, she leapt up and hurried over, all those golden locks swinging halfway down her back and her blue eyes shining with welcome. Clients didn't greet him with half the enthusiasm she did.

Kiss. Kiss.

The air over his cheeks felt warm. The blood in his veins ran hot.

"You can't work dressed like that." Like she was going to meet a date in the park. Instead of shaving money off his bid, she'd be adding to it.

"These are my weeding clothes." She glanced down at herself, presumably at her mouthwatering hint of cleavage, shorts that showed off her tan, shapely calves, and the cheerful, flowery Vans on her small feet.

Hank spun away, stalking back to his truck. It didn't take him long to return.

"What's this?" She stared at the items he'd thrust into her hands—a Green Gardening T-shirt and a pair of work gloves.

"You wear them or I'm raising your rates and hiring some real help." He would anyway if she so much as complained about breaking a nail.

"What's the big deal?"

Besides her being too beautiful to get dirty? "You need protection. If you get sunburned out here, you're no good to me. If the thorns on those vines pierce that delicate skin of yours, you're no good to me." If he kissed her—really kissed her—she'd be no good to him.

"You think I have delicate skin?" She beamed and tugged on the maroon T-shirt. It fell like a boxy mini-dress to her thighs. Or a sleep shirt if they'd had a sleep-over.

Dangerous thought, that. Hank grabbed a two-cup colander and a narrow cage with small mesh wires from the wheelbarrow. "We'll start by draining the fountain. The water will help loosen up the dry soil back here."

She followed him to the opposite side of the terrace. "What's the cage for?"

"The frogs. I'll take them to the park later and let them go."

"Why not just let them hop to someone else's yard?"

He got to his knees behind the fountain and loosened the plug. Almost immediately, water gurgled out nearly as loud as Kimmy's draining bathtub. "I have no problem with the snake eating them, but I thought that would upset you."

A frog leapt onto the rim of the fountain and then into the grass, taking charge of its own fate.

"The park sounds lovely." Julia sat on the lip of the fountain and covered her nose. "Pew. I'll be glad when this doesn't smell like wet garbage. Can we change the frog on top? He doesn't look very regal."

Hank stood firm. "Frogs are a symbol of abundance." People didn't normally look him in the eye during his work day.

But she did. With eyes as soft as a bouquet of blue hydrangeas. "You chose a frog for your logo."

"I grew up on a farm." He handed her the colander. "We had a pond which attracted all kinds of creatures."

Another frog hopped up next to her. She yelped and got to her feet with a shiver and a shake that robbed him of speech.

Not the frog. He blinked, croaked, and leapt deep into the grass.

"Don't get eaten," she called after it.

Common sense was telling him to back out of the project while he still could. She wasn't going to pull her weight. And he would have left if she hadn't kissed him. "Look, I need you to scoop out the frogs and put them in the cage while I bring in the rest of the equipment." The water was going down rapidly, swirling over the drain with a continuous suck and gurgle.

"I thought I'd be weeding."

He fought the urge to roll his eyes. "If you don't want to take orders, I have five different guys I know are looking for work. Just scoop. If you catch anything, dump it in the cage." He wasn't a total brute. He opened the cage door for her.

She looked pale, but began half-heartedly sweeping the colander through the mucky water.

Trusting her to catch any remaining frogs, Hank brought in the rest of the equipment from his truck. "Catch anything?"

"No. There were a lot of jumpers with death wishes." She sounded relieved. "The water's drained out and there's nothing but piles of mud and algae." She tucked a strand of golden hair behind an ear. "Wait. There. It's a baby frog."

She was looking, not scooping. With a weary sigh he had no right heaving at 8:30 in the morning, Hank came to stand beside her, leaning over to place his hands on the rim of the fountain. The frog was barely bigger than a quarter.

A small flat face shot out of the drain, mouth open, fangs bared, ready to eat a froggy snack.

"Snake!" Julia screamed. She dropped the colander and leapt back and then leapt onto Hank's back for a piggy-back ride. "Snake-snake-snake!"

The snake in question—the two-foot long garden snake he'd met last week—didn't have enough spare length to catch the leaping froglet. The snake twisted and tensed as it tried to free itself from the drain. The little frog leapt about in the corner. Safe. For now.

Hank straightened. Julia's legs were still wrapped around his waist and she was babbling unintelligibly. Every other word seemed to be snake.

The snake in question was nearly free.

"If you want me to save that frog, you need to put your feet on the ground."

Her long legs dropped to the ground (pity, really). And then she did a snake-inspired salsa dance next to him, similar to the one she'd done the day they'd met. "Hurry. Save the little guy. Hurry."

A swipe of the colander and the frog was rescued.

Although the frog was safe, Julia didn't stop dancing. "Ew. Do something about the snake."

"I can either put the frog in the cage or the snake. Not both."

She stopped dancing, eyes worshipfully-wide. "I have a vase. But only for the frog." She ran inside and re-appeared almost instantly, dumping a dried flower arrangement on her chair and holding out a standard, clear glass eighteen-inch vase. "Here."

Hank scooped the frog into his hand and deposited him in the vase. "Give him some water and put him out of the sun."

"Right." Julia stared at the frog.

"Looks like you have a pet."

"I'm not keeping him." Her gaze dropped to the snake swishing through the puddles at the bottom of the fountain. She retreated a few steps.

"Put the frog inside in the shade and I'll get rid of the snake." If this was any indication of the production pace they'd achieve together, Hank was in trouble. Once more, he considered backing out of the deal.

"You'll take him all the way to the park?" She turned those sweet blue eyes toward him again. "Promise?"

His feet remained firmly planted, not backing anywhere. "Promise."

"My hero." She kissed him.

On both cheeks.

CHAPTER THREE

Julia was hot and it wasn't because there was a hottie capturing a snake in her fountain.

She'd jumped him. Granted, it was from fear, not overwhelming desire. But she wouldn't be surprised if he thought she was a nut job.

The eggs sighed heavily, as if she was a lost cause.

"I'm not going to mess this up," she told them, holding the vase at eye-level. "You're my good luck charm, Kermit." And just like that, her frog had a name. She put a small amount of water in the vase and set it on the kitchenette counter. And then because she wasn't an amphibian person (or a snake person), she put a strainer over the top of the vase. "To keep you safe." And from hopping out into the shop and scaring the customers.

After getting herself some water, Julia went back outside to find Hank had returned from the park. "Kermit's an orphan, abandoned by his family."

"Circle of life." Hank was as basic as they come. Farm boy. Comfortable with critters. Broad shoulders. Strong back.

She hadn't broken him when she'd panicked. "I'm sorry about earlier. Hopping on you and all." All being the embarrassing panicky part.

The snake and cage were nowhere to be seen. The park was two blocks away and had a nice little stream with lots of tasty frogs. Kermit would not be one of them.

"We're weeding now." He was all business, pretending she hadn't invaded his personal space. "I'll loosen up the roots with a shovel. You pull them out and toss them into the wheelbarrow."

"Right." She wasn't going to disappoint him again. After all, Lesson #4: Find things to do together where you can talk. And Lesson #5: Compliment him on his skills. "You handle slimy things really well."

He shot her a look that told her he suspected she might be a little slimy herself.

"I mean, you're an expert at what you do. I can see that." Better. Definitely better.

The eggs sighed, lost-cause like.

I am not messing this up.

The eggs' silence was damning enough.

He began creating a shoveled line through the weeds, and then paused to look at her. "Ready, princess?"

"I'm not a princess." Her head came up. "I'm a city girl." She'd never pulled a weed in her life. "I grew up in a high rise apartment in San Francisco. I'm a hard worker when I know what I'm doing."

He went back to loosening the soil. "Princess… City Girl. Either way, the weeds are awaiting an audience."

Julia stomped over to the corner where he'd started working, grabbed a handful of grass, and gave it a big tug. Given the now-swampy soil, the weeds offered no resistance. She tumbled back on her butt, the muddy grass landed on her legs. "I'm okay…I'm okay…." If she said it often enough, she'd forget how much her butt hurt. "I'm…I suck at this."

Agreed, the eggs said.

A shadow loomed above her. Hank. A smile—*his first*—and a warmth in his eyes she'd never seen before. A hand extended toward her. "You'll get the hang of it."

If he had've made fun, she might have ran back inside. As it was, she returned his big smile, took his hand and came to her feet smoothly.

"I guess I learn by failing." She grinned up at him. This little red book had powers.

He grinned back. "You're running out of ways to fail."

She hoped that was true about a lot of things—not just gardening, but love. Or really, really strong like.

In no time, Julia's flowery shoes (so cute!) were covered in muck. Her legs were splattered with mud and her hair was a straggly blanket about her sweaty (not glowing) face. But she wouldn't give up. There was that smile of his. And so she wrestled with the vines Hank was cutting back, trying to get them into the wheelbarrow. Those thorny ropes just loved to snag on Hank's borrowed shirt and Julia's freshly-shaven legs.

"I'm here to spend my gift card." The Love Lady poked her head out the door, a red scarf fluttering at her neck. "I see the book is working."

Hank turned to toss another six-foot, thorny trailer at Julia's feet. "You look familiar."

"I've seen you at the farmer's market." The old lady smiled kindly. Her apple red lipstick didn't seep into the wrinkles at her mouth or stain her teeth. Talk about aging gracefully.

Paula appeared from behind her, très chic in a purple sheath and gray shrug. "Has Hank talked to you? At your table, Miss Uh…"

"Never." The Love Lady didn't provide a name. "I've seen him with a little blonde at the apple cart."

What? The eggs shrieked. *What about that smile?*

Julia's gaze made a hard right. Hank stood without an iota of guilt at being outed as having a girlfriend.

"My gift card won't buy anything in the shop," the Love Lady said. "Nothing, but Kermit." She held up the vase.

"But…" Julia forgot about eggs and blondes and potentially lost lovers or sperm daddies. "How did you know what his name was?" She hadn't told Paula.

"Kermit told me." The Love Lady turned to go, calling over her shoulder. "Don't forget Lesson #10."

Lesson #10? What was Lesson #10?

Ah, yes. Lesson #10: Don't be honest about what you want in the first seven days. Chances are he'll give you what you need for a lifetime if he's the one.

Lie? To Hank? Her gut rebelled. Her head, however, had an agenda no amount of gut-clenching could put off. "A blonde, huh?"

He surveyed the vine and admitted, "My daughter," the same way one might admit they had a haircut appointment at four.

What? If eggs could faint, hers did.

A child meant a mother. Ring or no ring. "So… you're married?" Had she kept butt-crack's telephone number?

"Divorced. I have custody." Matter-of-fact. Farm boy straightforward.

What? The eggs sat up.

"Oh, that's—" *Wonderful.* "—too bad."

"She…uh…. My ex was an addict." He hacked at the vine. "And a thief. She's in prison." His efforts increased in intensity. "But the thing she excelled at—the one thing they didn't convict her of—was lying."

Lesson #10….

If she lied to him, she'd be no better than his ex-wife.

"I know where I've seen that woman in red before." Hank turned to Julia, comprehension in his eyes, which was better than ridicule, if truth be told. "She sits at the Love Advice table."

"Yes."

"You paid for her advice."

Lesson #10….

"Yes."

He looked dubious. "Was it worth it?"

"Yes." It'd brought him to her. In a day, she'd come to like his straight-from-the-hip personality. It didn't hurt that he had broad shoulders and a killer smile.

His dubious gaze turned distant. "So you're looking for someone?"

"I'm thirty." The statement shouldn't make her want to squirm. If she held to the book's advice to the letter she wouldn't admit any more. A man should understand the importance of thirty to a woman. "I…uh…"

Shut up, said the eggs.

"I want children and my eggs…. Because cancer runs in my family, I've been advised the best chance for me to avoid the Big C is to…." Follow in the footsteps of Angelina Jolie.

"Oh."

A smart woman would stop the bleeding there.

Be smart, be smart, be smart, chanted the eggs.

"I'm going to harvest my eggs. I plan to fertilize the ones without the cancer mutation and carry at least one baby to term before I have to lose all my original equipment." She gestured from breasts to hip. "Men probably won't want a shell of a woman."

"Oh." Not: *Oh, I'm your man. Let me carry you off on a white steed and save you from being barren in a snake-filled garden.*

"Hey, Julia. I need a signature." Rick, the FedEx man, was standing in the doorway if his voice was any indication.

Julia didn't look. She only had eyes for Hank, who looked as if he'd eaten a bite of sour lemon cake. Or as if he thought the Love Lady sold mumbo-jumbo or love potion perfume. That look and his daughter stopped her from saying: *I was hoping to fall in love with a man who wanted a family immediately, just like me.*

Hank was just another frog.

Julia felt hollow as she trotted up the steps and greeted Rick with air kisses (because he was single, even if he was the town Casanova), signed for the package, and then put it on the chair.

When she turned around, Hank was busy cutting back the vines.

CHAPTER FOUR

Julia claimed to be looking for love, but it seemed she just wanted a sperm donor.

Hank wasn't on the market. Not for love. Not for any more progeny.

Love was messy. And unreliable. And heartbreaking.

Not only was Hank too busy to date, he also had a rule about Kimmy. He didn't want to begin seeing a woman and have her disappear from Kimmy's life if things didn't work out. When Nicole fell into addiction and robbed the credit union she worked for, his life had fallen apart. He hadn't seen the signs. But he had seen the fall out.

Julia greeted him to the job the next day in blue jeans and an Elvis T-shirt, looking more garden-worker-ish than princess-ish. He respected that. And her smile. It was golden, that smile. It said: *Forget being a hermit and take a chance.*

Hank had used up all his chances with Nicole.

"What's on the agenda today, boss?" Julia asked with forced enthusiasm. They hadn't talked much yesterday after her revelation that she was looking for a man and a family on a timetable with a fast-ticking clock.

Hank was here to do a job. Julia's personal issues could not come into the picture. "We need to pull up the flagstone and prep for concrete."

Julia stared at the flagstone patio. "These stones look heavy."

"They are." As heavy as his heart. Julia's impetuous idea would probably never come to fruition. She'd never know the joys of being a parent to a child of her genes. But he couldn't help her. "If you want to have a fashion show back here you can't risk your models twisting their ankle on uneven stones."

"I suppose that's logical." When everything about her dreams weren't. "Flagstone in the wheelbarrow?"

He nodded, handing her a screwdriver. "Use it as a pry bar."

She bent and got to work.

That was it? She wasn't going to bring up the topic of sperm donor or love interest? She wasn't going to look at him with a grin that invited him to focus on his needs for once instead of Kimmy's?

Glory hallelujah!

"I wonder how Kermit is doing with the Love Lady." There was a sad note in her voice.

Hank sat back on his heels. "If you wanted to keep the frog, why didn't you say so?"

"I've never had a frog before." She shrugged. "I wouldn't know how to take care of it."

"You've never had a baby before, but that hasn't stopped you from wanting one." He regretted the hurtful words as soon as he spoke them.

Julia's wistful expression and sad tone didn't change. "My sister had two children before she developed cancer and learned she had the mutated gene. Her boys aren't carriers." She glanced at him with eyes brimming with sadness and hope. "She's not alone at night, although she's divorced."

"It's exhausting being a single parent." And lonely, even if you weren't alone.

"I know." Julia's gaze dropped to her gloves. She plucked at one finger. "But...I used to play house when I was a girl. I always carried around a baby. I've always imagined being married and having a houseful of rambunctious, loud kids."

He should stop the conversation now. He didn't. "Did you also imagine a husband?"

"Not always." Her smile was tinged with regret, the way people smiled when they realized they'd lost dreams. "What about you? Guys don't seem to dream of much but being a sports star."

That was the problem with asking people questions. You opened yourself up to questioning right back. "I wanted the family and the picket fence. The whole nine yards." He'd thought Nicole was his soulmate.

"What happened?"

"We got married young. And my wife never grew up." Hank hesitated, the sense of loss and failure bitter in his throat. "She went from recreational marijuana to smoking meth. That drug stole the soul of our marriage. That drug compelled her to steal from the credit union she worked for. She's not getting out of prison for a long, long time."

"She cheated on you." Julia touched his cheek.

When had she moved so close? "That was the drugs, too."

She withdrew her hand. "I went to the Love Advice table because I wanted the love of a child. I'm willing to settle for less with a man in order to have that."

Hank wasn't the right man to be having this conversation with her. He had all he could handle with the business and Kimmy. And yet, something in his chest kept spewing forth words, words that made it appear he was open to a relationship with Julia. "Have you ever thought instead of considering it settling for less, you should consider dreaming of more? Of love without children of your own blood?"

"That's enough about my dreams." She swallowed and looked away. "What do you dream of, Hank?"

"I have to put my daughter first. I no longer dream."

Julia soaked in her bathtub after a long day in the garden with Hank. She was on the verge of giving up. On daddies and sugar daddies and sperm daddies.

Hank didn't dream. He didn't risk. He was living only to make his daughter's life a good one.

The same thing she'd do if she couldn't find love and had a child on her own. She'd put her child and Consignment Couture above having a personal life. It was what she wanted, even if it wasn't what her mother wished for her.

Hank made it seem so grim. Didn't his daughter fulfill him? Wasn't she enough to fill his heart with love? Is that the way Julia would be if she had a child alone?

The eggs were oddly silent.

On the final morning of work at Consignment Couture, Hank drank coffee and stared at his tiny condominium patio. It was filled with pots growing tomatoes and flowers. Someday, he'd like to have his own nursery in addition to his gardening business. He hadn't slept well last night. His heart had ached that Julia might never carry a child of her own. She might never even realize that adoption or fostering would bring her the same joy.

He liked working with Julia. She had what his grandmother used to call gumption. But with money as tight as it was it was best not to dream big.

His cell phone rang. It was Miss Clark.

"There's been an outbreak of chicken pox at the center." Her carefully modulated tones would be good over a P.A. system in time of crisis, because she sounded as if she had no heart, no deep love for the lives in her care. Nothing to lose. No loves. No dreams. "Since it's Friday, we thought it best to close for a long weekend. We're sanitizing the school. I'm sorry it's such late notice."

And Hank had no backup plan, except to bring Kimmy to work with him. A four-year-old in a garden. A four-year-old who was still so very full of dreams. How bad could it be?

"No school. No school." Kimmy clomped into Julia's garden wearing her yellow rubber ducky boots, a pair of jean shorts, and a pink Minion T-shirt. She carried a pail with a toy shovel, rake, and trowel. "We'll have ice cream for lunch and cupcakes for dinner."

"That sounds heavenly," Julia said. She wore blue jeans, work boots, and a floppy sun hat. She'd come a long way from Monday. But she didn't come to kiss Hank's cheek.

A pang of longing struck. He'd miss those kisses.

"Come meet my immortal frog." Sitting at the fountain, Julia held out one hand to Kimmy and the pointed at the frog statue behind her with the other. "His name is Kermit."

Kimmy's boots planted roots in the new curving sidewalk. She spoke not a word.

Julia glanced up at the fountain frog catching a dragonfly. "Don't be put off by his tongue sticking out. I've come to like Kermit." She looked back over her shoulder, smiling weakly at Hank. "Even if he isn't green."

Kimmy glanced up at Hank and whispered, "She looks like Mommy."

Julia heard. She'd been reaching up to pat the stone Kermit when she froze.

"Just her hair," Hank said. Nothing about Julia was the same as Nicole. Nothing. Julia was honest and kind and sober. "It's not her." He gave Julia an apologetic glance. "Kimmy was only two when Nicole went away."

"She's coming back." Kimmy regained some of her chutzpah. "And when she does we're going to go to Disneyland and the circus and the moon." She crossed her little arms over her chest, daring anyone to contradict her.

"That sounds fabulous," Julia said with an undisguised note of sadness.

"Do you have a little girl?" Kimmy came closer, still deciding if Julia was to be taken in her chatty inner circle, one not open to Miss Clark.

"No." The light faded from Julia's eyes. "I don't. I don't think I ever will."

"Do you have a dog?" Kimmy sidled closer.

"No." A defeated word. Spoken by a woman who'd given up on dreams.

Hank's chest felt tight.

Kimmy stopped. "No pets?"

"I had a frog." Julia glanced up at the frog on the fountain. "But he found a better home."

Was Hank the reason she'd given up on having a child? Had she decided a woman who gave up her birthing equipment was any less a woman? What could he do? What could he say?

Nothing.

The farmer's market would be opening in a few minutes. Maybe the Love Advice lady would have an answer.

"Can I leave you two ladies alone? I need to get something…somewhere…." At Julia's nod, Hank hurried toward The Local Grinder and the Love Advice table.

The old lady saw him coming. She was wearing a red gauzy blouse and matching scarf. There was a small terrarium sitting on her table. It had plants and rocks tucked around a low bowl filled with water. And of course, Kermit. "I was wondering when you'd arrive. Sit, sit."

He sat carefully in her folding chair. "I don't have much time. I need to know why Julia came to see you."

"Why she came is no concern of yours." Her voice was as high-pitched as the small bell charms on her bracelet. "Why are *you* here?"

"I'm here…um….I'm here to…"

Bob Millar, one of Hank's corporate clients, walked by, staring at Hank with open curiosity.

"I don't have time to date. I'm here for Julia's frog." So she wouldn't be alone.

Her brows rose. "Kermit is mine. I've given him a good home."

"You should have seen her this morning. She's given up." When the old lady didn't respond, he leaned forward and said urgently, "She needs someone."

"A frog isn't someone." Her voice gentled. "Do *you* have someone?"

He sat back in the chair. "I have my daughter."

"Now there's a girl who could use another someone in her life."

She was wrong. So very, very wrong. Love was risky. For both his heart and Kimmy's. "I'm not here for me. I'm here for Julia. She needs her frog."

"She has a frog in the fountain." The old woman's plump finger tapped the leaping frog on his shirt. "You understand about frogs. They're happy creatures. And happy creatures bring—"

"Prosperity." Yes, he knew.

"No." Her smile was patient. "They bring more happiness. With their song. With their loyalty. With their tremendous ability to support one's difficult decisions." Her gaze pierced, delving deep down where he hid things like hurt and loneliness. "You haven't made any hard choices for a long time. You've been in limbo."

"Yes." Because providing a stable environment for Kimmy was the most important thing in his life.

"Sometimes, frogs find the perfect place. And they stay for years. Like Julia's fountain."

Hank's glance strayed to the terrarium.

"Kermit has found a forever home with me." She tapped the frog on his shirt again. The one over his heart. "Your frog needs to find a forever home."

Don't say it. Don't say it.

"With Julia." She touched the top of his forehead, and then slid her fingers down to close his eyes. "A wise frog can close his eyes and see the life he wants. A wise frog is brave enough to sing long and loud about what he wants." Her voice dropped to a whisper. "What do you see?"

With his eyes closed? Was she crazy?

Except…. In his mind's eye he saw Julia. Holding Kimmy's hand. Smiling.

He saw Julia's face as he leaned in to kiss her.

He felt Julia's hand in his as they drank coffee in the morning and looked out on the terrace behind her shop at stone Kermit on top of her fountain.

He opened his eyes, mind filled with questions he couldn't voice. The most important being: *Could he risk Kimmy bonding with another woman when he didn't know for sure if Julia would stay?*

"You know the answer," the old woman said. "That will be forty dollars."

CHAPTER FIVE

"Do you have a sister?" Kimmy sat on the edge of the fountain, kicking her rubber ducky booted feet out.

"Yes." Julia's chest felt hollow and at the same time full. Kimmy was a joy. Hank was jaded when it came to love, but he had to be happy with his daughter.

"You are so lucky." Kimmy pounded her fist on her leg. "Madison has a little sister. She's a baby, but someday when she grows up, they'll play Barbies together and have light saber fights and build Lego castles and play princess."

We could be like her, the eggs said. *Don't give up.*

"You can do all that with your dad." Your wonderful, wonderful dad.

"I'll tell you a secret." Kimmy leaned in closer. "Daddy is sad a lot because we don't have Mommy anymore. Or a little sister. You could be the next best thing."

"Which would be…"

"A big sister!" Kimmy clapped her hands.

The eggs huffed.

"Hey." Hank appeared at the gate, looking like he'd just received some very bad news.

"Hey," Julia and Kimmy said.

Paula's face appeared in the window of the back door. She smiled encouragingly.

Julia sighed. "I'm waiting for marching orders to get started." May as well keep this business-like. One more day, and then Hank would be out of her life. Her heart would be broken, and a hard lesson would be learned: Always listen to your mother, not the Love Advice lady.

"Can we talk first?" Hank tried to smile, but oh, that smile looked like the break-up face.

How could he have the break-up face? They weren't even an item.

Retreat! Retreat! Cried the eggs.

Paula opened the back door, apparently having decided she couldn't eavesdrop as easily with it closed.

"Kimmy said you brought plants. Why don't I dig some holes?" Julia grabbed a shovel, positioned it in the middle of a flower bed, and jumped on the flat ends. The blade sank into the loose, composted soil easily. That's what Julia needed—something easy in her life.

"Daddy likes to play 'what if' with the plants before he digs," Kimmy said. "Sometimes he plays 'what if' for hours and hours."

"Julia." His palm came to rest on her shoulder. He took her shovel with his other hand. "I didn't like it the other day when you kissed the FedEx man."

The eggs shimmied with hope.

Julia wasn't as easily fooled. "Those were just harmless air kisses."

"I didn't like it when you kissed Mr. Jamison from the bank when he collected your deposit." Hank's voice was bankerly-serious. His gaze as unreadable as a loan officer's.

"Air kisses." Her hands fluttered in the wind. "You have to kiss a lot of frogs, you know."

"Sounds like you kissed a ton." Kimmy came to stand in the dirt at her feet. "I got into trouble kissing boys at school. You should stop."

"I didn't like it this morning when you didn't kiss me." He moved his hand from her shoulder to her cheek.

Gasps filled the patio. Julia's. Kimmy's. Paula's.

"I couldn't sleep last night because of the thought you might not be able to have the child you dreamed for...." Hank's voice fell out of banker territory and into uncharted territory. "I thought I might help… somehow."

Julia couldn't move. What did he mean?

Everything, the eggs whispered.

Hank locked his gaze on Julia. "But today I realized that I couldn't imagine you raising that child without me. And Kimmy." Hank smiled down on his daughter.

Oh, my. The eggs fainted.

"A little brother or sister?" Kimmy began doing a hoe-down in the flower bed, stomping feet and clapping hands. "This is my lucky, lucky day! The stork is coming. Wait until I tell Madison."

If he was offering to fertilize her eggs and then be a part time daddy, Julia wasn't interested. Somehow, over the course of the week, she'd fallen in love with him. Part-time Hank just wouldn't do.

Feeling a bit surreal, Julia covered his hand with hers. "You're a great guy, but I don't want you to feel obligated to participate."

Good thing the eggs were still passed out cold. They wouldn't approve of the out Julia was giving Hank.

"This isn't a business negotiation." He shook his head. "I'm willing to be your frog. The last frog you ever have to kiss to find your happily ever after."

"What are you saying?" Julia didn't dare hope or breathe or wake the eggs.

"I went to see your Fairy Godmother." He grinned. "I'm saying stop air kissing every man who walks in the door in the hopes he'll be your Prince Charming." He set the shovel aside and took both her hands in his. "I'm saying I'm your prince and your frog and the future father of our children, as many as you want as long as your life isn't put at risk."

"But…but…I haven't even gotten to Lesson #18."

"Throw away the book, girl," Paula chimed in.

"No books today. No school." Kimmy twirled around the fountain. "Just frogs and babies."

"I have no idea what book she means," Hank said. "But if you feel that we could have something together, it's time to take a leap of faith."

"I've kissed enough frogs," Julia murmured, allowing him to draw her into his arms and kiss her.

Copyright © 2015 by Melinda Curtis.

Petronella Glover is a multi-genre author whose work has been translated into a dozen languages, including the Catalonian Romance language, where she has won two awards for Best Translated Story. A little quirky, very geeky, and unabashedly romantic, she hopes to one day visit the City of Love, find a bustling café where she can sample their hot chocolate and write her first New York Times *Bestseller.* This is her sixth appearance in the magazine, and you can find out more about her at www.petronellaglover.com.

QUEBEC ROMEO VICTOR

by Petronella Glover

Please Note: This beautiful love story written by Petronella Glover appeared in issue four only a few short months ago. Speaking with Petronella, I found out that the story had been printed with one of the characters mis-gendered. Namid is a female name in indigenous First Nation Canadian culture, not male, but the magazine had not yet published same-sex romances (which is a change we are making from this issue forward) so she sold the version of the story to the magazine where the couple were heterosexual. The sexual orientation of the characters were never discussed in the original, so the tweak was minor. But as our dear romance fans know, love takes many different forms, so I've asked Petronella if we could have permission to reprint her story with the correct genders in place. The story is clever and beautiful in its original form. It goes to show that a love story is a love story, no matter the gender of the characters.

—Tina Smith, Editor

"RAoISS, NAiSS, this is KiTTI. Anyone out there?"

Ugh. Even I could hear the slight desperation in my tone. *Class it up, Kitty.*

I opened up a block of Lindt Dark Noir Coconut Chocolate, popping an oversized piece in my mouth, and grabbed the handheld microphone attached to my Yaesu FT-2900R amateur radio. Using the keypad on the microphone, I changed the frequency from 145.825MHz to 144.49MHz. While the former signal was used by the handheld Ericcson radio in the Columbus module of the International Space Station, the astronauts were more likely to switch one of their other radios to the latter uplink frequency at this stage in their orbit; they had just started their pass over the Americas, which that signal covered.

I've been trying for a few months to reconnect with Namid Carpenter—once my school chum, now a celebrated Canadian astronaut—during several of the sixteen passes the ISS makes over America each day. Towards the latter half of her 126 day stint on the Space Station I had found out she had taken particular interest in using the amateur radios in the various modules *outside* of the Station's regular appointments with student groups. That alone had sparked the idea to renew our acquaintance in the most unexpected, and even sentimental, way. We used to communicate with each other via HAM radios when we had first gone to our separate ways to different colleges, following graduation. Then Life interrupted, and, well…we have not talked in nearly a dozen years.

Up until around a couple of months ago I had sometimes heard a ghost of a reply from the International Space Station. I had even thought I'd heard Namid's voice once: "NA1S—*Crackle*—ere. November Alpha One Sie—*Crackle*—eaking." But, by the time I responded, either someone else was using the bandwidth to talk to the astronaut, drowning out my weaker connection, or it appeared the ISS had moved beyond the range my circularly polarized crossed-Yagi antenna could handle.

I grabbed another piece of chocolate and shoved it in my mouth, grimacing at the cramp searing across my lower belly. I knew my emotions were more heightened because of my period, but, following the recent media frenzy over the hushed up incident on the ISS two months ago, and whispers of assassination attempts on the astronauts from Expedition 63 whom had since returned back to Earth, I've grown genuinely concerned for Namid's safety. After literal radio silence from the International Space Station for the better part of two months, it was a relief to read on various ammeter radio forums that people were starting to hear chatter on the Station's regular frequencies again.

I was determined to find out if my former best friend was well.

While I hadn't seen the then-girl, now-woman, in the last twelve or so years, my memories of our friendship were warm ones. She once asked me to be her date at the Homecoming prom, in defiance of the outdated expectation that a girl wait until a boy asked her to attend. Up until then I had been a delightfully geeky but awkwardly tall and gangly girl whom only the thoughtful boys had wanted date, except they were too shy to ask. I would hunch over in an attempt to appear more petite, but all it did was make me appear round-shouldered and even more awkward.

Namid had told me to stand tall and embrace the elegance of my lithe build: "The boys are idiots if they cannot appreciate your inherent beauty."

At the time I thought her words were motivated by kindness, not from any true belief that I was beautiful. That's what friends are for; to offer home truths for the most part, but also white lies when opinion becomes biased because of friendship. But she didn't ditch me when she had become more popular in school and I was still trying to work through my intense shyness. Upon discovering my love of writing science fiction, she had even encouraged me to join the science fiction club and school newspaper by joining alongside me. She never cared that increased the probability of being considered uncool. She had always been more forward thinking, long before our classmates had considered that brains and personality were more important than their appearance and what they were *seen* to be doing.

I heard some static interruptions in the background buzz of my current frequency band, a sign that someone was online, just outside of my antenna range. I repeated my call to the International Space Station, in the hopes that one of the astronauts could connect me to Namid, even if she wasn't the first responder. While I could have simply emailed her, or looked up whether she was on Facebook, I couldn't shake the urge to renew our connection in a way deserving of the unique and special friendship we had once shared.

I pulled up AMSAT's online Satellite Pass Predictions website, and input my longitude, latitude and elevation details, and saw that the ISS was indeed passing over my neck of the woods. But even that wasn't a surety of contact. Even knowing the astronaut's waking hours were between 7:30-19:30 UTC, that they were more likely to tune in during the hour-or-so down time they have before and after work, and then mapping when those times coincide with them passing within *my* horizon-to-horizon antenna range, there was still only a ten minute window to be heard.

"—llo. This is NA1SS. QRZ?"

My heart thumped in my chest. They were asking who was calling them. Were they talking to me?

Answer, stupid. You have no time to be tongue-tied.

"K1TTI calling. Kilo One Tango Tango India."

I held my breath.

"Receiving you K1TTI. *Zdravstvujte*, Earthling. Where are you from?"

Oh god—they *were* talking to me!

Or at least *he* was talking to me. The voice was male.

"QHT Bellefontaine, Ohio."

"QRN. Can you—*Crackle*—peat answer?"

"Noise interference here, too." I told him, before repeating my location: "Bellefontaine, Ohio."

"Ohio. The *serdze*…eh, the heart of the—" His connection broke, but I knew what he was trying to say. Ohio was known as heart of the United States, because of its position in relation to the rest of the country.

I grinned. I was talking to an astronaut!

"How are you tonight?" I asked, then realized how lame that was. I only had ten minutes, tops, to communicate with them, and I might as well have asked how the weather was. Not that they actually experienced weather up there....

The astronaut took a moment before replying. "It has been a…interesting day, thank you."

This time I noticed the pause was not due to noise interference. Nor did it appear to be due to a language barrier. Interesting, indeed.

"Your name?" I asked him.

"Alexander Shvartsman. Yours?"

Ah, that confirmed it. Russian, second time on the ISS. "My name is Kitty."

"Oh—*Crackle*—nd's like your call sign."

My grin turned into a smile. "Yes. Very similar. It's a nickname I got while I was still in Mississauga at—"

I was interrupted.

"Kitty-Kat! Is that you?"

I was stunned silent. I would recognize that voice anywhere.

"Kitty?" the female astronaut repeated.

I found my tongue. "Yes," I replied simply, my heart in my throat.

"Oh, how small Space is! Sasha, this is my best frien—*Crackle*—om school. We used to write science fict—*Crackle*—tories together, and dream of visiting other stars."

"I still do. Write, that is." *And reach for the stars.*

"Oh, you are an author?"

I nodded, then realized she couldn't see that. "Yes."

"I *knew* that you—*Crackle*—even back then!"

She knew what? That I had promise? Was insane? Both were likely true.

I flexed my hand around the microphone, not surprised to discover my grip was sweaty.

"When did you move—*Crackle*—e U.S.?" she asked.

I paused, taking my time to piece together what she was trying to say. "Oh, two years ago. I needed a roommate after the second book in my series didn't sell as many copies. So I utilized my dual citizenship status and moved in with Jae."

"Sorry. QSB. Who?"

Crap. Fading signal. She was losing my connection.

"Jae. Juliet Alpha Echo."

"Ahhhh, your friend fro—*Crackle*—iversity?"

"Yes." The sound of another earthbound radio with a stronger signal chimed in, causing interference on our connection. I had to be quick, concise. "QRM."

"Your signal is being interfered wi—*Crackle*—here, too. QSY?"

I shook my head, eyebrows furrowing. "I don't think changing the frequency will help. We're about to lose our ten minute window."

"QRX on 144.49MHz tomorrow at—"

I sucked in my breath, waiting for her to supply a time, hoping that she was still in range, but she never finished that sentence.

"Seventy-three," I said finally, closing off our call with the traditional message of kind regards, bouncing between elation at having been able to talk to Namid in Space, of all places, and sadness at having lost the signal before we had a chance to really reconnect.

But she wanted to talk to me again, tomorrow, on the same frequency. That much I was able to glean before the signal cut out. And the advantages of working from home meant I could just leave the radio on while I worked. If she came in range, and reached out, I would be here to answer.

I saved my manuscript file, checked my Yaesu FT-2900R radio was on, for about the fiftieth time, and picked up the microphone, repeating my call to the International Space Station.

No answer, for the third day in a row. What if she didn't try contacting me back, because I had not heard when she had wanted to call me the other day, and missed it.

I put the microphone back on the receiver and walked over to the bay window, looking out at the night sky, imagining the International Space Station passing overhead.

It was still surreal that I had been able to talk to Namid while she orbited above Earth, but in hindsight I never even reacted in surprise when I had first found out she had been accepted for the astronaut program, four years ago. She had always been destined for the stars, her name literally meaning "star dancing" in Ojibwe, the language of the Anishinaabe people.

It had been a comfort, over the years, to imagine her dancing out there, among the stars. She had always shone so brightly in my world.

"K1TTI, this is NA1SS, Namid speaking. QRV?"

I turned to look at the radio, stunned. *Yes, of course I am ready!*

"Kitty-Kat?"

Oh, idiot. It helps to grab the microphone before answering. I rushed back to my desk and did just that.

"K1TTI receiving. Sorry about that."

"FB?"

I laughed while the signal was open, to make sure she could hear. "No, I was not doing any 'funny business'." One day someone was going to get confused by our deliberate misconstruing of the 'fine business' call sign if we inadvertently used it with other HAM radio operators. "I was just in my own little world, literally."

Now it was Namid's turn to laugh. "Touché."

"How is it in your very own Space, today?"

"Great! I worked on our latest vegetable crop experiment, answered some fan mail on my break in the *Cupola* observatory module, so I could spend some time gazing at Earth, then it was finally my turn to be abl—*Crackle*—o go into the *Destiny* module, to—"

The sound of someone clearing their throat, deliberately, cut Namid off. Presumably it was the Russian—what was his name again? That's right: Alexander. Or rather, Sasha, for short.

There was silence for such a long moment that I despaired the connection had broken for good.

"Sorry about that. Security Procedures," Namid eventually replied. "I'm still so distracted by being able to talk to you, again, and in this manner. But, no matter how nostalgic I am feeling, I shou—*Crackle*—not forget that we're not in university anymore, telling each other all our dirty little secrets."

"Ah," I replied, remembering that module was the primary operating facility for U.S. Research in a sterile pressurized environment. "Got you, loud and clear."

She decided to take me literally. "The connection *is* a lot better toda—*Crackle*—n't it?"

I nodded, loving the warmth in her voice. "I've missed you," I added, quietly.

Pause. "QSB. QRO?"

"Nope, no need to increase power. My voice was fading, not the connection."

"What did you say?"

"Doesn't matter," I replied, again shy.

I heard whispering in the background, Sasha to Namid: *Ya Skuchau po tebe.*

"Oh, Kat—I have missed you, too!" she replied, suddenly, with such enthusiasm I felt a blush spreading from my cheeks down into my chest.

I grabbed my discarded chocolate bar, and broke a new piece off, shoving it in my mouth. I don't know why I was feeling so bashful. It was natural to miss a friend I had not seen for a dozen years.

"How are your parents?" I asked her, by way of distraction, as I chewed on the chocolate.

There was no reply. Shit.

"Repeat?" she asked finally, and I let go of the breath I didn't realize I was holding.

I wondered if my signal was fading, for real this time. "QSB?"

"No. QRN."

"Ah." There wasn't much I could do about atmospheric noise, unless we changed frequencies. We didn't have enough time for that, so I asked her again how her parents were doing.

"Oh, they are still trying to match me u—*Crackle*—ny guy that's of our people. They've just given up on him being specifically Anishinaabe. Apparently, as long as he's a full-blooded member of *any* of the First Nation races, that's good enough for them."

I snorted. Some things never changed. "I remember your brother was more enlightened. In fact,"—I thought back to conversations we had when I had flown in to visit her on college break— "when I saw you last, didn't Animkii say that at the rate you were rejecting men, you would soon run out of them, and one day the only person you could tolerate dating was me."

There was a long pause. And this time I think it was Namid not knowing what to say, rather than the ISS passing over the horizon and out of my range.

Then, finally: "Would you like to be there when I take the Soyez bac—*Crackle*—to Ea—*Crackle*—ext week?"

"Be on the Space Station?" I asked, the interference confusing me. "Alas, I do not have the clearance for off-world visits."

She laughed, as I had expected her to, but then clarified her statement for me: "I mean, would you want to be waiting nearby, for the landing party…as my, ah…person there? When I come back to Earth."

My first reaction was shock. She wanted *me* there? Me, and not a family member?

My second reaction—slower coming, but no less intense—was: *Hell yes!*

I didn't know how to put my happiness into words; I didn't want to presume. I finally muttered something mildly appropriate, only to hear a smattering of Russian in response.

"Okay. That's settled then…. But now I have to go. Sasha says tha—*Crackle*—meone from Houston is trying to contact us."

I was a mixture of elation and disappointment—our conversation was ending too soon!—but I told her my email address, so she could pass it on to The Powers That Be to organize my flights and transport to the landing site.

I was jotting down my own reminders when I registered her goodbye sign off: "Eight-eight, Kitty-Kat. NA1SS clear."

For a second I brushed off her goodbye statement as heightened emotions due to finding each other again. But eighty-eight was traditionally used as a much more intimate sign off than seventy-three—both numbers part of the 92 code system adopted by the Western Union in 1859. While the latter number essentially meant "kind regards" and was used much more often on the radio waves, eighty-eight was used by couples to mean "love and kisses".

However, I didn't so much care how *other* HAM radio operators used the numbers….

What did Namid mean by her sign off?

I bit my lip, and then smiled, reaching for another piece of chocolate. Time to dust off my passport; I had a trip to plan.

Thinking of Ekaterina kept me preoccupied during the tedious three hour wait until the clamps released the Soyuz, and the springs in the docking mechanism pushed the Russian capsule away from the International Space Station. After the first three minutes the Soyuz performed a 0.5m/s burn to increase the separation distance, then maneuvered to nominal flight attitude.

Throughout it all I was performing my assigned checks, but couldn't keep my mind off the woman who was waiting for me at Karaganda, near the designated landing site in Baikonur, Kazakhstan.

Nine minutes later, the Soyuz performed a retrograde burn to ensure it was outside of the ISS's sphere, and started its last full orbit before the Descent Timeline software was initiated.

"Excited?" Sasha asked me in Russian, nudging my arm with his padded elbow.

"Of course. It is always a bit of an adrenaline rush returning home, especially the last part of the journey."

"No," he drawled. "I wasn't meaning *that*…. I was talking about your Russian Kitty."

I laughed. "Technically she holds a dual U.S./Canadian citizenship."

"But her name is Russian," he pointed out.

"Yes. One set of grandparents did indeed come from your Mother Country."

He said something about Russian women having more fire—*ogon*, as he called it—and I couldn't disagree. While Kat had been painfully shy when I had known her in school, she had always felt things with a deep passion, and was fiercely loyal as a friend.

It remained to be seen if that *ogon* translated into….

I shook my head. No. It wouldn't do me any good to make assumptions that could bite me in the ass later on.

I tried to focus only on the tasks at hand, and two hours, twenty-seven minutes, and a handful of seconds after undocking, the deorbit burn started, changing the capsule's trajectory in preparation for atmospheric entry. While I was aware the Soyuz separated into three distinct parts, twenty-or-so minutes after the burn was completed, my thoughts were already on the ground. I was performing my responsibilities like a well-trained robot, but Sacha had to prod me to regain my attention.

"Earth to Namid," he teased, using a popular Western term. "Not long now."

I turned to him, smiling, then grimaced when the Deorbit Module slammed into the atmospheric boundary four minutes later, the drag on the capsule slowing it down as it endured extreme heating over the next six minutes.

Focusing my attention on a graph depicting the velocity/g-load, I watched as Sacha used the PYC Descent Control Stick to tweak the descent, making sure the module was performing within prerequisite parameters. Then the parachutes began to deploy, the heat shield was jettisoned, and I let myself loosen up, giving myself permission to get excited.

The last fifteen minutes passed by me, quite literally, in a blur. A thruster fired downward to decrease our velocity in the instant before impact, and just like that I was Earthbound again with a resounding thud.

While part of me couldn't help but feel sad Expedition 64 was now officially completed, this time Kat was going to greet me once I was medically cleared. It was a giddying thought, despite the unfamiliar tug of gravity weighing me down.

The capsule was opened minutes after landing, an overly bright light shining into our confined space. Then NASA support personal and Russian recovery crews gently pulled me, and then Sacha, out to hand

us over to the medical staff, the sensation of being weighed down draining our energy fast.

Carried over to nearby recliners to be medically debriefed, we reassured everyone we felt no headaches, unusual chest pains, or any kind of constrictions in our limbs. But, despite exercising a minimum of two hours a day on the ISS, our muscles had started atrophying in the absence of gravity, especially after being in Space for stints of six months or more.

I grimaced when I realized how ungainly I would appear when seeing Kat again, and the flight surgeon asked if I was in any pain.

I laughed, telling him I was fine—"I'm just ready to see my loved ones."—and after the obligatory waves and comments to people viewing the live NASA stream, we were picked up to be taken over to the helicopter.

Keeping my eyes closed—I hated being manhandled by strangers—I opened them when we reached our transport to see a swarm of security surrounding us, checking the underbelly of the helicopter. Shocked, I glanced over at Sasha, who nodded grimly. Both of us remembered being briefed on the assassination attempts on Elanora, Babirye and Raine—astronauts from Expedition 63 whom had returned to Earth on the last Soyuz trip.

We also knew the importance of keeping the secret housed within the ISS *Destiny* Module exactly that: a secret. It was why I had organized a certain level of security clearance for Kat; so she could be protected under the NASA umbrella as family. I was so shocked and delighted to talk to her on the HAM radio, and in our many emails since, that I didn't recognize at first that public association with me could also put her in danger, too, if the unscrupulous used her to get to me.

And, I suppose keeping her safe was a good excuse to keep her close…

I was lowered directly in front of the helicopter, and reached up to clasp the hand hanging down from the cockpit to pull me up into it.

Our grasp secure, the hand squeezed mine with a warmth Kat's had used to have when—

Shocked, I looked up, my eyes widening.

She was stunning. Waist length blonde hair cascaded over her shoulders as she leant down, her body still lithe, but now supporting the curves of a mature woman.

Kat looked down at me, her eyes dancing and her smile warm, and squeezed my hand again. "You always knew how to dress to impress," she said, finally.

Confused, I looked down to see my flight garments in various stages of undress, and grinned. "I thought you were going to be waiting in Karaganda!"

"I wanted to surprise you, and it turns out for security reasons it was better to have me tag along." She shrugged. "Something about concentrating their security measures."

I opened my mouth to respond, only to be interrupted by a polite cough and the inescapable sound of someone clearing their throat.

I turned around to see Sasha supported between two men, grinning shamelessly. "Well, I'm feeling a little under the weather"—he coughed again in an overly exaggerated manner—"and believe I should take the medical personal with me in the *second* helicopter."

Then he winked, completely destroying the effect.

Kat laughed. "*Spasibo.*"

He grinned, unrepentant. "You are welcome, Russian Kitty."

Kat returned her gaze back to me, the twinkle in her eye softening. "QRV?"

My heart melted at her use of radio code. "I definitely am ready." *In more ways than one.*

She pulled me into the cockpit, another medical assistant helping me into my seat.

I turned to thank the staff for their assistance, instructing them to close the door, and then focused my attention on Kat.

She leant forward to help strap me in. "I just learnt this less than an hour ago, but I'm hopeless at these things."

Her hair smelt wonderful (oh god, how I was looking forward to taking my hair out of my braid and wash it in flowing water) and I couldn't help but reach forward to touch that golden waterfall.

She stilled, her breath catching.

Did that mean she was reacting to my touch? Or reacting *badly* to my touch, and was not sure how to tell me?

What if I screwed everything up, and lost our newly rediscovered friendship, too?

I waited for a long moment before sliding my hand up to cup her face, tipping it up until she looked at me.

"*Ya Skuchau po tebe.*" She said finally.

I smiled, loving the way she reverted to Russian when she was more emotional. "And I have been missing you, for far too many years," I replied.

She studied me for a long time, as if internally grappling with something. Just when it reached the point where I was about to panic, her head darted forward and I felt her lips fall on mine.

I gasped in surprise, and the kiss deepened, alternatingly tender and passionate.

I tugged her closer, until she moved to sit beside me, her arm brushing my breast unintentionally; I moaned into her mouth.

The kiss deepened, my lips opening to the onslaught of her tongue—*ogon* indeed—and she slid her hand up my neck to slide her slender fingers into the braid at the back of my head.

There was a polite knock on the cockpit door, before it opened.

We pulled apart, laughing in happiness.

"Well, your brother was right, after all," my Kitty-Kat teased, as she scooted closer to me on the seat and strapped herself in.

I reached for her hand, lacing my fingers with hers as the pilot hopped into his seat and started the rotors. "Yes, you are right. I think we're in for one hell of a ride."

Copyright © 2017, 2018 by Petronella Glover.

Meghan Ewald was born and raised in northern California. She now makes her home in Texas with her husband, their two children and one very happy rescue dog. Meghan writes fiction in the wee hours of the morning before going to her full time job playing with NASA space suits. She loves good coffee, reading, working out and writing. When not writing fiction, Meghan blogs over at http://gettingthewordswrong.com/. She loves to hear from readers. You can reach her at gettingthewordswrong@gmail.com.

IN SEARCH OF A PEACEFUL LIFE

by Meghan Ewald

Samuel Moss fled back to the Siskiyou mountains in a remote region of northern California after The Great War, not feeling like the sharp-shooting war hero the medals on his chest proclaimed him to be. But his return did bring life back to his father, Daniel.

When Samuel saw his father for the first time, he shot a questioning look at Charles, his older brother. Charles's own smile was tight and there were lines around his mouth and eyes that hadn't been there when Samuel had left for the war. His father's smile looked the same on the right, but the left was slack and frozen, and his once-strong legs looked like two sticks covered by the thick brown blanket over his lap.

Daniel hugged Samuel around the neck with his good right arm, Samuel bending awkwardly over the wheel chair.

"It's good to have you back, boy," Daniel said. His ruined mouth slurred the words. Samuel breathed in his father's wood and flannel scent and shut his eyes against the burn of tears.

After a supper of thin stew, and Daniel was seen to his bed, Charles and Samuel settled into the twin rocking chairs on the front porch, each with his own mug of coffee. They talked of this and that. The sun set and crickets chirped in the dark before the conversation circled back around to what was really on Samuel's mind.

He sipped his coffee. "How long has he been this way?"

Charles sighed. "Since the last stroke. I guess it's been three years now." Charles looked into his cup and swirled his coffee.

"Your letter said he had a stroke. You didn't say how bad it was." Samuel gripped his mug to keep the anger from his voice.

Charles sighed, and said, "What was I supposed to tell you, Sam? You were off trying not to get shot. Did you want to hear the worst of it? When I had to feed him? When I had to put him in a diaper and clean him like a baby? You had your fight. I had mine."

"You should have told me."

Charles nodded slowly. "Maybe I should have. You couldn't have done nothin', but maybe I should have. But you're here now. And I'm glad to have another hand bringing in money." Charles shot him a look from the corner of his eye, and a slow smile curled his lips. "I ran into Patwin Super yesterday. You remember his daughter Elizabeth, don't you?"

Samuel grunted noncommittally.

"She asked about you."

"She's probably married with a couple of kids now."

"Nope." Samuel heard the grin in Charles' voice. "She's been waiting for you to come home, Sam."

"It'll never work, and you know it. Karuk's don't like their girls marrying white boys. We're trouble, remember?"

"Patwin always liked you."

"He always liked Dad. They've been friends for years."

Charles pushed himself out of the rocking chair and poured the rest of his coffee over the porch railing. "Well, just so you know, she asked after you. I'm going to go check on Dad and go to bed."

Samuel rocked and listened to the familiar night sounds of home. He thought of Elizabeth until the moon rose high overhead.

Though Samuel left the War, the War did not leave him. He drank too much, got into too many fights. One night, deep in the heat of July, he fought the wrong person.

Josie Butler, a local girl working as a singer in a smoky bar, had tried to put off the advances of Henry Douglas. The son of a wealthy rancher, Abel

Douglas, Henry had been a mean kid when they were growing up, always pushing around smaller children. Samuel had been one of those smaller children. Not much had changed—Henry was just bigger now.

He watched Josie push Henry's groping hand away as she swayed between tables, saw the Deputy Sherriff's badge flash as Henry laughed. Anger pulsed in Samuel's temples. He'd despised men like Henry in the war. They hurt people, sometimes got them killed when their true cowardice was exposed.

Swallowing the rest of his whiskey, he pushed away from the table. He tapped Henry on the shoulder.

"We have something to talk about. Outside."

"I ain't got shit to say to you," Henry said, and turned back to his uniformed companions.

"Well, I have something to say to you," Samuel said. He grabbed Henry's collar and hauled him out back.

A broken nose convinced Henry to leave for the night. After closing, Josie expressed her gratitude in the bedroom upstairs.

Ten days later, Samuel set his pitchfork against the barn door and armed sweat off his forehead. The sound of booted feet thumped across the beamed floor and he looked up. Samuel's greeting died on his lips. He recognized the grim set of the rancher's face. Samuel straightened to his full height, steeling himself.

"Afternoon, sir," Samuel said.

"Samuel." The gray haired rancher nodded in greeting. He made a show of inspecting his barn. "You've done good work here, son."

"Thank you, sir." Samuel heard the 'but' coming.

"Yes, a good job," the rancher repeated. Samuel waited as his employer looked around. Finally, it came. "Listen, son, I'm going to have to let you go."

Samuel thought, *there's the first boot. Three jobs in ten days.* Samuel forced himself to exhale slowly.

"Sir, might I ask why?" Samuel kept his voice carefully modulated. He knew why. He wanted to see if this man would say it aloud. The other two would not.

The rancher stuck his hands in his pockets and scuffed his boots. "Times are hard, son." He did not look Samuel in the eye when he said it.

"Right," Samuel said. He spat tobacco juice onto the neat floor. "Times are hard."

The rancher flushed. "Listen here, you ought to keep clear of the Douglas's. They'll make nothing but trouble for you."

There's the second. Samuel did not argue. The first two firings had shown him arguing changed nothing. It only prolonged the moment. Instead, he collected his meager earnings, converted them to whiskey and poured them down his throat back at the bar.

"My brother could help," Josie said. She pulled a battered chair up to his table and sat down. The bar was quiet, only a few die-hards nursing drinks in the corner. A gramophone played ragtime softly from a small table near the stage.

Samuel narrowed his eyes. "Help what?"

Josie rolled her eyes. "You got fired again today, right?" Samuel felt his eyebrows climb. He opened his mouth to say something, protest maybe, but she cut him off. "Everyone knows the Douglas's have it in for you ever since you whipped Henry Douglas. You're not going to keep a job around here if they can stop it."

Samuel wanted to argue, tell her everything was fine. But the lie wouldn't come. He knew how much influence the Douglas family had. He tipped his tumbler to his lips and relished the burn of the whiskey.

"How can your brother help?"

Josie lowered her voice. "My brother dabbles in a small scale…operation."

Samuel heard the pause and frowned. "What do you mean 'operation'?"

Josie leaned over the table giving Samuel a healthy view of cleavage. She smelled of cigarettes and perfume. She whispered into his ear. "Rum."

Samuel sat up straight and looked over his shoulder. The bartender polished glasses and watched them from behind the bar. Josie grabbed his hand and said, "Smile now, and look at me like I just said I was going to make your night."

Samuel forced a smile and leaned in, attempting to ignore the bartender's eyes watching him. He tried to let go of Josie's hand, but she held tight. "Rum running is illegal."

"What's worse? The law or starving?"

Samuel sat back, pulling his hand out of hers, and considered his options. As he saw it, he didn't have any. "How small an operation?"

Josie pulled her chair around the table and sat next to him. She leaned on his shoulder and whispered more into his ear. He breathed in the scent of her. Not entirely unpleasant, he decided. *We must look like two lovers.*

The bartender went back to minding his own business.

When she'd told him all he needed to know, Samuel shrugged.

"A man has to eat," he said, and knocked back the remaining inch of alcohol.

The jail door rattled shut. *So much for Rum bringing good fortune,* Samuel thought bitterly.

He lay back on the hard bed and put his arm over his eyes. His stomach rumbled, but he ignored it. A sneering deputy would either be along with a tray of slop or they wouldn't. Unshed tears burned his eyes and he pressed his arm down harder. What right did he have to be hungry when he was worrying his father into an early grave? He thought back to a simpler time, and Elizabeth's brown eyes flashed in his mind. He pushed the thought away. He'd never have that either—not the way he was going now. After a while he slid into a restless sleep.

Samuel awoke to the sound of voices.

"You're wasting your money, Patwin. That one there's trouble."

"He's just going through a rough patch."

Samuel knew that deep rumble. Samuel got up from the bed and walked to the bars. Patwin Super stood at the front desk down the hallway, his wallet open, handing a fold of bills to the deputy.

Samuel's heart lurched. Elizabeth stood behind him, hands folded meekly in front of her blue dress, her brown eyes downcast. Samuel had to look twice. Meekness looked odd on her.

"He's been in here three times in the last ten days. That ain't a rough patch. That's a pattern," the deputy said as he counted the bail money.

Behind her father, only Samuel saw the angry look that flashed across Elizabeth's face. He suppressed a grin. Apparently she'd only learned to feign meekness.

"Maybe," Patwin said. "Or maybe he just needs another option."

The skinny deputy shrugged and put the money into a drawer. "Your money," he said. "Follow me."

The deputy led Patwin and Elizabeth down the short hallway to Samuel's jail cell. Samuel stood back as the deputy pulled out a jangle of keys and unlocked the door. "I'll leave you to it," the deputy said and went back to his desk.

"Patwin," Samuel said. He had to look away from Patwin, and his eyes shifted to Elizabeth's face behind Patwin's shoulder. The worry in her dark eyes, so like her father's, made his stomach roil and his cheeks hot. He wasn't sure which he wanted more: her to stay so he could look at her or for her to leave so she wouldn't see him this way.

"Hello, Samuel."

Samuel shifted his feet beneath Patwin's dark gaze. The silence stretched out until Samuel could no longer stand it.

"Patwin, I—"

Patwin held up his hand, cutting Samuel's words off. "I know what you're going to say, Samuel. I don't want to hear how sorry you are or how it won't happen again."

"Papa, that's not fair," Elizabeth said. "He didn't mean to—"

Patwin rounded on her, a bear angry with his cub. "He didn't mean to what? Get caught? Worry his father into an early grave?"

Samuel gave a start to hear an echo of his own thoughts.

Patwin's angry gaze silenced Elizabeth. She looked down at her feet, two spots of color high on her cheeks.

Samuel swallowed the lump that had formed in his throat. If he hadn't been such a screw up Elizabeth wouldn't have had to stand up for him.

"Sir," he pleaded, no longer feeling in good enough esteem to call him Patwin, not after his multiple mistakes. "I appreciate your help, but I can't accept it."

"I didn't do it for you," Patwin said, and the anger went out of him like air from a balloon. "I did it for your father. He's been a good friend to me, Samuel. If it weren't for him my lumber business would never have survived. The white folks in this county didn't

want to compete with a Karuk. If not for your father's support on the city council, I wouldn't have the life I do now. He deserves better than what you're doing to him, Samuel."

Samuel opened his mouth to say his father didn't know what he was up to, but Patwin rode over him.

"He might not know exactly what you're doing, but sitting in that wheel chair doesn't mean his mind doesn't work. You've been fired from too many jobs, and you're out most nights. Every few days you don't come home. He knows you're mixed up with the Fosters and it's killing him."

Samuel grimaced. "What else can I do? No one will hire me. Not since the fight with Henry Douglas. I have to bring money in. We have to eat."

Patwin pinched the bridge of his nose and shut his eyes. "There's another way, Samuel."

Samuel narrowed his eyes. "How?"

"Come work for me. I need someone to run lumber from the reservation into town. It's not a lot of money, but it's honest work and it'll keep you out of here." He gestured around to the jail cell.

For a moment, Samuel's tongue forgot how to work. He swallowed hard and said, "You would do that for me?"

"No." Patwin shook one thick finger in Samuel's face. "I'd do that for your father. And you better not make me sorry I did."

A small flame of hope burned in Samuel's chest. "Yes, sir."

"I need you to start right away." Patwin's next words sealed the deal in Samuel's mind. "Take Elizabeth with you," he said. "She'll show you what to do."

Elizabeth flashed a grin at Samuel. The small flame in Samuel's chest blazed into a forest fire.

Samuel and Elizabeth's truck bumped along the mountain road, a rocky outcrop of mountain on their right, and the slope of the mountainside on the left. The September sun shone through the windshield of Patwin's old pick up heating the cabin to a pleasant temperature. Samuel rolled his window down and hung his elbow out the side. Elizabeth toyed with the end of her thick braid, wisps of her dark hair breaking free and floating gently around her head in the breeze. Samuel scrambled for something to say.

"Nice of your dad," he said, looking at her sideways then quickly back to the road. "Giving me a job, I mean."

"He'd do anything for your father," Elizabeth said. She fiddled with the end of her braid, not looking at him.

"Still," Samuel said. "Nice. He didn't have to—"

"Sam, why did you leave?" Elizabeth broke in, twisting around in her seat to look at him. "You weren't drafted. You could have stayed. But you left me. *Why?*"

Samuel caught his breath in alarm to see tears standing in her eyes. "Elizabeth, I—"

But Elizabeth wasn't finished.

"I waited for you. And when you came home, you went with that woman from the bar. These runs, I was so excited to get to be with you. But the closer we got to the truck, the more I questioned myself. Why would I want to be with you when you left me?"

"I had to know," Samuel said. He gripped the steering wheel until his knuckles were white. "I wanted to see the world. I had to know what was outside this place. But the world isn't what I thought." Anger made his voice tight. "*War* wasn't what I thought. I thought I was going to fire a gun, get to march around. Instead I saw the worst of people. I saw looters picking through pockets of dead soldiers, my friends. When the looters were gone, I saw rats crawling over their faces." Samuel took a breath to say more but stopped himself when he saw Elizabeth's wide eyes.

"I'm sorry," he said. His heart pounded too fast. "I shouldn't have told you that." Samuel wrestled his anger back down. It felt huge inside him and his body thrummed like a live wire. His throat burned for a drink.

The back of Samuel's hand grew warm and he turned to Elizabeth, eyebrows raised in a question. Elizabeth blushed and gave him a shy smile, but she did not remove her hand from the top of his. His anger dissolved, and Samuel smiled. The movement was unfamiliar, as though the muscles had forgotten the sequence of movements needed. Samuel curled his hand into hers.

"I won't leave you again," he said.

"Good."

A cloud of dust rose from the road up ahead and Samuel slowed for the oncoming car. He saw too late up ahead a Sheriff's car pulled parallel across the road. Samuel's breath caught and he slammed on the brakes, but he was too late to stop. The truck fishtailed and Samuel gripped the wheel fighting for control, but the truck tires rolled over the edge of the slope.

Elizabeth screamed as the truck careened down the hill at a breakneck speed, brush and brambles scraped the underside of the truck. Grimacing, Samuel gripped the wheel and pumped the brakes to slow their descent. The truck slowed some, but the hill was too steep. Samuel's stomach flipped as the truck rolled over once before fetching up hard against a thick pine tree.

When the dust settled, Elizabeth slumped over in her seat, her long dark hair half tugged loose from her braid by the impact of the fall.

"Elizabeth," he said, and gasped in pain. It was hard to breathe. Why was it so hard to breathe? He gingerly patted his sides. He hissed when his prodding found the hurt ribs on his left side. Broken or bruised, he couldn't tell.

Elizabeth did not respond.

"Elizabeth!"

Nothing. Her chest rose and fell, so she was alive, but how badly injured he could not tell.

Samuel turned the handle on the driver's side door. At first it wouldn't open. The door caved near the foot well. He threw his shoulder into the door, and cried out in pain from his hurt ribs, but the door squealed open.

Samuel limped around to the other side of the truck. Something under the hood of the truck poured out steam that made him cough. Samuel pressed his right hand into his left side. It seemed to ease the pain a bit. He needed a doctor, they both did, but he had to get Elizabeth out first.

On the other side of the truck he saw Elizabeth's face through the pane of dirty glass. Her eyes were closed, blood trickled down the side of her face.

"Elizabeth," Samuel pounded a fist on the glass, "Elizabeth, wake up!" Samuel tugged at the door, but it was stuck, another dent caving in her side of the truck.

Elizabeth did not move, and her eyes did not open. Samuel wrenched mightily the door open, pain from his ribs making sweat pop out all over his body from the effort. Minding his injuries as best

he could, Samuel got one arm around Elizabeth and hauled her out of the truck. She was alive and breathing, but badly hurt. He had to get them both to a doctor.

He looked up. Silhouetted against the blue sky, the deputy looked down from the rim.

"Help us," Samuel called. "Please! She's hurt!"

"Good," the deputy said, and Samuel forgot how to breathe. He would know Henry Douglas's voice anywhere.

The silhouette man sat back against the hood of his Sherriff's car. The shift in light confirmed Samuel's fear. Henry folded his arms across his chest. He smiled. "I hope she dies."

"You hope...*what?*" Samuel shook his head trying to get the words straight. They didn't make sense. "You have to help us. Elizabeth, she's hurt. Please. She needs a doctor." Samuel knew he was explaining what was plain to see, but Henry didn't move off his perch on the car.

"You know, I hoped I'd find you two up here. When you were bailed out, I did some checking, found out who posted bail. Cash isn't easy to track, but it's a small town, and I have my ways." He shrugged. "I was hoping to just catch you, but your filthy Indian woman is a nice bonus."

The meaning of Henry's words sunk in. "You *meant* to do this?" Samuel's breath sawed in and out of his lungs. "You ran us off the road on purpose? Why would you do that?"

Henry lunged away from the car and leaned over the edge, glaring down at Samuel. "No one makes *me*," he stabbed one finger at his chest, "look stupid. No one acts like they're better than me. You should've left me alone in the bar that night, Hero."

"In the bar," Samuel said, mostly to himself. He remembered the fight, but it was shrouded by the haze of too much alcohol. "You ran us off the road because of a bar fight? Elizabeth is hurt. She might be," he had to swallow a lump in his throat before he could go on, "she might be dying."

Henry shrugged and sat back against the car again. "One more Indian dead. No great loss. Long as I get to see you go, too. In fact," Henry tipped his head to one side in thought before unholstering his sidearm, "I might help you along with that."

Henry raised the gun and years of training and war experience took over. Samuel shoved Elizabeth behind the shelter of the truck and rolled away to the right just as the gun cracked. Something sounding like a bee buzzed past his ear.

Samuel lay panting behind a thick bush. The sharp smell of juniper cleared his head a little. He had to get that gun away from Henry.

"Come out, Hero," Henry said, his voice echoing down the side of the mountain. "Or do I need to start taking shots at your whore?"

Samuel's gaze shifted to Elizabeth, lying on her back in the dirt beside the ruined truck. Fury doubled Samuel's vision and for a moment there were two Elizabeths.

"Not her," Samuel said, forcing himself to take deep breaths. "You should have left her alone."

Samuel heard laughter and looked up through a hole in the juniper.

"You talkin' to yourself, Hero?"

Samuel ignored the taunt.

"I'm just gonna wait right here until she dies, Hero. Then I'll radio it in." Henry laughed. "It's a damn shame, isn't it? The War Hero and his filthy Karuk girlfriend die tragically on mountain road. And was the Hero drinking?" Henry pulled a flask from his hip pocket, tipped it up to his lips to drain it and tossed the empty flask down the hillside. It clattered to a stop beside the driver's side of the truck. "I bet you he was."

Samuel only heard one important word from Henry's little speech. *Radio.* If he could get to the car at the top of that slope he could use the radio to get help.

Staying behind the hillside's thick brush cover Samuel propelled him up the slope, digging in the toes of his boots. His ribs hurt like hellfire, and the rocky ground tore his palms and knees, but he had no time to think of it.

"You get out here, you coward," Henry said. "You get out here and face me like a man. Or I put holes in your girlfriend."

Keep him talking, Samuel thought. *Have to keep him talking.*

"Why didn't you join up when the war started, Henry?" Samuel cupped a hand over his mouth to redirect the sound toward where he'd been. "You missed all the fun. Or maybe you were too scared."

Henry gave a small choked cry and Samuel heard the gun crack again. A puff of dirt kicked up from the first bush he'd hidden behind. Henry didn't know he'd moved.

Samuel crept from bush to bush, keeping low. "You know, we talked about guys like you. When we were sitting in the trenches at night, waiting for the Germans to maybe shoot us, maybe blow us up. We talked about the cowards who stayed behind, leaving us to do the hard work. Cowards like you, Henry."

Henry fired two more shots into the brush, closer now to where Samuel crouched and Samuel knew Henry was projecting his path through the bushes.

Samuel's shoulders sagged. He'd run out of brushline. He only had another fifteen feet or so to the road, and to the radio, but it was all uncovered ground. He'd be an open target.

Samuel glanced back toward Elizabeth. He could just see the top of her head from this angle, her bedraggled braid dragged on the ground. Guilt racked his body and he hunched over his hurt ribs. He gritted his teeth against the pain. He had to get her out of this.

Samuel took a deep breath and bolted up the rest of the slope, running full out, ignoring the tearing pain in his side. Henry gave a cry of surprise and fired wild, ill-aimed shots.

The echoes off the side of the mountain made Samuel's ears ring. He reached the edge and lunged for Henry, tackling him to the ground, wrestling the gun out of his hand.

Henry punched Samuel in his ribs and agony exploded in his side. He cried out, but didn't let go of the gun. The deputy reached up, wrapped his hands around Samuel's throat and squeezed. Before the blackness could take him, he brought the butt of the gun down hard on Henry's head.

Henry's hands fell away and Samuel sat back, panting. His ribs radiated pain, making him dizzy. He crawled to the driver's side of the Sheriff's car, pulled open the door and reached inside. He pulled the radio to his lips, depressed the button and spoke into it.

"Accident. Deputy Douglas's car up on Three Mile Lane. Send medical help."

The radio crackled and a voice asked him to confirm, but the pain was too much and blackness took him.

Samuel awoke on a familiar hard cot. Before even opening his eyes the wet concrete smell and the nearby rattle of closing bars told him where he was. His body hurt in more places than it didn't. Samuel opened his eyes and sat up not at all surprised to find himself in a jail cell. He wasn't wearing a shirt, and someone had bandaged his ribs while he slept. He probed the tight dressing gently.

"Got yourself some broken ribs, I heard them say." Samuel looked up in surprise. Josie Butler sat in the adjacent cell on a cot just like his, resting her chin on knees drawn up to her chest, her arms wrapped around flaring skirts. "Been watching you. Guess you and your little girlfriend got into some trouble with the law."

"What the hell are you doing here?"

Josie shrugged. "Public drunkenness. As if half the town doesn't do it."

"Did you hear if Elizabeth is all right?"

Josie snorted lightly, a small, mean smile curving her lips. "Heard about her, too. When they were bandaging you up. They took her to the hospital."

Samuel wanted to growl. He said again, "Is she all right?"

Josie shrugged, her eyes growing wide and innocent. "Don't know. Sounded like she was pretty bad." The small, mean smile came back. "Sounded like she might die."

Samuel's breath caught. "You're lying."

"Am I?" Josie batted her eyes, all sweet innocence. Then the tight smile returned. "You never should have left me, Samuel. We could have been good."

"Good?" Samuel snorted. "Leaving you was the best decision I ever made."

Josie opened her mouth, perhaps to argue, when a skinny deputy walked up to the cell, keys jangling.

"Shut up, Josie," the deputy said, "or you'll stay in here longer."

Josie stuck her tongue out at the deputy, but the deputy ignored it. Samuel shook his head in surprise. How had he not seen this side of her before? And she wanted him to go back? Not a chance.

The deputy's face tickled a dim memory. Samuel subtracted the uniform and the mustache from his mind and came up with a name.

"Clayton Perkins?"

The skinny deputy nodded. "Hi, Sam." He plucked at the sleeve of his uniform. "Been a few changes since you left."

"I see," Samuel said. "Look a little different since the last pasture party I saw you at."

Clayton gave him a rueful smile. "Yeah, but you're in the same place now as then."

"Got yourself in here a few times, if I remember right."

Clayton shrugged. "Kids," he said. "Just being dumb kids."

Behind Clayton stood Patwin Super. Samuel stood up with no small effort, ready for the berating—or worse—that Patwin would surely give him for getting his daughter killed. It was no less than he deserved.

"See me when you're done," the deputy said to Patwin. A meaningful look passed between them. "What happened to your girl wasn't right. I'll see you get the time you need."

Patwin nodded to Josie. "And the girl?"

Everyone looked at Josie, sitting on her bunk in the next cell. The deputy sighed. "Yeah, you're right. It won't do for her to hear." He walked over to her cell and with another jangling of keys unlocked her door. "Come on, Josie. You're coming with me."

"I'm not going anywhere." Josie all but snarled the words. "Whatever they've got to say, they can say in front of—"

Josie jerked in alarm when the deputy extracted a pair of handcuffs from his belt. "You're really gonna make me do it this way?" He sounded bored, but a light in his eyes said he might enjoy the struggle.

Josie pursed her lips.

"Just go with him, Josie," Samuel said. "It doesn't have to be a fight."

After a moment, Josie sighed dejectedly. "All right." She glanced at handcuffs dangling from the deputy's hand. "You don't need the pretty jewelry. I'll behave." Samuel and Patwin watched as the deputy escorted Josie away to another room.

When they were alone, Samuel asked, "How is Elizabeth? Josie said she d-d—" He couldn't get the word out.

"She's not dead," Patwin said. His shoulders slumped, as if exhausted. "Though she wasn't far from it when she came in."

Samuel burned with shame. Elizabeth was hurt and it was his fault. He only nodded and let go of a breath he didn't know he'd been holding.

"Listen, Samuel, this was not your fault."

Samuel blinked in surprise. That was the last thing he'd expected Patwin to say.

A bitter smile flitted across Patwin's lips. "You thought I was coming here to hand you your own skin. Well, I might have, if I didn't know what I know now. Elizabeth is hurt bad. She's got broken ribs and a concussion."

"But she'll live?"

"Yes, son. She'll live."

Samuel knees suddenly felt watery and he sank down to his cot. Patwin went on.

"The official police report might say Deputy Douglas stopped to assist an accident on the side of the road, but I was there when Henry woke up." Patwin grimaced. "I went there to thank him for saving my daughter. He was waking up but still in that twilight stage and muttering to himself."

Patwin fell silent, and Samuel saw his jaw working. He realized the man was trying not to cry. Noticing the heavy bags under Patwin's eyes, he wondered when the last time the man had slept.

Samuel prompted Patwin gently. "What did he say?"

"Enough," Patwin said. "Enough that I know what really happened." Patwin gave Samuel a level look. His eyes were dry, but flashed with anger. "You saved her life, Samuel. I know that, even if the records will never show it. I want you to make sure this doesn't happen again. I want to walk out of here with a *plan*." He studied Samuel, as if finally seeing him for the first time. "I love my daughter, and I want her to have a good life. Can you give her that?"

Samuel nodded. "Yes sir, I believe I can."

"Good. Then let's figure out how to get you out of this."

Samuel was released from jail on Patwin's bond the same day Elizabeth and the deputy went home from hospital. His jail-time had done him good. It gave him time for his rage to cool.

He visited Elizabeth once at her home to explain. The bandages covering the sutures on her head set his stomach in a furious roil. Tears rolled down her cheeks, when he explained his plan—their plan—but she nodded.

Samuel walked away from his father's house, aware of the two sets of eyes on his back. The weight of the linen-wrapped Colt revolver his father had pressed into his hands felt heavier with each step. The gun repulsed him. He pushed the feeling away and replayed the conversation with his father and brother telling them of his plan.

"Why do you want it, Samuel?" Charles sat next to their father at the kitchen table. In the middle of the table lay a bundle. Samuel could just see the gray steel of the barrel of his father's old Colt Walker Revolver peeking out of the white linen. "More trouble?"

"I don't want more trouble," Samuel said. Samuel traced the wood pattern of the table top with one finger. He remembered doing this when he was a kid, too, sitting at this same table. The thought made his heart ache. "But trouble is coming my way whether I want it or not."

"You know no one has fired that thing in twenty years," Charles said, gesturing to the gun. "It might not even work."

"I'd go buy a new one if I could afford it. But it'll fire. It has to." Samuel prayed he was right. He made himself fold his hands and look up at them. "It's a small town. I've heard the rumors. Henry hates me as much now for living after that wreck as for humiliating him in that fight. And now he wants Elizabeth dead, too." Samuel took a breath. Now for the hard part. "I have to go away for a while. Maybe forever"

"Go away?" Red crept up Charles's neck and face. Samuel almost smiled, though that would have been disastrous. Charles had never been one who'd been able to hide his anger. "You're leaving us again? And where would you go to?"

"Up to the old hunting cabin. There's water and shelter, and I can kill game for food. We won't starve."

"We? Who is we?" Then Charles' eyes widened in shock. "You mean to take Elizabeth with you? You're insane. Patwin will never agree to that."

"He already has," Samuel said quietly. "It was his idea."

Charles opened his mouth to argue further when Daniel put a hand on his arm. Charles fell silent as Daniel worked to get the words out. His speech was slurred and slow from the stroke, but Samuel understood every word.

"Henry hates you. I've heard it, too. But it goes deeper than the fight and living after the wreck. Henry hates you because he wants to *be* you. He is a coward and a bully and something inside him is broken, so he means to break you." Daniel sat forward with effort and pushed the linen wrapped gun toward Samuel. Its rasp across the wood sent a chill up Samuel's back. Daniel's voice thickened with emotion making it slur more. "He will not stop until you are dead, Samuel. And I do not want you dead."

Samuel gathered the bundle into his hands. He folded the linen so he would not have to touch the gun.

"Thank you," Samuel said softly.

Walking away from them now, Samuel wanted to drop the gun and leave it in the dirt. He never wanted to pick another one up or to kill again. Samuel kept the image of Elizabeth's broken body lying outside a wrecked truck in his mind and straightened his back for the two men watching him from the porch.

Samuel stowed the gun and his packed bag in Patwin's new truck. Then he went back to hauling lumber. And he waited.

The fight Samuel had been waiting for came two weeks after his release. Samuel bumped along the same mountain road in Patwin's truck, his elbow stuck out the open window. The ruined vehicle had been hauled up and junked. Samuel was just appreciating the smoother ride when around a bend in the road he found three Sherriff's vehicles parked across the road, one behind the next.

A grim flash of gratitude raced through him that he was alone this time. Elizabeth had not ridden with him since the accident.

Samuel slowed the truck, then stopped. Henry Douglas stepped out of the first car. Samuel suppressed a satisfied grin at the crooked set of Henry's nose. *That'll never be the same again*, Samuel observed. The thought twinged a tiny amount of guilt. He did not like hurting people, but Henry had deserved it.

Two more deputies stepped out of the other cars. Samuel noted their guns already drawn. Samuel pulled his father's gun across the seat so it would be close.

With a start, Samuel recognized one of the deputies. Clayton Perkins, the skinny deputy with a mustache from the jail. Clayton's eyes darted nervously from Samuel to the other officers back to Samuel and he chewed on the end of one mustache.

"Well, it's a small world. Samuel! I didn't know you were back to work." Henry did not have his gun drawn. He stood with his thumbs in his belt loops.

"Then move the cars, Henry, and we can go our own ways," Samuel said from the cab of the truck. With his right hand Samuel unwrapped the cloth around his father's gun without taking his eyes from the four men. "We don't have to do this."

"Sure, Moss. Come on out and we'll talk about this." Henry spread his hands in a look-how-harmless-I-am gesture. "I ain't gonna bite."

Samuel's gaze flicked to the other deputies. Two of them appeared as stolid as ever, and made no move to put up their side arms. Clayton looked like he wanted to sick up.

Samuel opened his truck door and stood behind it, holding his father's Revolver at his side.

"All right, Henry. I'm out. What do you want to say?"

"This," Henry said. He drew his gun and Samuel ducked behind the truck door. A loud report echoed off the mountain side, followed by a screaming hiss of air. Samuel looked beneath the truck. Henry had shot a hole in one of his tires. Samuel waited for more gunshots. None came.

"You see, Moss, here's what we're going to do. You're going to come out here and I'm going to whip your ass for every time you made me look stupid. Then, I'm going to roll your truck down the side of the mountain. Mountain roads are dangerous places to have a tire blow out. It'll look like an accident."

"Sure, Henry. Whatever you say." Samuel pulled the hammer back on the Revolver. It made a satisfying ratcheting sound. "I'm coming out now."

Samuel stood and walked around to the hood of the truck while Henry and the two deputies watched him. Samuel kept his hands behind his back, the Revolver ready to fire in his right hand. Samuel met Clayton's horrified gaze.

"Whatcha got behind your back, Moss?" Henry said. His words were casual, but Henry's hand twitched toward his own weapon.

"This isn't right," Clayton said, his voice shaking. "This isn't why I joined up. I can't—" He didn't finish what he couldn't do. Clayton ducked back into his car and haphazardly backed the car away.

When the dust settled and the car was gone, Henry said, "We'll handle him later. I need to deal with this first." Without preamble Henry aimed and fired his gun at Samuel.

Samuel felt the wind of the bullet as it went past his head. Samuel pulled the gun from behind his back. He aimed at Henry and pulled the trigger. Nothing happened. Samuel ratcheted the hammer again and pulled the trigger again.

Nothing.

Samuel flung the gun away and rushed at Henry. He hit him in the stomach with his shoulder and wrapped his arms around the deputy's waist, lifting the bigger man off his feet and onto the ground.

Henry bared his teeth at Samuel, like a feral animal would, and punched him in his still tender ribs with his free hand.

Samuel winced, telling himself ignore the pain and wrestled the gun away from Henry.

"I don't want to do this, Henry," Samuel said.

Henry wrapped his hands around Samuel's throat and squeezed. Black spots danced in front of Samuel's eyes. He aimed Henry's gun as best he could and squeezed the trigger. The report of the gun made his ears ring. Henry's hands fell away.

Samuel scrambled away, gasping for breath. Rough hands grabbed him and hauled him to his feet. One of the remaining deputies, angry and red in the face, was telling him something. Samuel couldn't hear through the ringing in his ears, but he saw the deputy's lips form the word 'jail' and 'life'. The other deputy jerked Samuel's hands behind him and cold metal bit into Samuel's wrists. He was bundled into the back of one of the cars. As the car pulled away, he twisted around to see the remaining deputy talking into his radio.

Samuel knew how this would look, and he thought he might see the death penalty for killing an officer.

Samuel stood in front of the judge, his hands chained at his waist. He did not recognize the man.

Judge Simmons was in the hospital after a heart attack, and this judge had been brought in from out of county to sit for Samuel's case. He'd already listened to the testimony of the other two witnesses. Both deputies told a similar version of the same story: how Samuel had cornered Henry on the mountain road, ruthlessly shot an upstanding citizen and fellow lawman. Samuel's own testimony had sounded weak in the face of the credibility the badge leant their version.

The air in the full courtroom was tense. It was the story of the year. Hometown war hero on trial for killing a sheriff's deputy.

Samuel glanced over his left shoulder and saw a clutch of Sherriff's department employees staring daggers at him from their side of the courtroom. Among the faces were the two deputies who had stood at Henry's side. They flanked Abel Douglas, Henry's father, who stared steadfastly at the judge. Clayton Perkins wasn't looking at Samuel either. His head was bent, his gaze on fidgeting hands. He chewed on one corner of his mustache and did not look up.

Samuel turned around in his seat to see the only kind faces in the room. Charles sat next to Daniel's wheel chair. Daniel looked stoic in his best suit, even with a blanket covering his withered legs. Patwin sat between Daniel and Elizabeth.

Samuel met Elizabeth's eyes. She gave him a reassuring smile, but there was worry in her eyes.

The judge banged his gavel and Samuel turned back to face him. The judge waited for the muttering crowd to settle before speaking. "Samuel Moss, after hearing all testimony related to the death of Henry Douglas, this court finds you—"

"May I say something?"

There was an audible gasp around the courtroom. Samuel turned to see the speaker.

Clayton Perkins had gotten to his feet. Someone Samuel could not see tried to pull him back to sitting, but Clayton shook them off and stepped out into the aisle. "Your honor, I would like to testify."

The judge frowned. "You have testimony that will contribute to this case?"

"I believe so, Your Honor."

"Then don't waste our time standing in the aisle, son. Get up here."

Clayton strode up the aisle and took the witness stand. A bailiff gave him a Bible to swear on.

The judge waited for the swearing in to be done before asking, "Now what is it you'd like to say?"

"I was there for some of it," Clayton said, and the story tumbled out of him.

Samuel hardly dared to breathe as Clayton told a rapt audience how Henry had bullied him into coming along that day, how Henry had cornered Samuel and forced a fight. Clayton's face reddened when he talked about the part where he'd fled.

The judge eyed the two deputies when Clayton spoke of how they'd chivvied him into silence afterwards.

"It was self-defense, Your Honor," Clayton concluded. "Henry cornered him and Samuel fought back."

Clayton was excused from the witness stand. He did not go back to his seat; he took an open seat beside Elizabeth. Tears rolled down her face as she threw her arms around Clayton's neck and sobbed into his shoulder. Clayton reddened again and patted her on the arm.

The courtroom buzzed with conversation, and the judge had to bang his gavel a number of times before the room silenced. "In light of new testimony," the judge said, "I have reconsidered my original verdict. Samuel Moss, I find you not guilty of the murder of Henry Douglas. And," he said, looking hard at the cluster of Sherriff's department uniforms, "I intend to begin an investigation into the nature of this cover up." The judge banged his gavel. "Courtroom dismissed."

The bailiff unlocked the shackles around Samuel's wrists. Elizabeth gave a whoop of delight and rushed into his arms.

Samuel sat beside Elizabeth at the Moss kitchen table. A turkey he had shot a few days before was roasted to perfection. Side dishes that made his mouth water steamed beside the bird.

Elizabeth took his hand beneath the table and squeezed.

Samuel looked at her and smiled. "It looks wonderful," he said.

She laughed and said, "Just don't expect it every day."

"Samuel, will you say the blessing?" The question came from Patwin. "Make it short," he added. "I'm hungry." Charles and Daniel nodded their agreement.

Samuel looked around the table at the people most important to him, at the lady he had already asked to become his wife. He swallowed hard and bowed his head. "Thank you, God, for this life."

Copyright © 2018 by Meghan Ewald.

Called a "legendary erotica heavy-hitter" (by the über-legendary Violet Blue), Andrea Dale writes sizzling erotica with a generous dash of romance. Her work—which has been called "poignantly erotic," "heartbreaking," and "exceptional"—has appeared in 20 year's best volumes as well as about 100 other anthologies from Soul's Road Press, Harlequin Spice, and Cleis Press. Her latest release is novella Kiss on Her List. She finds passion in rock music, clever words, piercing blue eyes, the wind in her hair, and the scent of the ocean. Visit AndreaDaleAuthor.com for more information.

HOUSE OF DREAMS

by Andrea Dale

"Do you want to drive?" The keys jangled from Vince's fingers.

Stefanie smiled around the single, hard thump of her heart. She knew why he offered. It would take her mind off the sadness, the heartache of watching their baby girl bound up the stairs to her freshman dorm room at Pepperdine.

A cool wind from the ocean below teased her hair. "Thank you," she said. Their hands brushed as she took the keys, and if he'd squeezed her fingers she might've cried, but he didn't, because he knew, and she appreciated that, too.

She'd scoffed at the idea of empty-nest syndrome, the same way she'd scoffed at "getting older"—although after a bout with sciatica two years ago she'd taken up running and Pilates and healthy eating, and dropped forty of the pounds that had crept up during three kids and all those years of marriage. They'd turned Geoff's bedroom into a workout room, because he was already married and unlikely to be returning home.

The older two had had already fled the nest, and seeing Lauren off to Pepperdine should have been easy, but Lauren had been her precious girl (after two precious, but somewhat alien, boys). Lauren had been her Mini-Me, and despite the usual teenage rebellions had still been loving and filled the house with laughter.

Stefanie turned the car left onto Pacific Coast Highway, to head south down the coast towards Santa Monica and then inland to home. At least Lauren had chosen a local university. There'd be visits—when it didn't cramp Lauren's college lifestyle.

Bright sunlight glinted off the ocean, and she couldn't resist cracking the window to inhale the scent of the surf.

Vince's hand was warm on her thigh where her skirt had ruched up, comfortable and comforting. She was startled when she'd eased to a stop at a red light and he squeezed and said, "Look, hon, there's an open house up there. We have time before lunch. Maybe we should check it out."

She laughed. "What, you want to *upsize* now that all the kids are gone? That's what we call 'cross purposes.'"

He laughed, too. "Yeah, we probably don't need a bowling alley or a gift-wrapping room. I just figured we had some time to kill…and it's been a long time since we imagined what we'd do with a house like that."

It was a game they'd played, before the kids were born. They'd go see houses for sale that they could never, ever afford. They'd wander through, discussing how they'd arrange their meager living room furniture in the cavernous great room, come up with crazy ideas for how to use the eighth bedroom.

They'd also…. Her breath caught. They'd also done things she'd almost forgotten about. The game they used to play.

The light turned green, and she turned left up into the canyon.

Vince squeezed her thigh again, and now she was squirming in her seat, trying to focus on the hairpin turns as the GPS squawked its disapproval at their detour.

The house was in a gated community in the hills, not quite tony enough for mega-celebrities, but still mind-numbingly expensive for the average buyer. A place to see D-list celebs, producers, the one-hit-wonder pop star who hadn't burned through her money yet.

They went in, put disposable booties on over their shoes to protect the floors, and signed their names and addresses (fake) in the guest book. The entryway could best be described as cavernous, with two staircases on either side curving up to meet in the center. The floors were marble, the banisters and chandelier wrought iron. Mediterranean traditional, meet Hollywood chic.

The previous owners had moved out, so all the furniture and artwork were beautiful but staged. There weren't many people viewing the house right now, and the agent let them wander at will.

Stefanie did feel a pang when she saw the enormous professional-grade kitchen, and then another pang when she thought about the amazing meals she could cook here for the whole family.

Then she reminded herself that she really wasn't all that fond of cooking, and herding her family to do clean-up was a lost cause.

"If this were our house," Vince said, using the almost-forgotten phrase, "we'd have a maid." It was as if he'd read her mind.

Hand-in-hand, they went out to the patio. The views were stunning, and the outdoor kitchen by the pool was bigger than their kitchen at home.

"If this were our house, we'd host amazing parties," she said. "And you wouldn't set anything on fire when you grilled."

"Look at how private this is," Vince said. "If this were our house, we could swim *naked*."

She didn't remind him that before the kids, they'd walked around naked all the time.

"We could," she agreed, but somehow, she didn't feel it anymore.

The master bedroom had a walk-in closet the size of Lauren's room at home, and the soaking tub in the bathroom looked out over the hills to the Pacific.

If this were their house…. The thought came unbidden. If this were their house, she'd crawl into that tub right now and not come out for several days.

She was actually looking at a landscape of mountains over the bed and pondering taking up painting again when Vince stepped up close behind her and growled in her ear, "If this were our house, I'd bend you over the foot rail and fuck you so hard you wouldn't have the breath to scream when you came."

His words made her breath catch in her throat, and her thighs literally went weak, her groin suddenly heavy and aching and wet. So much for not being in the mood anymore. She hadn't gotten this horny this fast in…far longer than she wanted to ponder.

She grabbed hold of one of the turned-wood mahogany bedposts for support. Vince moved even nearer, and she could feel the bulge in his pants against her ass.

"No," he went on, his voice low and hot in her ear, "even better, I'd bend you over the foot rail and spank your ass until it turned that pretty shade of red it always does, until you're begging me to fuck you. And then," he put his hand next to hers and gave the bedpost an experimental shake, "since these seem sturdy enough, I'd tie you down spread-eagled, and *then* fuck you senseless."

This, *this* is what they'd played at before kids and mortgages and crazy work hours. A few times Vince had managed to get her off without anyone walking in on them…and in one glorious instance the real estate agent had gone down the street to make a call (in that dark time before cell phones) and they'd done it standing up in front of an enormous window that looked out over the Hollywood sign.

They hadn't wanted to mess up the bed. It wasn't until afterwards, too late, that they saw the smudges they'd left on the plate glass.

They'd snuck out before the agent returned, laughing triumphantly and still, despite their mutual orgasms in the house, had barely made it home before they fucked like bunnies again. Twice, come to think of it.

How could she have forgotten? It was as if it'd been another part of her life—so long ago, so distant, that it seemed like a movie she'd once seen, a book she remembered reading.

Now it all came flooding back.

Almost literally, judging from the state of her panties.

"Vince…" she managed.

"I want to do you in every room of this house," he went on as if she hadn't spoken. "In the kitchen, that granite countertop cool on your bare ass. In the wine cellar. In the screening room while we watched porn."

His hand was under her skirt now, moving determinedly up her thigh, and she wanted to tell him no, tell him to stop, that someone might walk in.

That had been the thrill before, hadn't it? The chance of being caught?

But somewhere along the line, that had changed. Now she felt honestly worried about the repercussions. They were upstanding members of the community. They had careers on the line. They had *children*.

Then, it was as if a switch flipped her brain.

Well, screw that, she thought.

She swallowed the laughter that bubbled up in her throat (only because she didn't want someone to hear and interrupt them). The kids could bail them out, right? Wasn't that the point of having kids, to have someone to take care of you in your later years?

"Sex in the, uh, formal dining room that we never use," she said, her brain melting under the feel of his fingers stroking against her panties. "And, um…oh god, yes…."

The last words hissed out of her because he was already beneath the panties, pressed hard against her as he stroked. He took over the story, his lips against her ear, but she barely heard the words. Just the sound of his voice and the feel of his hand and the slow, steady climb towards climax that drove all thoughts out of her head.

Footsteps snapped on the marble staircase, growing louder. The real estate agent didn't have to wear the stupid booties.

"Vince…." Stefanie meant to say it as a warning, but it came out as a moan. The sound of her own voice, husky with arousal, startled her—and helped send her over the edge.

She swallowed her moans of pleasure as she ground against Vince's hand.

By the time the clipped footfalls arrived and the agent smiled and chirped, "How are we getting along? Any questions?", Stefanie was standing in front of Vince to hide the tent in his pants. He had one hand comfortably on her waist—the other, the one that smelled like her, he'd stuffed in his pocket.

"Everything's great," Stefanie said with a smile, sure she was flushed and sure the agent's return smile was knowing. "The view from the soaking tub is amazing."

As the agent turned to go, and they moved to follow her out, Vince murmured, "Thank you."

It hadn't occurred to her until now, because she'd been so wrapped up in her own goodbye, that he'd needed this, too.

❖

Later—much later, after they'd gotten home and gotten their clothes off and gotten off again—as they waited for their heart rates to subside, Vince said, "You know…we could always turn Lauren's room into a play room…."

Stefanie snuggled back against him. "Let's at least wait until she graduates and finds a place of her own," she said. "In the meantime, though, that furniture store near the Galleria is having a sale. We could look at getting a new bed—a nice, sturdy, four-poster one…."

She wasn't ready, not quite yet, to say goodbye to her last child. Some changes had to be gradual.

But she was ready to embrace and welcome back the dreams and desires she and Vince always had as a couple.

Copyright © 2018 by Andrea Dale.

Alia Mahmud has loved reading and writing since she was a child and is especially interested in the power of storytelling. She is a big fan of comic books and video games, and practices short-form improv on a regular basis. Though she often tries to seem cool and tomboy-ish, she has a secret sappy romantic side that she is happy to now share with you.

HOT CHOCOLATE

by Alia Mahmud

Sighing, I glanced down at my phone. No notifications.

I should have known, I thought, sipping my tea. *Nothing ever works out that easily.*

I looked around the café. There were happy couples, a group of teenagers, and a young family scattered around the open room. And me.

Normally I don't mind being alone, but for whatever reason today my feelings were more… complicated.

Against my better judgement, I read back over our conversation. It seemed like Dean had been genuinely excited to meet me, but I guess that's easy enough to fake over text.

Texting him one more time can't hurt, can it?

I mulled it over as I swallowed the last mouthful of tea. Why not?

Hey we were supposed to meet like 30 mins ago…. You coming?

There. Sent.

The waitress approached to take my mug away and refill my water glass.

"Thanks," I mumbled, still scanning the room as if I hadn't already looked over every inch multiple times.

"Would you like anything else? We have some pretty great hot chocolate here."

I looked up at the waitress for the first time since arriving. She was smiling warmly at me.

"S-sure. Hot chocolate, yeah."

"Coming right up!" she beamed, before turning and walking away.

I turned back to my phone. Still no notifications. I opened up the conversation, wondering if Dean's phone was dead and he had gone to the wrong place. I mean, it's possible.

√ *Seen.*

I groaned and put my head down on the table. He had seemed so nice, too. So much for online dating.

I heard a *clunk* on the table. I looked up and the waitress had set down a steaming mug of hot chocolate, topped with whipped cream. I turned to thank her, but instead of stopping, she sat down across from me and set another mug in front of herself, smiling sheepishly.

"Sorry…I just got off work and it looked like you could use some company," she said. "If you'd rather be left alone, um, just let me know."

She looked up at me, a faint blush coloring her cheeks. I glanced at my phone one more time (still nothing), and put it away before taking a sip from my mug.

"Yeah, I could use some company. My name's Alex," I said.

"Carrie. Nice to meet you!"

She stuck out her hand for me to shake. The moment I touched it, I felt a surge of electricity race through me. I hesitated letting go, and it seemed as though a million years passed before she finally withdrew her hand from mine.

"So, there's a movie theater next door," Carrie said. "If you're interested, we could maybe…I dunno… go see something? If you want to, of course." Her blush deepened.

At that moment, I got a notification from my phone. I excused myself and opened it up. Dean had finally messaged me back.

Oh shit I forgot we were meeting. Do you still want to meet up?

I looked up at Carrie, who was still waiting for my answer. I smiled at her.

No thanks, I texted. *I've got another date.*

Copyright © 2018 by Alia Mahmud.

Our columnist, Julie Pitzel, has been a receptionist, radio DJ, bill collector, telemarketer, administrative assistant, community college instructor, and an expediter (aka professional nag). She's been involved in the Houston writing community for many years including two years as President of a local Romance Writers of America Chapter. She writes paranormal fiction from a geodesic dome south of Houston, where she lives with her husband and a pair of cats. Most recently, her story "The Dance" was published in The Death of All Things *anthology.*

YOU READ *THAT?* COVER STORY

by Julie Pitzel

"You can't judge a book by its cover."
Really? Have you bought a book lately?
Okay, I know the phrase is metaphor and not about actual books, but maybe it's time to retire the idiom. Because when it comes to books, I judge them by the cover every time. We all do.

I looked up the origin of this saying, expecting it to be from a time of plain leather bindings and block font titles. To my surprise, it originated in the 1940's. By then, the book-buying public was already accustomed to choosing books based on vivid pictures and lurid titles. It was introduced well after dime store novels, pulp fiction magazines, and mass market paperbacks displayed sensational covers.

As early as 1935, Penguin began color coding books. Red for Drama included Shakespeare, Bernard Shaw, some Orwell, and P. G. Wodehouse. It merged into the Orange for Fiction with titles such as *1984*, *Jane Eyre*, and *The Great Gatsby*. Crime Fiction included Agatha Christie and Arthur Conan Doyle. There was a color for Essays, World Affairs, Travel and Adventure, and Autobiographies. Yellow served as the catchall, Miscellaneous.

But even without the Penguin color spectrum, artwork and font provide giant clues to genre. Picture the following three covers, all with the image of a distant city. One is bright, harsh colors with hard angles and straight lines, and the title is a digital font. The second is soft, muted colors, lots of curves, sweeping lines, and a swirly font. And the third is dark silhouettes and shadows, with red highlights

and a newspaper font. Without looking at the titles or authors we'd guess the first is science fiction, second a fantasy, and third a mystery or thriller.

If we picked up those books and the descriptions didn't match our expectations, we probably wouldn't buy them because the premise didn't live up to the promise of the cover.

Romance covers are a little more nuanced, but still give clues regarding time period, sub-genre, and sexual content. A woman in a sweeping ball gown is obviously a historical romance. If we see cleavage or even a bit of leg, it's going to be more sensual. If there's a wolf or pentagram or batwings, we expect to find a paranormal twist. Whether we're browsing physical book shelves or an e-reader, we are drawn to certain books because the clues are there, showing us that this is our type of book.

When I started reading romance in the eighties, I chose books with sensual embraces—bodice rippers. I knew just looking at them that I'd get a sizzling historical, filled with bold characters and hot sex. I didn't bother reading descriptions on the sweet-looking contemporaries. That wasn't the story I was looking for.

My tastes have changed a bit over time. I still love saucy historicals, but I've discovered I enjoyed contemporaries also, especially if they're humorous and a little spicy. And I adore paranormals. Brooding vampire? Check. A hot Alpha wolf? Yum. And while I'm drawn to covers showing off a little man-candy, I'm more apt to pick up books with a "take-charge" woman on the cover.

If it's a passionate embrace, the woman will be the obvious instigator, the seducer. On a historical cover, maybe she's wearing pants or carrying a sword. Usually she has a very direct look that tells me she intends to control her own destiny.

The premise I'm looking for, regardless of subgenre, is heroines acting as their own heroes. And many romances today follow through on that promise.

According to Sarah Maclean in a recent[*] *Entertainment Weekly* article, "The larger arc of the romance novel is the arc of the women's movement. Women fighting against a dominant, gendered

---

[*] Romance as Resistance: How the happily-ever-after genre is taking on Trump *http://ew.com/books/2017/11/03/romance-novelists-resistance-trump/*.

misogynistic culture, and ultimately triumphing." Cover images have begun to reflect that arc. In books from the 80's, many of the women look slavish. In today's covers—even in an impassioned clinch—the woman might look orgasmic, but she doesn't look like she's paying him homage.

The article pointed out that romance pushes the boundaries of society. You'll find stories with same sex romances, and people of mixed races coming together because we can't control who we fall in love with. The pages of romance stories are filled with resistance and political activism. And we see some of that diversity when we look at the choices for romance on our e-readers: male/male, female/dinosaur, Highlander/Sassenach.

Not all authors will share their opinions on Facebook and Twitter, but writers put their passions and beliefs in the stories they tell. They may not be in your face with their thoughts on the current administration, but their views and beliefs will be reflected in their plots and characters.

Over the years, romance covers have changed, but not quite as much as the stories inside them. The rapey heroes from the 70's and 80's went away years ago. Our protagonists started using condoms and promoting safe sex when that became the norm in modern life. Romances have been dealing with issues of consent for many years, but in today's climate I'm sure we'll see many story lines dealing with concerns of pressure and coercion.

The romance genre is based on happily-ever-afters. Its core message is about hope and overcoming hardships. Some people dismiss the genre because of the happy endings, because they think fiction should be realistic. (But those same people probably don't have a problem with James Bond or Frodo Baggins.) In many ways they're judging romance by its covers. They're missing the clues that promise feminism, activism, and diversity.

While we *can* judge a book**, a genre, or a person by their cover, it doesn't mean we know the whole story. For that you have to open the book.

Copyright © 2018 by Julie Pitzel.

** To see a roundup of 2017 Romance covers, check out Houston Bay Area RWA—Judge a Book By Its Cover Contest *https://jabbic.hbarwa.com/*. They open it up for Readers to choose their favorite covers the first week of February.

Alice Faris grew up in a small community in Northern California that proudly boasts of having more cows than people. She raised guide dogs for the blind, is dyslexic, and can shoot a gun or bow and miraculously never hit the target (which at some point becomes a statistical improbability). Alice worked as a school psychologist and counselor for local schools. Alice also writes paranormal romance as Tina Gower. She won the Writers of the Future, the Daphne du Maurier Award for Mystery and Suspense (paranormal category), and was nominated for the Romance Writers of America® Golden Heart®. She has professionally published several short stories in a variety of magazines.

PUTTING SEXY IN CONSENT

by Alice Faris

Tell me again: why isn't consent sexy?

Since the #MeToo hashtag has become the biggest news event of the year—so huge that it took the *TIME* magazine spot as the Person of the Year—it's been on the lips and ears in serious discussions online, in person, and at work. Men and women are reevaluating and thinking back on every interaction and wondering what *is* appropriate and what is sexual harassment.

And I've noticed an interesting discussion around it, whispered in romance circles. Will all this talk of proper interaction between romantically interested partners kill the romance? Will our Alpha heroes flatten into emasculated husks of their former glory? Instead of sweeping heroines off their feet, will heroes now need to stop and ask permission? Won't this *kill the mood*?

My opinion? Consent is sexy.

Yes. It is. Believe me.

If you have a "but, what about…" on the tip of your tongue, hold that thought. Let's talk about where this instinctive reaction comes from.

We know through research that women have been conditioned to act a certain way, be treated a certain way, and react a certain way. As a psychologist I've read study after study that shows women talk less in meetings, yet are perceived to talk too much when asked about their behaviors by peers. This perception becomes so internalized that some women become self-conscious to speak out more often than men.

It's no wonder given this toxic mix of expectations that women are harassed as often as they are in the work place. We are expected to keep it quiet to save our jobs. We're expected to give a firm no, but also be polite, but also keep the door closed to further attempts, but also not hurt his feelings, but also take some of the responsibility for wearing that form fitting shirt—as you can see it's maddening!

To see where this has seeped into our perception of romance we don't need to look back too far to find evidence of men's role to be the protector, the decision maker, the one who knows all. Transfer this belief into the role of someone in a position of sexual power over someone else and we start to have a concern.

In the beginnings of romance, readers saw reflections of these behaviors in men. I vividly remember reading one of my mother's romance books by a well-known author where the woman protagonist becomes pregnant unexpectedly, is left by her fiancé, and then cue unknown rich dude with an interest in her to come in and buy all her baby items now that she's down and out. Arguably, this is a fantasy. Someone coming in and taking away the financial stress of the situation for the heroine isn't common and *who wouldn't* want that? But let's be honest: if this were a real-world scenario and a guy we didn't know well came in and bought all your baby clothes, and took a sudden interest in you, it would be creepy.

It's creepy because today's women have slowly gained independence. We are taught to guard our safety and protect ourselves from predators. It's a common tactic for abusers to buy their victims things in exchange for good behavior or sexual favors. This is why I think the secret admirer trope with these scenarios has died out in recent decades. It can be really hard to pull off with readers who are searching for these red flags.

It's not that those books written in the 70s, 80s, or 90s were meaning to feed into the problematic beliefs; they are highlighted as even more concerning now only because the context has shifted and shined a light on these micro-red-flags. Added together, they make for the beginnings of an unhealthy relationship. Yes, romance is fantasy. We are making the perfect match for our love interests. They are not real people. These are not real scenarios. I don't expect my boss to fly me around in his private helicopter. Readers know this. We go into the novel knowing that it's not true to life and we just want to be in that other world for a while. We look past the "is this real" to see the story of a relationship blooming underneath. But we want that relationship to have a sturdy, realistic foundation. Our characters consenting to the activity is key. Context of the character's interaction is important!

What about the same scenario, but the love interest isn't consenting and he or she doesn't have any sexual interest or interest in a relationship? Then can you imagine that being sexy at all? I can't. When the element of fear and lack of trust enter the picture, that's no longer a fantasy. It's a horror.

The situations we're talking about in the real world are not the same as the ones we've seen in romance. They're not even close. How often has the hero whipped out his penis unexpectedly? Usually our love interest is pining for that moment to happen. There has been talk and behavioral cues of interest, secret smiles and looks. We know the characters are consenting. That is building the anticipation. That is creating the amazing chemistry we know and love.

I've read so many books that feature the alpha male characters doing what alpha males do—being the decision maker, the one who jumps into danger at the call of duty, the one who gets hot and bothered and takes his love interest by the waist and brings him or her close. Most times he looks and checks to see if his actions are okay. A little nod. He or she nods back. That is consent. And it's sexy as hell.

A few of those times the big, strong, ultra-manly man will ask his love interest "Is this okay? Are we really doing this?" Oh my. He jumps from buildings, he's held a live grenade in his hand, *and* he's asking for permission? That window into his vulnerability is hot, hot, hot.

I've lost track of the number of readers I've talked to who admit that well-written, consensual romance is what saved them from an abusive relationship and directed them into their true love's arms instead. THAT is amazing. That is power in writing. If you ask most engineers or astronauts, they'll tell you they watched or read science fiction, Investigators read mysteries, and lawyers were inspired by *To Kill A Mockingbird* or John Grisham books. The story, sure, is fantasy—but it can inspire people to better themselves. So why *wouldn't* romance books inspire relationships?

We can all agree harassment is awful and needs to stop. We've all read a character that we just can't stomach. Someone who reminds us of an ex, or a toxic best-friend, or is too one dimensional, or not someone we'd see ourselves with or even be friends with. And we put those books down like they're hot potatoes. Or we toss them across the room in disgust. Sometimes this is personal preference and sometimes the writer missed the cues of a problematic personality. It's hard. These issues are ingrained into our society.

If the characters I'm reading were not attracted to each other, and not in a hate-to-love kind of goodness (a trope I LOVE), then I don't really want to read it. There is too much of non-consent in the real world. We shouldn't expect non-consensual relationships (verbal or non-verbal) in romance and we don't get them today. I've rarely read a book where the character is thinking in their heads they don't want to be having sex with the love interest, but oh well, "I guess I'll think of England." Doesn't happen.

So, is consent going to kill our romance? No. It's not. It's going to make it a thousand times better. The fantasy in romance can be forward thinking into what we'd like to see from our love interests in real life. Healthy relationships are the new fantasy. The new romantic ideal.

All those men on social media asking how the heck they're supposed to interact with women now in the age of harassment awareness? I have a small suggestion for them. Pick up a damn fine romance. We can provide you with a list if you like.

Further Reading on this topic:

- Why Women Talk Less Than Men at Work
  http://time.com/money/4450406/men-interrupt-talk-more/
- Do Women Talk More Than Men?
  https://www.scientificamerican.com/article/women-talk-more-than-men/

- The Unusual Phenomenon of Men Interrupting Women
  https://www.nytimes.com/2017/06/14/business/women-sexism-work-huffington-kamala-harris.html
- Beyond Bodice-Rippers: How Romance Novels Came to Embrace Feminism
  https://www.theatlantic.com/sexes/archive/2013/03/beyond-bodice-rippers-how-romance-novels-came-to-embrace-feminism/274094/

Copyright © 2018 by Alice Faris.

Lezli Robyn is an Australian multi-genre author and Assistant Publisher of Arc Manor, living in the US with her mini-Dachshund/Chihuahua, Bindi. Her love of books led to her meeting her future collaborator, Mike Resnick, on eBay. Since that serendipitous event Lezli has sold to prestigious markets around the world and is in the process of finishing too more small press books while writing her first two novels. Known for her bittersweet and heart-tugging writing technique, she has been a finalist for several prestigious awards, including the 2010 Campbell Award for Best New Writer. In 2011 and 2014 she also won the Catalan Premi Ictineu Award for Best Translated Story. You can find her at www.lezlirobyn.com.

IN SEARCH OF
THE *SASSENACH* CONNECTION

by Lezli Robyn

Outlander Opening Title

I f you haven't been swooning over Jamie Fraser, aka actor Sam Heughan, aka sexist-Scot-in-a-kilt, then you clearly haven't been reading or watching *Outlander*—either the first in a (soon-to-be) nine book series by Diana Gabaldon, or the Starz television show, which just concluded its third season. More importantly, you haven't been watching one of the best in the current crop of television showcasing female empowerment. Its other lead Claire Randall, played by Caitriona Balfe, shows us how strong a woman can be, even if she was from the 1940's, a time when women were empowered by WWII to step up alongside men to contribute to the war effort, but then expected to return to a submissive "housewife" role upon its conclusion.

Not only is Claire a forthright, forward-thinking lass who cusses like a sailor, fighting the inequality experienced by women during her time, but she is thrust two hundred years into the past, where she has to use her keen intelligence and war veteran grittiness to help her survive a time where woman effectively had no rights and were *owned* by their husband.

And therein lies the beauty of this couple. Because while Jamie and Claire are from different times, different cultures, and born with very different role expectations upon adulthood, they challenge each other to better themselves, to become more equal partners. The lead characters are from time periods 270 and 70 years in the reader's/viewer's past, yet Diana Gabaldon shows us a couple that are often more enlightened in their beliefs and their trust in each other than many representations of romance set in the modern age.

Now, that doesn't mean this couple doesn't have problems—theirs often seem insurmountable. For one thing Claire was already married when they met, to the liberal-for-his-times Frank Randall. But they put the effort in...as does the Starz Network. Diana Gabaldon's words are beautifully reflected on the screen, and the locations filmed are often as breathtaking as the relationships depicted.

Outlander Season 1 Poster

The scene where Frank proposes to Claire was filmed in Glasgow's bustling George Square. While most fans of Outlander are Jamie/Claire shippers, you can't help but be swooned by the gorgeous locations that play backdrop to Frank and Claire's romance, too. The scene was wonderful in giving us a glimpse of the 1940's Glasgow, and is probably one of the easiest locations for fans to access.

George Square, Glasgow

When Claire is given her marching orders by the military, she leaves on the train, in uniform, as her husband Frank watches her carriage pull away, his heart in his throat. The historic Bo'ness and Kinneil Railway near Falkirk stood in for the bustling 1940's London station, one of its locomotives being used to depict her departure. While it was an important moment showing us another facet of Claire and Frank's relationship, the scene also flipped the gender norms; the traditional "leave for war" moment is usually depicted with the *man* in uniform hopping on the train, with his lady love waving a teary farewell from the platform.

The Bo'ness and Kinneil Railway

If you were to visit the station with *your* love, you could take one of the scenic tours, which helps raise money to keep the trains serviced, but if you truly want to go to one of the most pivotal season one locations between Claire and Frank, go no further than Falkland, Fife, which is a picturesque town that stands in for the bigger city of Inverness in the show. Fayre Earth Gift Shop became Farrell's Hardware and Furniture Store, where Claire daydreams about how her life might be different, if only she had have bought that vase. And down the road is The Covenanter Hotel, which stands in as Mrs. Baird's Guesthouse, where Frank and Claire are dedicated to rediscovering each other, biblically and otherwise, on what they determine to be their second honeymoon. Not only can you stay at the hotel with your own significant other, making it a romantic night away, but you can go outside to see the majestic Bruce Fountain, where one of the most important (and unexplained) encounters of *Outlander* happens, when Franks sees Jamie (his ghost?) looking up into their hotel room window at Claire.

Bruce Fountain and Covenanter Hotel

are fictional, alas, but you can take a nice stroll with your partner through the surrounding scenery; pack a picnic, and you can have a romantic lunch on an *Outlander*-inspired tartan blanket on the very spot Claire leaves her tartan wrap to explore the 1740's.

Clava Cairns

While the author has still has not revealed *how* Jamie came to be standing at the fountain in the 1940's, around two hundred years passed his time (Diana recently told fans on her Facebook page that this mystery will be solved in the *last* scene she ever writes for the series) if you travel up Rannoch Moor, in Perthshire, you can see the location of the Craigh na Dun stone circle, through which Claire travels into the past to meet the love of her life. The stones themselves

The nearby Clava Cairns are said to have provided inspiration for the more Stonehenge-like Craigh na dun—especially the tall rectangular slab that could represent a stone door. The ancient standing stones are around four thousand years old and one of Scotland's most evocative prehistoric locations. Two parts of the site, Balnuaran of Clava and Milton of

Rannoch Moor

Outlander Season 3 Poster

Clava, are open to the public and contain a range of burial monuments and what remains of a medieval chapel, so you can brush up on the burial beliefs of the Bronze Age society. Not only that, you could do a mini photoshoot with your significant other to recreate *Outlander*'s third season promotional poster. If you pose on each side of the tall rectangular stone—maybe even in clothes that match Jamie and Claire's respective time periods—you and your loved one can create the visual that you are separated in time. But I digress….

When Claire first travelled through the stones, the location scouts used the sweeping area of Tulloch Ghru, near Aviemore and The Cairngorms, to depict the hilly, woodland journey Jamie and his clansmen take the bewildered Claire on after their run-in with Frank's ancestor, Captain Randall, and his English soldiers. (The location is also used quite extensively in the opening credits.) Their long journey leads them to one of the most significant locations of the first season: Doune Castle, in Perthshire, which stands in for Castle Leoch, home to Jamie's Uncle, Colum MacKenzie, and his clan.

Doune Castle, Stirlingshire

We first see the castle when a bedraggled Claire and an injured Jamie ride up to the entrance after successfully evading the English. But Claire is not in the mood to admire the 100ft high gatehouse. While today Doune Castle can host everything from large wedding ceremonies in its remarkably-preserved stone-walled Great Hall to more intimate affairs in the thirty-person-capacity kitchen—both of which were used extensively in scenes throughout the first season of *Outlander*—all Claire wanted to do is

escape, to return to the Craigh na Dun stones and, through them, her husband, Frank. (The castle also featured heavily in the first episode when Claire and Frank visited the ruins of the castle during the 1940's and use the opportunity to get reacquainted…in the most intimate way possible.)

Doune Castle Interior

Interior of Doune Castle, Stirlingshire

It is during Claire's stay at the fictional Castle Leoch that she meets Geillis Duncan, a somewhat conniving and mysterious woman who is immediately interested in discovering Claire's secrets. While Glasgow's Pollok Country Park doubles as the grounds surrounding Castle Leoch, playing host to the scene where Claire and Geillis look for herbs to treat the ill in the 1740's, the Royal Burgh of Culross, in Fife, with its cobblestone roads, stands in for the village of Cranesmuir, where Geillis lives. Not only is the Royal Burgh managed by the National Trust, which helps it maintain its historic condition, behind the impressive Culross Palace you can find an exquisite garden filled with herbs and vegetables, which doubled for garden Claire works in during her stay at Castle Leoch. It is a real treat for fans, because it appears unchanged from what you see on the screen compared to real life.

Culross Castle Garden

Claire's early excursions outside of Castle Leoch were often not of her own volition, with Claire regularly being teased or bullied by the Scottish clansmen (who believed her to be a spy), until she proved through her own acerbic wit, on their tax collection tour through the MacKenzie villiage, that she is no pushover, nor weakling female. The Folk Museum in Newtownmore features replicas of traditional turf-roofed Highland crofts, which made it an ideal setting for the fictional MacKenzie Village. While there were no romantic scenes filmed there to channel into a date with your loved one, if you visit the Folk Museum, you and your significant other can see what it was like to live the Highland life, how they built their homes and how they dressed and

tilled the soil in a warm welcoming environment. You could see for yourselves what it was like for Claire to be thrust several hundred years into a more rustic past.

But if you are looking for a much more romantic location to take your partner, then you can go no further than Glencorse Old Kirk in Midlothian. The 17th century church rests near the foothills of Pentland Hills, and it is the spot where Jamie and Claire are married to protect her from Captain Randall, who catches sight of her again when the English intervene in the MacKenzie's tax collection tour to "rescue" her, believing (somewhat correctly) that she is not travelling with the Scotsmen of her own volition. The location is breathtaking with it's beautiful ancient church, old graveyard, lush parkland and atmospheric garden, and it is the perfect location for a marriage proposal—or indeed, to get married yourself.

Glencorse Old Kirk

Speaking of locations to get married, Blackness Castle is often a popular venue to tie the knot in Scotland. The ex-artillery fortress is often referred to as "the ship that never sailed" because of its seavessel shape, and the 15th century castle offers couples a breathtaking view over the Firth of Forth, the beautiful backdrop for many a romantic occasion with your loved one. It also stood in for Fort William, in *Outlander*, where "Black Jack" Randall's headquarters were based in the series (and where Jamie rescues Claire, after she is kidnapped by Randall lfollowing their marriage) so you would be able to experience what it would be like to visit one of the show's more unusual filming locations.

Blackness Castle

If you were wanting to go all out on romance, you could do no wrong then visit Hopetoun House in South Queensferry, on the outskirts of Edinburgh, which is owned by Adrian, Marquis of Linlithgow. It is a beautiful grand stately home that doubles as the residence of the fictional Duke of Sandringham in *Outlander* (played by the brilliant Simon Callow), whom Jamie and Claire visit in order to obtain a pardon for Jamie, after his latest encounter with Jack Randall at Fort William reinforces how precarious their position is. The estate is open to the public in Summer, and many a couple have taken over the splendid estate for their wedding day, saying "I do" in the stunning Adam Stables before having their reception in the House's main ballroom. (Don't be surprised by the size of Hopetoun House, as the *Outlander* special effects team digitally erased some of its outer wings for the show. One of the rooms also doubled as the spare room in Jamie and Claire's Paris apartment.)

Hopetoun House

If you prefer to get married in a church, and Glencorse Old Kirk was not to your tastes, or you needed a venue that could seat more guests, try Tibbermore Church, which played host to Claire and Geillis's trial after they were accused of being witches while Jamie was away performing a task for the Laird MacKenzie. Even though the church played host to one of the ugliest scenes in the show, it also emphasized the true friendship that had developed between the two ladies and many a Jamie fan were swooning upon his late but timely arrival and the declaration that he would defy all—including God—to protect his wife, as he rescued her from the whipping leading to her execution. (What girl doesn't want such devotion? *swoon*)

Tibbermore Church

Tibbermore Church has a fascinating history. The earliest monument in the church was a large stone tablet inserted into the aisle wall in 1631 by Sir James Murray of Tibbermore, as a gift to his family. Then in 1632 the church was significantly rebuilt when the local lairds altered it to the medieval east-west alignment, proving a church was dedicated to St Mary during the late middle ages. In 1789 James Stobie, architect and surveyor, removed an aisle at the east end and stretched the church 10 feet eastwards, making other changes including adding a new door and porch on the west gable, installing new galleries at each end to add extra seating, and rearranging pews to face the pulpit, which now was positioned in the traditional Scottish Presbyterian location between the central windows. The south windows were made symmetrical and then in 1810 a north aisle added transformed the church into a late T-plan making it capable of seating 600 warm bodies. In 1874 the present pulpit (with its rarely-surviving stenciled decoration) and the horseshoe seating with recessed celtic crosses were installed (the seats in the galleries and aisle were left alone), and in 1920 a marble First World War I memorial was added as well as stained glass inserted into the two central windows to commemorate women who served in the War.

Tibbermore Church Interior

While the church is in serious need of repair, many of these fascinating alterations could be seen during the witch trial scene, following which Claire reveals her remarkable origins to Jamie— who believes her! They head to his ancestral family home of Lallybroch (also known as Broch Tuarach), which is represented in *Outlander* by Midhope House. Unfortunately, the 16th century tower house near Edinburgh is in serious disrepair, so if you visit it, please admire from a distance, as the interior is not entirely safe.

Linlithgow Castle

Linlithgow Palace, on the other hand, in West Lothian, might be ruined, but it is entirely safe to explore. Once the royal seat of the Stewart Kings of Scotland, and the birthplace of Mary, Queen of Scots, the 15th century site was used to represent Wentworth Prison, where Jamie is taken to Jack Randall and abused after he is captured outside Lallybroch. Maintained by the Scotland Trust, this majestic venue would make for an intimate outing with your significant other, despite its representation in the TV show as the location of a brutal prison. In reality the Palace hosts many a marital occasion with couples saying "I do" in an open air ceremony in the Great Hall, or beneath the Undercroft's cosy, vaulted ceiling in the palace's charming courtyard.

Linlithgow Castle Interior

After you have proposed to your significant other, or maybe even married them, go visit Balgonie Castle, which was built in 1296-1300, and located on the South Bank of the River Leven, several miles east of Glenrothes, Fife, in Scotland. Also mostly in a ruined state, the castle is where Claire goes when she left Wentworth Prison to plan Jamie's escape, and excepting the recently-restored keep and tower (the later of which is used for residential purposes), the rest of the castle are roofless ruins and considered a Scheduled Ancient Monument.

Aberdour Castle, on the other hand (also in Fife), is arguably one of the two oldest standing stone castles in Scotland. Built around 1200, the beautiful building, with a stunningly well-preserved early 17th century painted ceiling, stands in for the Abbey of St. Anne de Beaupré in the show, where Claire takes Jamie to recover from the horrific abuse he suffered at the hands of Jack Randall. While obviously not a monastary in real life, you can see why the location scouts of the show thought the castle a soothing and romantic setting for the reacquainting of Jamie and Claire, as you stroll through its beautiful gardens and halls.

Aberdour Castle

If it's a sea change you and your partner are after, then visit the Troon coastline and stroll hand in hand, barefoot, down the sandy beach in the exact location Claire, Jamie, and his mentor, Murtagh, leave Scotland for France in order to sabotage the Jacobite Rebellion's efforts, to prevent the slaughter Claire knows will happen if the Battle of Culloden occurs. Or alternately, you can visit Historic Dysart Harbour (also, yet again, in Fife), and the Reaper Tall Ship, which is berthed nearby, both of which were used in the scenes depicting the trio's arrival in France.

Dysart Harbour

Dysart Harbor was once part of a wider estate owned by the St. Clair or the Sinclair family, whom were responsible for gaining burgh of barony status

for the town towards the end of the 15th century. Following a swift decline of the town's harbor traffic in 1930, caused by the closure of the Lady Blanch Pit, the harbor and attached town were amalgamated into the royal burgh of Kirkcaldy under an act of parliament. It was only through the protests of local residents that part of the historic town (specifically the 16th and 18th century houses of Pan Ha' opposite the harbor) were protected and preserved for future generations.

Outlander Season 2

Dysart Harbour isn't the only Scottish location that doubles for a French location in the second season of *Outlander*. Located on the banks of River Teith, eight miles from the historic town of Sterling, Deanston Distillery stands in for the winery in France that Jamie's cousin owns and loans to Jamie as a place to operate from while he is staying in France. Known (in real life) as being the largest distillery owned by Scotch whisky producer Distell Group Limited, Deanston Distillery started its life in 1785 as a cotton mill designed by Sir Richard Arkwright, and it wasn't until 1966 it was converted into producing whisky which is handmade by ten local craftsmen, unchill-filtered, natural colored and bottled at a hearty strength of 46.3% ABV.

Claire also works while the couple are in France, at L'Hôpital des Anges, a charity hospital run by the imperious Mother Hildegarde. But there is no need for you and your partner to sail over the Channel to go on a date at any of these season two France-set *Outlander* locations, because the hospital is represented in the show by the gorgeous Glasgow Cathedral (also called the High Kirk of Glasgow, or

Glasgow Cathedral

When you can tear yourself away from the ornate steeples and breathtaking stained glass windows of the Glasgow Cathedral (perhaps yet another great venue to get engaged or married?), travel to the Drummond Castle in Perthshire, to visit ornate formal gardens and the orchard that *Outlander* used as a very convincing representation of the gardens at the Palace of Versailles. Jamie and Claire's continued efforts to sabotage the Jacobite's ability to obtain funds to build a credible army for the Bonnie Prince Charles are thwarted time and time again, and it is at those gardens they are confronted by the reappearance of Captain Randall.

Drummond Castle Gardens

St. Kentigern's, or even St Mungo's Cathedral), which is located beside the Glasgow Royal Infirmary. Built from the late 12 century onwards, it is an exemplary example of Scottish Gothic architecture that served as the seat of the Bishop and later the Archbishop of Glasgow. It is also one of only few medieval churches (and the only one on the Scottish mainland) which amazingly survived the Reformation without being unroofed.

Seen as one of Scotland's—and even Europe's—most important formal gardens, the Drummond Castle estate dates back to the 17th century, with the gardens being redesigned and terraced in the 19th century and then replanted in the 1950's. While you take a stroll with your partner through the many hedgeways, or enjoy a picnic in the orchard, take note to spot the ancient yew hedges and remaining beech tree that was planted by Queen Victoria, commemorating her visit in 1842.

And if you are not *Outlander*-ed out by the time you have travelled to all these gorgeous locations steeped in history and romantic beauty, take some time to travel to the pivotal location of the Battle of Culloden, near Inverness, in the Scottish Highlands. It would not take long for you and your partner will realize the vast scope of the battle, where many clans, including the *real* Frasers and MacKen-

Glasgow Cathedral Interior

zies, fought in the final 1745 Jacobite battle alongside Bonnie Prince Charlie. You can learn more about the events leading up to, during, and after the Battle of Culloden at the award-winning Culloden Battlefield Visitor Centre, through watching a film they prepared, attending an interactive exhibition or by joining a tour of the battlefield.

Drummond Castle Gardens

Culloden is also where Jamie and Claire say their tearful goodbyes, before Jamie joined the Jacobite army to fight for the Stuarts, and Claire returns through the Craigh na Dun stones to the 1940's, and Frank, to raise Jamie's baby away from the threat and danger of war. It's heartbreaking, and evocative, and only adds to the experience of touring the Culloden Battlefield with your partner, as you have a better understanding of the scope of what it must have been like for couples to have been separated at the onset of battle.

Battle of Culloden

You can finish off your *Outlander* experience for now (I will be writing a second article to cover the filming locations in season 3 and 4 of the show) by heading into Beauly and visiting the 13th century Priory ruins where Claire meets Maisri the seer. It's associated with the (real) Clan Fraser of Lovat from whom the (fictional) Jamie descends, and you can take a romantic stroll up to the tomb of Lord Lovat, in the heart of Fraser lands, and see the burial cairn upon which the Fraser Clan's name has been carved—as seen in the show when Claire pays her respects to the grave in the 1960's and tells Jamie of how accomplished his daughter has become, and how much she still loves him.

Beauly Priory

Clan Fraser

It's hard not to be swept away by the beauty and romance of Jamie and Claire's love story. It's almost as if visiting real locations—even if they represent fictional scenes—makes the couple more real to us somehow; showing us that we, too, can have a love that profound, if we just reach out to our partner and hold on to them fast as we take the leap into uncertain futures, together.

Copyright © 2018 by Lezli Robyn.

Outlander *photos copyright © 2014-2018 by the Starz Network, and included in this article via their fair use policy. All other photos sourced on government tourism sites or fotolia.com.*

C.S. DeAvilla writes award-winning science fiction, fantasy, and romance under another pen name. She has been a romance fan since she sneaked a peek at her mother's massive historical romance bookcase and fell in love with all the characters. She reads every romance genre—as long as two people are falling in love, she'll give it a read. Her favorite authors are Jennifer Crusie, J.R. Ward, Darynda Jones, Suzanne Brockmann, Sarah MacLean, and Kristan Higgins. But she always has room for one more.

RECOMMENDED BOOKS

by C.S. DeAvilla

Title: ***Dating You/Hating You***
Author: Christina Lauren
Publisher: Gallery Books (Simon and Schuster)
ISBN: 150116581X
Release Date: June 6th 2017

I'd really fallen in love with *Hating Game* by Sally Thorne and I'd been searching for a similar book. As a reader, when I find a story I love I want to read more of it. And sometimes the author doesn't have anything else out yet so I'm sent on a long journey to find the book that will quench my thirst. *Dating You / Hating You* had shown up on several recommendation-lists alongside *Hating Game* and I'd recognized Christina Lauren's name on other books I'd been wanting to read, so I gave it a chance. It was amazing. Christina Lauren is actually two authors working together under one pen name. Their style is smooth and humorous with a lot of character depth. Though the storyline didn't deliver two feuding co-workers who fall in love, it did provide a lot of conflict between two agents who had instant chemistry suddenly finding themselves competing for the same job. Carter benefits from the boss being sexist, yet doesn't stand up against it until the end. Evie works hard with no complaints, but is stuck in a delicate position where she can't say much (not to mention her own personal vow not to gossip). By the end both come together when they realize someone in the office is possibly doing something illegal and Evie will take the fall if they don't pursue it. Overall a compelling story that had enough angles to keep my interest and crave more from this author.

Title: ***How to Date a Douchebag: The Learning Hours***
Author: Sara Ney
Publisher: Three Legacies
ISBN: 0999025333
Release Date: July 19th 2017

I've been reading Sara Ney's Douchebag series since the release of the first book. I'm a sucker for New Adult books. I think it's the best genre creation that has come out of the self-publishing industry. *How to Date a Douchebag* follows the members of a college wrestling team. Typical set up: a jerk jock gets paired with a nice girl who doesn't let anyone push her over. Love and hilarity ensues. That all changes in this third installment. *The Learning Hours* focuses on Rhett, a new recruit to the wrestling team who is actually a really nice guy. Trouble is he's targeted repeatedly as the new member of the team. The hazing begins right away when the team takes him out to dinner, orders over four hundred dollars of food and then leaves him with the bill. Problem is Rhett doesn't have the money to carry that kind of bill and his credit card takes a hit he can't afford. The team? They really don't see the big deal at all. To them this is something Rhett just needs to accept and get over. Laurel witnesses this event with a friend, but that doesn't stop her from calling Rhett when the team's next prank is to post his photo around school asking women to call him if they want to help him lose his virginity (he's not a virgin, but damn near close, having only slept with one girl). Laurel appears to play the part of the douche in this book with her repeated misleading as to her real identity. Even after she discovers he's a sweet guy. The problem is Rhett isn't classically cute or hot in the way she's come to expect in her other dates. Being gorgeous herself, she can't see herself with him, except he keeps surprising her at every turn. Though she judged him shallowly in the beginning, she soon falls for Rhett in the real ways that count. I recommend this entire series. It's taking bad boys to new levels, but the heroes still respect the women they attempt to woo. They don't actually turn out to be the jerks their reputations would make readers believe.

love. Sosa's writing style has echoes of Susan Elizabeth Phillips with her own stamp of originality.

Title: *Acting on Impulse*
Author: Mia Sosa
Publisher: Avon Impulse (HarperCollins Publishers)
ISBN: 0062690345
Release Date: October 31st, 2017

I knew I'd love Mia Sosa's *Acting on Impulse* from the first chapter. Her unexpected humor hits were a blast as was the pop-corn popping dynamic between her two main characters. Tori escapes to Aruba after her boyfriend announces on radio that he's single and there's nobody special in his life, which is news to Tori. But that paired with other relationship issues between the two means she's done. Actor Carter Stone, her seatmate on the plane, is instantly attracted to the spunky personal trainer. One problem? He's on the island to get some alone time away from the cameras and prepare himself for a new role. However, once at their destination he can't resist seeking Tori out and quickly building a flirty friendship with her. But once they get close enough to really experiment with the chemistry they both feel, Carter's real identity is outed and Tori freaks over falling for yet another guy in the public spotlight. They end their vacation not connecting again, but a harmless tweet by one of Tori's co-workers brings them back together. And *this* time Tori gets to take out all her frustrations by becoming Carter's personal trainer to prep him for his next role. This is a great book that readers will

Title: *Bountiful*
Author: Sarina Bowen
Publisher: Rennie Roads Books
ISBN: 1942444486
Release Date: October 20th, 2017

Sarina Bowen very quickly became one of my favorite authors this year as I swept through most of her catalog of novels. Each of her books get better and better, and *Bountiful* is the latest offering, meshing together two different books series: the Brooklyn Bruisers and True North. The Bruisers is a fantastic sports romance series through Berkley Publishing and True North, a self-publishing venture. Watching the two worlds collide effortlessly was part of the fun, having read through both series. Zara and Dave met two summers ago in a whirlwind romance that was supposed to just stay in the summer, but a surprise pregnancy makes that fun couple of a few weeks impossible to forget—for Zara. She searches for Dave, but, natch, she insisted they keep it first names only. She doesn't even know that he's a professional hockey star. Two years later he shows back up in her small Vermont town looking for more fun, never really forgetting the woman he left behind. He'd been expecting another summer hook up, maybe the option of something more, but discovering he's a father leaves him with a choice. Either embrace the family life he's sworn away from due to his own traumatic past, or pay child support and let Zara continue raising Nichole as a single mother. And she's totally willing to give him complete permission to walk away and not look back. It would be easy, though he cares for Zara too deeply to ever let her go. Bowen's style is compelling and fresh. Her characters are people I'd love to be friends with and the romance is always realistic and believable. The relationships between side characters gives it the feel that the town exists, and I could visit at any time. If you love sports romance, small towns, rural themes, and sizzling chemistry—then pick up any of the books from Bowen's series, mix it with a full three days to binge, rinse and repeat.

Title: *Hot Cop*
Author: Laurelin Paige and Sierra Simone
Publisher: Self Published
AISN: B01N6YE99C
Release Date: June 13th 2017

Hot Cop was one of those books I kept seeing pop up everywhere when it released. It had been recommended by a few of my favorite authors, ear-

lier readers of the book were praising it in reading groups, and it hit a fantastic number of reviews right out of the gate. These are all usually signs that I need to get my hands on a copy right away. According to my reading history both of these authors were new to me, so I read the sample chapter. It didn't take me long (maybe a few paragraphs) to realize that this book would be right up my alley. Livia Ward has turned thirty and her biggest regret? That she hasn't found the right man to settle down with and her biological clock alarm is ringing with no more snooze button. Enter our hot cop, Chase Kelly, who instantly is attracted to Livia after she steps in to help a protesting student at the high school. He goes in for his usual wine and handcuffs routine to get her into his bed, but she has a different proposition for him: let her have his sperm instead. Also? He can sign away his parental rights. No obligation to the baby after conception. All that responsible free sex is too good for Chase to pass up for various reasons of his own. This plot never gets old for me. I love the baby-making-plan-leads-to-love trope. My favorite part of this author duo is the steamy love scenes—hot chemistry for an equally hot cop. I read it in a few sittings even through a crazy busy week. This is one entertaining read!

Copyright © 2018 by C.S. DeAvilla.

USA Today and national bestselling author Anna J. Stewart writes sweet to sexy romance for Harlequin's Heartwarming and Romantic Suspense lines, but paranormal romance is her first love. Early obsessions with Star Wars, Star Trek, *and* Wonder Woman *set her on the path to creating fun, funny, and family-centric romances with happily ever afters for her independent heroines. Anna lives in Northern California where she deals with a serious* Supernatural *and* Sherlock *addiction and tolerates an overly affectionate cat named Snickers. You can read more about Anna and her books at www.authorannastewart.com.*

WARDEN OF MAGIC

by Anna J. Stewart

"Not another bookstore."

Grateful for the distraction given the day ahead, Clara MacQueen stifled a grin at her sister's tortured groan and gazed through the grimy, cluttered window of *Thistles and Thorns.*

It was only one of a dozen bookstores they'd come across since their arrival in Scotland three days before. The store had seen better days, with its crooked overhanging sign and rusted door handle. The crisp Edinburgh winter air swept over them and as Clara took a deep breath, she could all but smell the musty old pages and worn leather covers waiting inside. She tightened the plaid scarf around her neck and rocked back on her heels, determined to explore despite the snow that caked the sidewalks and continued to fall. "Give me five minutes, Nellie." Clara glanced down the street where their oldest sister had surrendered to her caffeine addiction on her way to pick up their rental car from the agency.

"It'll take you five minutes to stop looking in the window."

At Nellie's perfectly arched brow, Clara laughed. "Okay, a half hour. Stall Amber for me and I promise, I won't say a word when you find another castle to tour."

"Hey!" Nellie's green eyes sparkled like emeralds under a spotlight. "It's Edinburgh for crying out loud. What else are we going to do?"

"Visit bookstores?" Clara's eyes watered against the chilly breeze. "We made a deal. You get your castles, Amber gets her art galleries, and I get—"

"To buy another suitcase because you've already run out of space. How many antique books do you need, anyway?" Nellie let out an overly dramatic sigh and whipped her red curls out of her face. "Vacations are supposed to get you *away* from work. Don't you see enough books in that library of yours?"

"I don't know, *Professor.*" Clara fluttered her lashes. "Added any more history notes to that card catalogue brain of yours?"

Nellie smirked. "I'm not a professor. Yet. And my students love to hear about all the places I visit when we travel." She hesitated, some of the humor fading from her eyes. "Of course the one character trait we MacQueen sisters share is the talent for procrastination. We agreed we can't play the entire time. We have to go and see our mother some time."

Why? Clara bit the inside of her cheek and focused her attention on the beautifully decorated lampposts rather than the chiding expression on her older sister's face. Given the three girls had been abandoned by Shona MacQueen before any of them could barely say "Mama", Clara wasn't in any hurry to get reacquainted. It hadn't been Clara's idea to spend their annual vacation tracking down their long-lost mother, but for whatever reason, her sisters' yearning for healing old wounds had overridden her practical desire for the sun baked beaches of Hawaii. She'd been outvoted. Again. But at least she usually got her way when it came to bookstores.

"We promised Dad." Not that Nellie had to remind her. Again. "And it's not like we aren't having a good time. You have to admit that Christmas celebration at Edinburgh castle last night was pretty amazing. Nothing makes the holidays like bagpipes under a starry sky."

"There's nothing about Scotland that isn't amazing." From the second Clara had stepped foot off the plane, she'd felt as if she'd come home. And not because the entire city was decked out in all its holiday finery, from Princes Street to Georges Street. The German Christmas Market had given her chills while Calton Hill had given all of them some of the most gorgeous views of the old-world city possible. "I just don't see what good it's going to do, meeting her. She left us, remember?"

Clara's chest tightened as she remembered her mother driving away for the last time. And the unending toddler tears she'd shed on her father's strong shoulders. "There's no guarantee we'll actually find her. The address the private investigator found is more than a decade old."

But Clara knew. As did Nellie and Amber. Their mother was here. They could…*feel it.*

"Oh, hey, that's Amber." Nellie glanced down at her phone and the text message that appeared on her screen. "They can't find the reservation number. I need to resend her the contract. If I can find it." She tapped on the screen. "We'll come get you when we're done. In a half hour. Max."

"Yeah, yeah. Thirty minutes." Excitement pounded through Clara as she reached for the doorknob. "Ouch!" She jumped back, shaking her hand as the electric shock sparked along her fingers.

"You okay?" Nellie turned back to her sister at Clara's hiss of pain.

"Yeah. Fine." Clara stuck her index finger in her mouth. "Static build up I guess. Probably the wool scarf. I'll see you in thirty."

"Twenty-nine." Nellie grinned and headed back down the street, her brown booted feet clomping on the snow-caked sidewalk.

Cautious, Clara reached for the handle again. This time there was no shock. She pushed open the door and stepped inside. Ahhhhh. She always found the smell of paper and ink both calming and invigorating and the added aroma of nutmeg seemed appropriate given the season. The quiet reverence of the cluttered store welcomed her like an old friend as the door clicked shut behind her, and she unwrapped her scarf and tucked her purse behind her as she inched down the narrow aisle.

The dim light had her stomach jumping, as she confronted that life-long fear of closed-in dark spaces. A fear offset by the comfort brought by shelves stacked high and wide with books of every size and shape. Some had shiny new wrap around paper covers while others displayed embossed leather tomes layered with enough history to make Nellie drool. Not an inch of wall space wasn't covered in shelves that were in turn packed tighter than commuters on a subway train during rush hour.

"Ach. Customer." The muffled, female voice came across as irritated and confused. "Who is it then?"

Clara froze in her tracks as a plume of dust erupted from the end of the aisle. In reflex, she pressed a finger under her nose to stave off a sneeze attack. "I'd just like to look around if that's all right."

"Look and look, sure. All people ever do is look. Those who come in at least."

Clara stared at the small, stooped woman who seemed to float toward her. Silver streaked her hair, the same silver that shone in narrowed eyes. The long plain black dress was so big on her slight frame, Clara worried she'd trip on the hemline.

"Well." The woman wrapped arthritic fingers around the copper amulet hanging around her neck. "What be your name, young one?"

"Clara." Clara cleared her throat and dismissed the idea the amulet had begun to glow. "Clara MacQueen."

"MacQueen, you say?" Her knuckles whitened around her amulet. "Ah, yes, of course. Finally. Welcome, welcome. My name is Elya. Old name. Family name. Just like yours. You'll be wanting a special book then. Come, come. No time to waste." She waved her hand and a trail of silvery smoke danced from her fingertips.

Clara's toes scrunched in her boots. "Oh, no, really, I'd just like to look around." Her sisters' countdown clock was already counting down and she could hear the tick-tick-tick. Shrugging, she politely followed Elya toward the back of the store, curiosity pushing her forward. She almost knocked over a stack of old text books and did a spin and stoop to stop them from toppling. "Do you have a section on… oh." Clara stopped when she caught sight of the familiar cover on the shelf closest to the ceiling. *The Bruadarach.* Clara blinked and touched her fingers to her lips. Loosely translated from Scottish, the word meant dreamer or visionary. The author—unknown—had either been a fan of metaphor or unable to come up with an appropriate title for his—or her—stories.

Memories of late nights spent under the covers reading the stories of a trio of magical warriors—Bowen, Keane, and Rivalin—charged with protecting a Celtic goddess from her power hungry, evil enemies flooded back to her. Bowen had always been her favorite because of his unwavering loyalty to his family and friends. He'd sacrificed so much to fulfill his sworn duty.

Clara let out a long, sad breath. Books had been the only thing Clara's mother had ever given her daughters, other than her name. One book, one volume, for each of the girls.

How many hours had she spent reading about magic, adventure, and good triumphing over evil? Crazy magical creatures, characters with ulterior motives, mystery and honor. She'd been so silly about those stories, about those heroes, even believing they rewrote themselves every time she read them. As if books could change their plots with every new turn of the page. Never before had she ever encountered another copy, despite years of searching. She'd often wondered if that was what had attracted her to being a librarian where she could, as curator of one of the largest libraries on the west coast, be granted access to private and public collections across the country.

She'd long given up hope of ever finding another edition. But seeing the book now…the desire to dive back into those pages left her trembling.

"Oh, my." Clara breathed. "Are they all…first editions?" Her credit card was about to hit Def Con One if the illustrated trilogy was indeed original. What wonderful gifts for her sisters and the perfect reminder of their long-planned trip.

"In a manner."

"May I see volume one?" Clara moved in as Elya climbed onto a rickety step stool to retrieve the first of the three books. The old woman moved with far more ease than Clara expected and when Elya turned, she held out the coffee table-sized book as if presenting an honored offering.

Hands shaking, Clara accepted the book. Her fingers tingled as she blinked tears from her eyes. The thick leather cover was intricately embossed with threads of gold and silver, twining in a vine around an elaborate tree. The branches bent in on one another to form what Clara recognized as a Celtic triskele. She traced the image, marveling at the way the gold shimmered beneath her touch. The idea of seeing the original writing, in the original language—even if she couldn't understand it—was almost more than she could bear. She dropped her purse to the floor and drew the book close, her hopes of turning the gold-edged pages plummeting. "It needs a key."

"Aye." Elya left the other two books on the shelf and climbed down.

"Do you have it?" Clara turned the book over in case the key was somehow attached.

Elya stood before her once more and inclined her head. "Odd question coming from one of Shona MacQueen's daughters."

"I, uh, excuse me?" Clara might have gasped if she'd had any breath. Her heart hammered in her chest as the fleeting, familiar image of a tall, curvy woman with grief-filled eyes and a lying smile drifted through her mind. "How do you know my mother's—"

"We've been waiting for you. You and your sisters." Elya moved closer, peered into her eyes so deeply Clara could almost imagine her tapping against her mind. "You have her eyes. And your Gran's. No mistaking a MacQueen woman, that's for certain."

Hugging the book to her chest as if protecting it, Clara backed away. "I wouldn't know." Except she did. She and her sisters all had the same gold-sparked green eyes their mother possessed. Fate's eyes, their father had called them.

"What do you mean you don't know?" Elya couldn't have gotten any closer, and the frustration in her voice matched the hold she had on Clara's wrist. "You're here, aren't you? Something called you home."

"I live in California." Clara began to wish she'd resisted temptation to come into the shop. She'd come to Scotland to close the book on her mother once and for all, not begin a new one.

"Doesn't mean Scotland isn't your home." Elya turned and shuffled away, tossing, "Come, tea time. Your sisters may join us when they get here," over her bony shoulder.

"Oh, no, please." Clara shook her head as Elya turned around again. "I don't have time for tea and Amber went to get coffee," she lied. "I should probably go and…find…her."

Elya sighed, shook her head and looked up to the ceiling. "All this time, all this waiting. And fate sends us a clueless girl who knows nothing of her destiny." She turned around and straightened, the amulet around her neck flickering to a steady, blue white glow. An odd, controlled simmering energy pulsed around the room. The air in the store ruffled, as if a breeze had blown through an open door. "So be it."

Clara backed away, the book still in her hands as she looked for a safe place to set it down. The hair on the back of her neck prickled to attention as her fingers brushed over the brass lock concealing the pages from curious readers. From her.

A spark erupted, as if she'd struck flint against stone. Clara cried out and let go of the book, unable to do anything but watch it fall to the floor.

It fell open.

The light from Elya's amulet cast its bluish glow onto the illustrated page. She should run. She knew this as surely as she knew she was meant to breathe, but she couldn't look away. Not from the thicket of silver-topped trees on the exposed pages. Not from the obscured opening to a cave. And not from the solitary flickering flame moving through the image at her feet.

Her breath caught in her chest as something tugged her forward and moved her feet against her will. In the time it took her to blink, in the time it took for her booted foot to brush the bottom of the page, the room began to spin.

No. It wasn't the room that was spinning. It was her.

The bookstore faded behind a fog of brilliant yellow and white. A quick flash, a *boom* against her ears. Nausea swept over her. She couldn't move. Couldn't make a sound and only when she forced out a breath and released a fraction of the fear coursing through her, did her mind and vision clear.

She let out a breath and closed her eyes in relief. Whatever had been happening stopped.

Until she was sucked straight down.

And the cover slammed shut above her.

Bowen stumbled against the trunk of a Farrengold tree as the ground shook beneath his feet and the stag he'd been tracking leapt across the stream and out of sight.

The Farrengold's delicate, florescent silver flowers cascaded around him, bathing him in darkness-easing light. His calloused fingers tightened around his bow as a loud *wumph* ripped through the air; an unfamiliar sound which echoed across the expanse of the lush world that served as his prison.

He straightened, spotting a bolt of light in the direction of his dwelling. Bright enough to light the sky.

Bright enough to cause problems in the guise of the sentries that patrolled the woods.

Familiar energy shot through him. Beneath his touch, the tree shivered. The night air—neither warm nor cool—brushed across his face and ruffled the long-sleeved tunic he wore. The dark fabric not only protected him from the cold, but also kept him camouflaged in the darkness against well-sighted predators lurking in the woods.

The arrow he'd had poised at a stag large enough to provide meat for the season had lost its target. Frustration over wasted time almost overcame the unease circling inside him. He slung his bow onto his back and stalked through the knee-deep flora, shoving the arrow into its quiver. He made quick work of the woods, having traversed them every day since his arrival, his soft leather boots barely touching the ground.

He couldn't remember the last sight of magic he'd beheld let alone felt. But he felt it now, coursing across his body, caressing his soul before moving away and into the darkness. The longing for the powers he'd been born with nearly drove him to his knees. Powers that had been stripped from him the instant he'd arrived in this world. A world both familiar and foreign. A world that had stolen everything from him.

A world from which he'd never escape.

While the light in the distance dimmed…it continued to glow.

The rustling in the trees ahead had him pulling his dagger from the sheath at his waist and he crouched to scan the area. A dark shape shifted into his line of sight. Dark but…small. Delicate almost. He narrowed his eyes and let the moonlight aid in his evaluation. Arms and legs like himself. More slight—fragile, even—as the figure tumbled and stumbled along the worn path he'd created upon arriving in this place. Drunk, no doubt. Or soaring along the hallucinogenic waves of Lovara root.

He gripped the hilt, planning his attack, determined to rid this world of another of Dracha's soldiers. It would be a merciful death, Bowen told himself. Dracha was not known for his tolerance of wayward soldiers with a penchant for intoxicants.

Bowen shifted on silent feet, ready to pounce, waiting to see a telltale sign of stark yellow hair tied in intricate braids.

The odd squeal that erupted from the creature had him reconsidering. High-pitched, panicked, almost, and most definitely—

"Holly hell in a hand basket!" The squeal ended in a stream of words. "What in the crappety-crap just happened?"

A woman.

Bowen's insides tightened as he shot to his feet. Knife still in hand, he moved forward, every step deliberate. He'd never seen a female sentry before. "Who are you?"

The woman yelped and spun so fast her feet flew out from under her. She hit the ground hard on her backside, long red hair spilling around her head as her skull smacked the ground. "Well, that's just great. Ow."

Bowen crept closer, his grip loosening as he reexamined his prey. He stood over her, marveling at the odd fitted cloak she wore and the pants covering her legs. And that hair. He hadn't seen hair that color in…. What kind of magic was this? Where had this woman come from? "What are you?"

"Right now, I'm pissed off." She shoved herself up on her elbows and glared at him. "And who—or *what*—are you?"

She didn't seem intent on attacking him or defending herself. Either she was that certain of her power or she was completely out of her element. He would bet his last pelt on the latter. "I am Bowen."

"Yeah, right. Bowen." She snorted. "Next I suppose you'll tell me you're the Warden of the Eastern Realm."

Bowen gnashed his teeth as his past shot back at him with the speed of an arrow. So their sacrifice had not gone unnoticed? Their battle to protect the Goddess's daughter hadn't disappeared into the ether of history after their disobedience? Their families…his heart stuttered. Did their families know the truth? Did his family live?

He focused his attention back on the stranger. "You know me?"

"Only in my thirteen-year-old mind. Although, I gotta admit"—she skimmed her eyes up and down his body in a way that reminded him he was most definitely male—"I think adult me is appreciating you in a much different way." She dragged her feet underneath herself and pushed herself up. "Okay, Elya! Game's over! Whatever you've done—"

"Elya!" Bowen raised his blade, ready to plunge his knife into the heart of the one who had betrayed them. His body stiffened as he scanned the sky and tree line. "The traitor! You're one of hers! She's here? With you?"

"Woah, hold on." The woman scrambled back a step and held up her hands as he advanced on her. "I'm no one's but my own. And this Elya person poses no threat. She's probably older than that tree over there. So back up, Conan, and tell me what LARPG I've stumbled in to."

"*Ell-ay-are-pee-gee?*" Such strange words coming from her lips. Determined lips. The moonlight caught her in its beam and she blinked green eyes at him; alarmed green eyes that, in the next moment, almost had him dropping to his knees. Instead, he lowered his blade and braced his feet apart as any warrior would when facing his goddess. "Shona."

She stared at him and didn't move. For an instant, Bowen wondered if time had turned against him and slowed even more.

"You have got to be kidding me," she muttered. "I go twenty-seven years with barely a mention of the woman and the second I hit Edinburgh, I can't get away from her. Nellie put you up to this, didn't she? You know, I bet she and Amber planned this entire thing and they dropped some sedative in my tea this morning. Really good tea, which totally explains why I'm suddenly standing in front of a man who looks like he could rip that tree in two." She reached up and pinched her cheeks repeatedly. Hard. "Come on. Wake up. Wake. Up."

"Stop!" Bowen sheathed his blade and moved toward her, ignoring the flash of panic that shot into her face. "You are hurting yourself." He caught one of her hands in his. "Please. Stop. I will keep you safe."

Admiration speared through him as she inched up her chin and braced her feet.

"Right." She gave a slow nod and dropped her gaze to their linked hands. "Not sure we'd

agree on what you consider safe. Whatcha doing there, Robin Hood?"

These names she called him, they made him want to smile. Her fingers fit perfectly between his, the touch of her skin as smooth as the water that rushed over the rocks in the nearby river. He rotated his hand, rubbed his thumb over the pulse pounding unsteadily in her wrist. An unexpected—and most welcome—heat blasted through his body and settled heavily in his groin. How long had it been since he'd touched a woman? Seen a woman? Interacted with anyone who didn't try to kill or trap him? Or betray him to those who wanted him dead.

Which was why he lived alone. In the middle of nowhere. As far from the marketplace and central community as he dared. He'd all but arrived with a target on his back and a price on his head: a trophy to be won for Dracha, his men, or Bowen's fellow prisoners. Alone he only had to worry about protecting himself while not being surrounded by those willing to do—or say—anything to make their own existence more tolerable. Now his only companions were the knots of dread that had tightened in his belly upon his arrival.

As he inhaled, above the night aroma of lavender heavy thistle-ferns blooming beneath the moon he caught the scent of something spicy and warm. Much like the woman standing before him.

Her mouth opened and closed, as if she struggled to speak. Had a spell overtaken her? Had she brought magic back to him with her mere—and unexpected—arrival? He felt her tremble under his touch and with his other hand, he caressed her cheek, catching her chin in his fingers and angling her face up and into the light.

"You are bewitching." He couldn't help it. His hand moved to the length of her hair that tumbled in thick waves over and behind her shoulders. Even strewn with leaves and sticks, he'd never beheld a more beautiful sight than the pale-skinned woman with a small nose and sparkling, jewel eyes. Innocent eyes that looked to him in uncertainty. "Your name. Tell me your name."

"Clara." There it was, the melodious voice he'd worried she lost. "Clara MacQueen. And you're one hell of a welcoming committee."

He watched as she lifted a hand to his face, stroked his cheek, and had him resisting the urge to haul her into his arms and carry her into his dwelling.

"Remind me to thank my sisters for however they managed to pull this off." Her fingers curved around to the back of his head as she rose up on her toes. "No harm in playing along, is there?"

"Sisters." Her mouth was a mere breath from his. "You are of Shona. You and your…sisters."

She licked her lips, the tip of her tongue darting out ever so slightly; ever so tempting. "Shona Mac-Queen? Yes, she's my mother. But we can talk about that later—"

"Hell and hail fury." Bowen released her and stepped back, forcing the attraction growing inside of him back to its dormant state. He stepped back, shifting his hold so he grabbed her arms and kept her at a distance. Shona was not old enough to have a child of this age. "Dark magic enhanced by lies." Even as he uttered the words he knew—as certain as he continued to draw breath—this Clara was precisely what she claimed.

Shona, only reaming daughter of the Goddess, had birthed children? Had continued the magical line? Shona was…alive?

Relief would have driven him to his knees had he surrendered to it. Instead, all he could do was stare at the woman who had brought not only light to this dark world, but also…hope.

"Not the magic I was going for." Clara muttered. "Ease up there, Hercules. I'm not going anywhere. Yet." She kicked at the book at their feet as Bowen heard a crack in the distance.

He hauled her closer before shoving her behind him and this time, he drew the broadsword he'd not used in many cycles.

"If you're trying to scare me—"

"Quiet!" Bowen sliced the word as sharp as he could, angling his head as the sound of voices and booted feet echoed through the woods.

"Look, this has been fun and all and whatever theater group Nellie found you in, I'll leave you a great Yelp review. Totally authentic, really. But I need to get back. You hear that, Elya? You can wake me up any—"

"I said quiet!" Bowen reached back and gripped her hip. "Dracha's men are determined and cunning. They will not give up until they find the source of the fire that streaked the sky. We must go." He sheathed his sword. "Now."

"That's what I just said."

When he turned around he found her staring at him. Whatever fear she'd been displaying earlier had vanished and instead, he found nothing but muted humor reflected on her face. The woman didn't have any idea what was going on, did she? His stomach quivered as he found himself reciting the oath he'd taken all those years ago. The oath he and his friends had broken by disobeying orders. This woman, this Clara, was his chance for redemption.

"Just like a man to usurp a woman's idea for his own," Clara muttered. "You know, I have a good mind to just wait here for your friend Dracha and—Hey! What are you doing?! Put me down! Wait! The book!"

Her screams of protests cut off abruptly as he stooped down and threw her over his shoulder. She kicked her feet, the toes of her boots hitting disturbingly close to where he'd much prefer her hands. Her fists hit him hard at the base of his spine and he grunted. She was strong for such a little bit of a thing.

"Since you are not inclined to move on your own, I shall move for both of us." He made quick work of the twisting path to the mouth of the cave that lay deep in a clearing among a thicket of Farrengold trees and vicinta shrubs, a prickly yellow plant with thick stickers which burrowed under the skin.

She twisted her body around and her fists unclenched so she could grab at him. "Oh, no. Do not take me in there."

"I mean you no harm." What would it take to keep this woman quiet? "We must hide. You will be safe here." The inclination to hide went against every instinct raging through him. He was a warrior, a soldier, sworn to protect the Goddess and all her kin, but the only way he could fulfill that obligation was to stay alive. And taking on a battalion of Dracha's men was only going to be a fight in futility. Not without a plan at least.

"Put. Me. Down!"

Once inside, he did as she demanded. "Now will you be quiet?"

"Just tell me to do that one more time." She moved closer, planting her hands on her hips, and stared at him, eyes to chin. "I *dare* you."

Reminding him of a scared rabbit, she attempted to dart past him, which he prevented easily by holding out his arm. After shoving him proved fruitless, she tried the other side. He caught her around the waist and shifted her back. Then she attempted to

dive under him. He bent down and hauled her up. Finally, she stopped and crossed her arms over her chest and glared at him. Bowen's lips twitched. If only they had more time to play this game.

"If you don't stay still and be quiet, I shall be forced to restrain you." He reached over the entrance to the cave and untied the animal skin covering he'd fashioned soon after his imprisonment in this realm. The skin of the eloquine, a large animal normally used for transportation over vast distances, would reflect any light cast on it and make it appear as if the opening did not exist. At least that was the theory.

Bowen had only tested the curtain on intoxicated interlopers and never well-trained, let alone sober, soldiers. He could only pray it would continue to work.

"I'm all for hiding from…whoever they are." Clara's voice lowered but trembled none the less. "But not here. I can't do close dark spaces. Nothing I can do about it. Crap." She patted her hands on her sides. "Left my cellphone in my purse. Along with my sanity, apparently."

"It's not dark. I can see you." He could hear her breathing, ragged, short, shallow breaths that made the hair on the back of his neck prickle. He looked over his shoulder to where she stumbled over to the cave wall.

Frustration and sympathy intermingled as he reminded himself that The Forgotten Realm was a place of nightmares. Growing up, he and Keane and Rivalin had been warned of the prison world reserved only for those who had committed unforgiveable crimes or had dishonored themselves or their families. Half the lunar cycle was spent in varying degrees of darkness. Light was used as a weapon and could ignite curiosity from both man and creature. Advantage was often given to those who had been here longest, but his training had given him an instant reputation. That said, he'd lost count of the scars he'd accumulated proving he should be left alone.

If it had been difficult for him to adjust, he could only imagine how terrified Clara must be. Clara. His heart twisted in his chest even as a newfound sense of pride swept over him. This was his chance to prove himself worthy once more—to the Goddess, to his dead comrades. To himself. He would protect the woman to whatever end the Goddess deemed fit. And earn his honor back in the process.

He shifted position so he could see both outside the cave and keep watch over her. Even from the vast distance, he could see the outline of the book she'd arrived with lying on the ground near the underbrush. She was clearly not of this world. Her words, her attitude, none of this fit in the world he knew. But he knew there were far more mysteries in life than anything that had explanation. To discount something as unbelievable simply because he'd never seen or experienced it himself…the concept simply didn't make practical sense.

Had the book acted as a type of portal? In which case, Clara was right and he'd been wrong to leave it behind. Magic like that, power like that, in Dracha's hands would only mean more trouble for him and the others who dwelled in this realm through no choice of their own.

He shifted his fingers under the edge of the curtain, fisting the thick fabric in his hand as he debated his odds of being able to retrieve the book and return without being noticed.

His eyes narrowed against the flicker of torch flame as the soldiers came closer. Over the unnerving mumbling and whispers of Clara's unease, his fear was realized as saw one of the silver armored soldiers carry the book into the clearing and uttered an excited cry of triumph over his fellow men.

Bowen cursed and withdrew his hand from outside the cave as Clara let out a whimper. She had her arms wrapped so tightly around herself he wondered how she could breathe. A thin thread of moonlight trickled in from an overhead crack in the stone, enough for him to see well enough to move. Which he did. Toward her.

"Clara."

She started at the sound of her name as Bowen marveled at how it sounded coming from his lips. Clara. So natural, so beautiful. So…perfect.

He didn't know why, but he left his sentry post and moved toward her, held out his hand to guide him, only to find it caught hard in hers. The second she grabbed hold of him, that odd flame of connection shot through him and for the first time since he arrived in this realm, the knots of dread loosened inside him.

"I hope you have a paper bag around here somewhere, Tarzan." She squeezed his hand hard. "Because I'm about to have a major panic attack." The air in her lungs sounded heavy, as if she'd been caught in a rushing river's undertow. "Crap. Can't. Stop. It." She shook her head and he felt her hair brush against his face as the footsteps of the soldiers drew closer. "I'm sorry. Always. Had. Them. Can't—"

He silenced her the only way he could think of.

He pressed his mouth to hers.

The pressured panic twining through Clara's chest took a side route and shot straight to her toes which curled in her boots. His lips were softer than she imagined, stronger than she anticipated, and more tempting than reason dictated. Without a second thought she surrendered to the sensations coursing through her and rose up. Her hand flattened against his torso as she trailed fingers up toward his heart where she gripped his shirt. The weakness in her knees faded as the urge to draw closer to him overrode the confusion fogging her brain. She clung to him and surrendered to the power of his kiss.

The soft moan that escaped her throat didn't get very far as he angled his head and, after a gentle brush of fingers against the side of her face, deepened the kiss. She opened her mouth beneath his and their tongues brushed, relishing in the sudden tightening of his body as he moved forward and pinned her against the cave wall.

The clanging of metal against stone outside the cave had her gasping as Bowen tore his mouth away, but instead of abandoning her and letting her drop to the ground, he moved closer and braced her body against his, his leg sliding between hers to hold her up.

"What—" she halted her whisper at the sharp turn of his head. In the receding darkness she saw the flash of his eyes and marveled at their golden, shimmering intensity. She bit her lip, head spinning as she clenched her hands in the fabric of his shirt. How was any of this possible? How was she…here? With him. Part of her didn't want to know. Part of her just wanted to enjoy whatever fantasy this was.

Bowen shook his head, his long hair brushing over his shoulders to caress the back of her hand.

She ducked her head while she tried to ignore the heated pressure building between her legs. Never in her life had she experienced such an intense—and immediate—reaction to a man. *Any* man let alone one who looked as if he'd stepped out of every fantastical hero-centric book she'd ever read. He was blindingly gorgeous, intensely overwhelming and could no doubt short circuit any electrical outlet with a mere glance. If any outlet could be found here.

She let out a long, slow breath and tried to ignore the desire pulsing through her. Forget electricity. It was as if he'd struck a dormant match inside of her and set her aflame. The way his body pressed into her, the way his hands caressed her, or even the way his arms held her left her reeling. What had happened to her in that bookstore that took her dreams to a place of such intense reality?

Maybe it was the nutmeg. She remembered smelling it when she'd entered. Nutmeg had been known to cause hallucinations, right? That had to be it. She'd never had such vivid dreams before. Such physical ones. She gripped her fingers harder, felt the firmness of his arms and chest beneath her grasp. She couldn't explain a single thing that was happening including why she felt safe with him. So aroused with him.

The second the word slipped through her mind, Bowen eased away and her feet touched the ground once again. Had he read her thoughts and was offended? Did he not feel the same? Ridiculous. There was no mistaking his physical reaction to her. The flush that warmed her cheeks brought a shy, knowing smile to her lips even as the angry and frustrated shouts of men echoed beyond the mouth of the cave.

The light drew her and she moved in beside Bowen. He stood stone still in the center of the opening, as if daring those on the other side to attempt entry. This place was so odd. Where thick green brush and shrubs and draping tree limbs should be reflecting every shade of green, they glistened in reds, blues, and yellows, refracting against the moonlight. Flowers and blossoms glowed bright enough to cast light through the darkness which she only now realized was devoid of stars. Just a black blanket over hanging the space above the unending treetops.

She watched a group of armored men hacking their swords through the nearby brush. Flickering torches lit the area outside and cast panic-easing fragments of light into the cave. She looked at Bowen and pinched her lips tight to stop from asking how they weren't seen, especially with the way the men violently searched the area. She brushed her fingers against his arm and felt a slight relaxing in his muscles. As she trailed her hand down, his fist opened and he wrapped his hand around hers. Instantly, she calmed.

The sound of hoof beats echoed in the night. A large horse-like creature, as black as the surrounding sky and adorned with a saddle and bit of sparkling bronze, came to a halt at the edge of the clearing. The rider's muted command didn't make sense to her, but the men on the ground scattered and reassembled in a razor sharp line on either side of him.

Clara couldn't tear her eyes from the creature he rode. Iridescent scales covered its massive body and shimmered against the threadbare moonlight. The slick silver tail and mane glistened like liquid mercury and draped over the creature like a blanket. "Olappa," she whispered and jumpedwhen Bowen squeezed her hand as a reminder to remain quiet. She remembered the creature from the storybook—part dragon, part horse type creature, an Olappa blood-bonded to its rider at birth. They were, in essence, one being. If one were to perish, the other would follow. Loyal beyond fault, the Olappa was one of the few creatures she, Nellie, and Amber had always agreed would make the perfect pet.

Nellie. Amber. Fear Clara would never again see her sisters nearly choked the breath from her lungs.

"What is this?" The question exploded through the darkness and made Clara jump. She gasped and followed the direction the rider's sword had taken toward one of his soldiers.

The tension in Bowen's body returned. Clara stepped closer and wrapped her arms around his.

A soldier stepped forward and into the thicket. "It is a book, my liege." He clutched it against his chest and carried it over.

"Open it!" The rider ordered.

"Sir." The soldier sheathed his sword and removed his black glove. The second he touched the brass lock on the cover, he began to shake.

Bowen released her hand and slipped his arm around Clara's shoulders, turning her into him.

"Don't look," he whispered as he bent over her. He attempted to push her face into his chest, but she turned at the last moment, clinging to him as she peeked out.

Yellow flames exploded from the lock and into the soldier's fingers. He dropped the book and leapt back. Clara watched, horrified, as flames erupted inside the man's body, illuminating every vein, every vessel, every bone and muscle before engulfing him in fire. Clara cringed as the man's screams ripped through the night before falling heavily silent.

For an instant, Clara thought he'd survived. Until the ash of the soldier dropped to the ground and was carried away by the midnight breeze.

Nausea roiled inside her. Her entire body went cold as dreaded realization dawned. This wasn't some drug-induced dream or hallucination. She hadn't fallen asleep last night and neglected to wake up. Her fingers gripped Bowen's shirt as she inhaled the warmth of him tinged with fresh air and determined strength.

Whatever was happening to her, around her, was real.

The rider slung his leg over the front of his saddle and dropped to the ground. The bronze helmet covering his face glistened in the firelight of his soldiers' torches. Clara could hear the leathery squeak of his uniform as he moved. His men backed away as he approached the book.

He bent down and brushed his gloved hand over the cover to clear the remains, then traced a finger over the embossed image. With a shake of his head, he lowered his chin and removed his helmet.

Bowen's arms tightened around Clara; whether in reaction or in protection she couldn't be certain. Not until she looked up at him as shock crossed his handsome, scarred features.

She wanted to ask him who the man was; she wanted to ask him why he looked—for want of a better word—horrified. But voicing any question now would only add to his stress. Instead, she found herself reaching her hand to his face and brushing her fingertips lightly against his cheek.

Tears glistened in his eyes, but only briefly. So briefly Clara was certain she'd imagined them.

"Rivalin," Bowen whispered as a coldness draped his face.

Clara looked back to the rider as he carried the book to his charge and remounted. That wasn't possible. The Rivalin she'd read about was a hero, not a villain. He was good, pure of heart and one of the Goddesses' chosen warriors. Warriors closer than brothers. Inseparable since childhood; chosen by the Goddess herself as her personal guards and warriors. They were the only ones she'd trusted with her last living child, a girl, unnamed in the stories, but considered the last hope of her people.

Clara cringed and wondered what was going through Bowen's mind. How utterly betrayed he must be feeling. And yet….

How had he not known?

"Spread out and search the forest!" Rivalin ordered. "This book would not have arrived on its own. It came with someone. I want that someone found and brought to the keep to present to Lord Dracha. Move!" He bellowed. "Now!"

Clara followed Bowen's lead and remained frozen where she was. Rivalin disappeared into the darkness of the woods as the torch-carrying soldiers dispersed. Darkness descended once more, punctuated only by the still-glowing wilting flowers, pitching Clara into the panic attack that had nearly suffocated her. She squeezed her eyes shut, chanting in her mind that she was safe, the darkness couldn't hurt her. That in a few minutes Bowen would remove the covering to the entrance and she would once again breathe fresh, clean air in an open space.

Seconds ticked past. Minutes. Clara shifted on her feet, the hard soles of her boots little protection against the rocky ground of the cave. The ridiculousness of her situation began to dawn as doubt slipped free of its rational tether and floated away.

She was trapped *in* a book. With a warrior who had just learned one of his best friends had betrayed their oath. Clara giggled and tried to catch the sound behind her hand. Too late. She glanced up and found Bowen watching her, his expression furrowed to the point his eyebrows merged.

"If I start talking will you kiss me again?" She'd meant it as a question, not a request. But the second the words were out of her lips, she realized how easily he might misinterpret. Rather than wait for an answer, she stepped in front of him and reached for the covering to the cave.

"Wait." His quiet command had her doing as he requested, but not without a tinge of irritation.

Did he really think she was dumb enough to go gallivanting out there with those soldiers still around? Soldiers she knew were looking for her? Resisting the urge to salute, she moved aside so he could poke his head out. Yeah, great idea. Let him get himself killed and leave her all on her own to deal with this Dracha person.

"Dracha." Now it was Clara's turn to frown. "Who is he?"

"Overseer of this land." Bowen's voice was back to its normal timbre and made her shiver. He had a deep, baritone voice that a woman could feel from her toes to the tip of her spine. There was a fluidity to it that drew her in, like the welcoming tide of the ocean drawing tempted toes to the shoreline.

"And what land is that exactly? This isn't the Eastern Realm," Clara told him and earned an arched brow in response. "I've read *The Bruadarach* since I was a little girl. I know all about you and Keane and…Rivalin. Or at least I thought I did." She winced as he looked away and leaned further out of the cave. The air had warmed. Perhaps remnants of the torches? Or for another reason? "The three warriors charged with protecting the Goddess's daughter. Bowen of the East, Keane of the North, and Rivalin of the West."

"And what of the South?" Bowen asked.

"Alastrine, Goddess and Warden of All. The Southern Continent is a place of peace, whereas the other three are…not."

"The Southern Continent *was* a place of peace," Bowen corrected her. "Before we failed to protect Alastrine and all her people. Before our banishment to this prison realm. Before Keane and Rivalin were lost…"

He ripped the covering down and threw it inside the cave. His fists clenched and the muscles in his arms bulged. Clara could feel the rage building inside of him, like a fireball building to explosion and yet he couldn't release it. Not without bringing the soldiers back.

"So this is a penal colony." If only that information provided more answers rather than more questions. "How many prisoners are there?"

"I am one of thousands."

"Quiet for such a crowded place." The only sounds she did hear, other than the wind rustling through the leaves, was an odd growling sound as if a frog had a, well…a frog in its throat. "Where is everyone?"

"*Cosanta Baile*." At her arched brow, he thought for a moment. "A place of protection. Inside the stone walls, people are left to their own devices. Mostly."

That mostly didn't sound entirely convincing. "Tell me what happened to your friends." Uncertain what else she could do, she grabbed hold of his hands and slipped her fingers through his. He'd helped calm the panic inside of her earlier and while she didn't think it a good idea to repeat his method of distraction, the least she could do was attempt to quell the rage coursing through his body. "Tell me what happened to Rivalin. Why would he be on the other side of good now?"

"I cannot explain it." Bowen closed his eyes and took a long breath. "I saw him die with my own eyes. Pierced by Dracha's sword the moment he arrived…." He looked up into the sky. "None of this matters now. What matters is that you need to be taken somewhere safe while I set out on this quest."

"Somewhere safe?" Clara echoed. "*Cosanta Baile*?"

"Yes. Miranda will know what is best." He shook his head. "It is not safe there for everyone."

"Do you mean it's not safe for you or for me?" What possible use could anyone have with an ignorant liability like her? As far as Bowen was concerned, okay, sure—she could see where some might consider him threatening, but—

"We will find out." He stalked past her into the cave and after a few seconds, soft light erupted to illuminate the space. What she'd seen as grey stone now glowed an odd, deep purple, sparkling against the light like a geode. Caves normally smelled of stagnant water or moldy earth, but there were no suffocating aromas here. If anything, the air smelled a bit sweet. He'd fashioned a table out of chunks of wood, and she saw a collection of bowls, cups, and utensils lining a rudimentary shelf wedged into the side of the wall. A large, wide bed strewn thick with hand-woven blankets and rudimentary stitched cushions lay across the room as round, uneven candles flickered stronger rays of light than Clara would have thought possible.

But it was the sight of Bowen himself that stole what little breath remained inside her. Her earlier shadowed glimpses and imagination hadn't done him justice. She'd suspected he was handsome—what dream in her head wouldn't have provided a pretty picture?—but seeing him now, up close, the way he commanded the space he occupied with every long stride, the way the fabric of his pants and tunic stretched tight over his muscular form…she had to wonder if perhaps the Goddesses themselves had paid special attention to this man. The tiny scars that marred his angular face did nothing to detract from his good looks, framed by long, gold-tipped hair the color of rich espresso. Fearing she might be ogling a bit too much, she looked for something—anything—to distract her from staring.

"You have books." The small shelving unit beside the table drew her close and she plucked one of the tattered, worn hide-covered tomes free. She didn't recognize the language. To her it looked like a cross between runes and hieroglyphics. "Where did you find books?"

"The marketplace." Bowen dragged a satchel free from one of the carved out spaces in the wall. "It's a day's walk from here. I can find most of what I need and want. Provided I have something to trade." "I'm guessing they don't take PayPal."

Bowen stared at her.

"Yeah, bad joke. Sorry." She stood up and rubbed her hands down her sides. "So, what are we going to do about getting that book back? I'm assuming if that's how I got here, that's how I get home."

"We?" Bowen halted stuffing what looked like clothes into the bag and turned to face her. "This quest is for me alone. I will take you where you'll be safe."

"Oh, I heard you the first time. And no, you will not take me anywhere other than with you."

He shook his head. "I am not accustomed to my orders being disobeyed. You will allow me—"

"Let's put a pin in that male ego of yours for the time being, okay?" Clara struggled to maintain her patience. He had to be feeling a bit stressed out, but it wasn't as if she'd had a Shirley Temple Good Ship Lollipop kind of day. "Even after a few minutes of knowing you, I feel safe in saying you aren't going to leave something as powerful as that book in the

hands of some evil warlord. That's what Dracha is I'm assuming?"

"War. Lord." Bowen frowned. "An odd phrase but accurate. He has fought in many wars. And you are correct. I am going after the book."

"Huh. Wherever women go, misogyny follows. Even into other realms. Good to know."

"Who follows?" Bowen demanded and darted back to the cave's opening.

Clara grinned. Oh, she was really going to have fun with this man. "In a nutshell, it's a word that means sexism. The belief that men are superior to women and therefore are entitled to control their every move."

"A fallacy." Bowen's gold eyes glimmered dangerously in the cave light. "Women are not only equal, but in my experience, far superior to the male species. It is why they lead our people. Women are far more rational and reasoned than brute men."

"You don't say?" Clara took a seat on the bed next to the bag of clothes. "Well, if I needed proof this world is fictional, there it is. And yet I'm not allowed to go with you to find the book. The book I brought here, by the way. The book that apparently only I can open. Unless you're looking to be ashes in the wind."

"You need to be protected," Bowen said in a tone that made her think he thought her stupid. "You are of Shona. You are of the Goddess Alastrine and it is my obligation to keep you safe. I cannot do both that and retrieve the book from Dracha. That is the end of the discussion."

Whatever Clara had been expecting to hear in regards to her mother, it certainly wasn't that. "I'm sorry, what? I'm of the what?"

"The Goddess. Shona was—is—the Goddess's only surviving daughter. You are, if what you say is true, therefore—"

"Stop! Just…stop." Clara held up her hand. She might be willing to accept she'd been transported into a magical realm. She might be willing to accept an evil tyrant wanted to capture and maybe imprison her. But being descended from a Goddess?

Clara shivered.

Nellie she could probably buy. Her middle sister had a spunk and spirit that allowed her to make friends with everyone and anyone. Amber? Absolutely. She was never a woman to take no for an answer. But plain old librarian Clara who fell in love with fictional heroes rather than take a chance on a real man?

There wasn't anything Goddess-like about that. Or about her. Nevertheless, clearly Bowen believed it to be true and it was going to take some serious negotiating to convince him leaving her behind was not in his interest.

"Tell me something, Bowen. What would happen should someone discover who I really am? That I'm Shona's youngest daughter?"

"That would depend on who the someone is. The Goddess has many followers here, but she also has her enemies. There are many who blame her for the rise of Dracha and his brotherhood. They believe she has forgotten and abandoned them."

"Meaning you really can't trust anyone with that knowledge, can you?"

"I trust Miranda." He flipped the flap on his bag closed and faced her. "And it is to her I will take you. You should rest. We will leave come morn."

"What exactly was it that you gave me to eat again?"

Bowen glanced over his shoulder to where Clara trudged behind him kicking through the ankle thick brambles and vines covering the direction he'd chosen. He had attached a thick branch of Ferringold flowers to a staff to light their way through the seasonally dark sky. The normally glowing leaves were still huddled together and curled, hibernating until the moon rose back to its zenith.

"Tashiri eggs." They would have spoiled long before he returned to his dwelling—*if* he returned to his dwelling. Therefore he had cooked enough to feed them both and left the rest for the nika birds that would come scavenging in a few hours' time. "A bracing breakfast that will keep your energy up as we have much land to traverse."

"If that's your way of saying they'll stay with me a while, I'm about to prove you wrong."

Bowen stopped and peered at her as she covered her mouth and turned a bit green.

"You are unwell?" He pulled out the animal skin flask from under his pack and held it out for her. "Drink this."

"Unless that's Pepto, I don't think I…um. I'll be right back." Bowen moved to follow her behind an outcropping of deadened trees, only to stop when he heard her retching. Their quest to reach Miranda by nightfall was not looking promising. Especially as the old wise woman was in the opposite direction of the keep, Dracha and…Rivalin.

Rivalin…

"That's water, right?" Clara called weakly.

"Yes." He withdrew another container from his pack and walked it over to her. "Drink as much as you like. There's a river nearby and we can stop for more."

"Great." She held out her hand without looking at him. "Always good to stop on the road for a pick me up." She gagged. "Give me a few more minutes, here. Go…away." The retching began again.

Bowen reluctantly took up a post a few feet away, unwilling to let her too far out of his sight. This time of day, far earlier than he normally rose, most everything in the forest would be asleep or at the least, not prowling for prey. Creatures and animals he could manage easily. It was forest dwellers like himself they needed to be wary of. One reason he'd chosen a spot closer to the keep. Fewer people dared to come within a day's distance of Dracha and his men.

He'd been grateful Clara had fallen asleep after he was certain the soldiers had moved beyond the borders of his cave. Since he knew he would never do the same, he'd given her his bed and stayed awake, standing guard and listening to her soft breathing.

It had felt good, invigorating, life affirming, to slip back into the role of protector. A role that had brought him both accolades, gratitude, and eventually, disgrace. He would do whatever it took to erase the latter. And make certain he was remembered for his devotion to the Goddess and her kin.

But…he was out of his element. He needed guidance. Miranda would know what to do. If anything, he could count on the former high priestess to talk Clara into staying with her. Bowen shifted uncomfortably. And if she couldn't, he'd insist the old woman use whatever magic Miranda had at her disposal to…convince her.

Once on his own, he could fulfill his duty. Not only to retrieve the book.

But to save Rivalin..

Even it it meant he had to kill him.

Anger and confusion continued their battle deep inside him as he wondered what had happened to his friend. To be in service to Dracha meant one of two things: either Rivalin had switched allegiances or he was under a spell. Either way, Bowen owed it to the man he'd called brother to end Rivalin's disgrace and return his honor—by allowing him to fight to the death. He could only hope Rivalin had been forced to live this way, to have betrayed the oath he took, the promises he'd made. After all they'd been through together, he owed his friend everything. Including an honorable death.

"Well, since I think I just puked up my esophagus, I should be good to go for a few miles." Clara stumbled out from behind the tree into the dimness of the morning. The forest had been cast in its graying silver splendor, illuminating the thick colorful foliage and blossoming trees. The pink had returned to her cheeks and she drank greedily from the soft flask.

"You appear to be feeling better."

"Just no more eggs. Of any kind." She patted a hand against his chest as she passed. "You hear me?"

"I do indeed." He let her take the lead this time. Not that she gave him much of a choice. While independence and stubbornness were ingrained in the fabric of the matriarchal society he came from, strong-willed women weren't necessarily qualities he found appealing in those he wanted to bed. But there was something intriguing, not to mention intoxicating, about Clara MacQueen that had him thinking she was more than worth the challenge of exploration.

He watched the gentle sway of her hips beneath the odd sleeved cloak she wore. He enjoyed the way she whipped the edges of the fabric together and clutched it between what he knew were full, round breasts. She was a lush woman, with curves that tempted a man's fingertips and electrified a man's desires. Kissing her had been both the greatest pleasure he could remember and the worst mistake he'd ever made. Because all he wanted to do now, aside from protect her from Dracha, was tip her into his bed and make love to her until she cried out his name.

Her red hair flashed against the reflection of the glowing florescent flowers dangling over his head. As if he needed a reminder she was off-limits to him. A woman like Clara, descended of the Goddess herself, a daughter of the girl he'd sworn his life to protect…he would have been unworthy even if he hadn't failed in his duty.

"You're awfully quiet back there, Bowen. You trying to figure out a way to ditch me and go on this quest alone?"

"I am quiet because I don't wish to attract attention. And I promised to take you to Miranda. From there it will be up to you if you continue on my journey," he lied.

"What exactly is this place, anyway? One of the realms?"

"The Forgotten Realm, yes." Bowen nearly tripped over her when she stopped.

"If I remember my bedtime reading, that's like your version of hell." She craned her neck and looked above them. "How can something so beautiful, even in all this darkness, be considered hell?"

"It's each person's individual hell." Bowen seized the opportunity to regain the lead. "Upon arrival, it robs us of that which we prize the most. In my instance, it was my magic that vanished. My connection to whatever world I inhabit. My control over… everything." He flexed his hands around the staff as if he could reignite the flame inside of him. How he missed the simple task of thinking to light a fire, or being able to slip into an enemy soldier's mind to avoid detection or anticipate a battle maneuver. Not so long ago a snap of his fingers would have provided enough light so the darkness receded permanently, at least around him, or provide him a meal with little more than a flicker of thought. The only reason he was still alive was because of the extensive training he'd undergone upon taking his oath. Magic, he'd been told, can be fleeting. Skill and strength would always light the way, even in the darkest of times.

Words he realized too late had been all too prophetic.

"What did you do?" She asked. "Why are you in this place?"

"I disobeyed my orders. We all did." It was the first time he'd spoken of his misdeeds out loud. "We went against our commanders and took Shona where we believed she'd be safe. Once she was, we found ourselves here. Keane was taken immediately, captured by a cherellian water beast and dragged to his death. Rivalin and I were attacked soon after by Dracha's soldiers. The last thing I remember was seeing a blade being driven through his heart by Dracha himself."

Clara rushed to catch up with him and Bowen prepared himself for the sickening sympathy he was certain he'd hear in her voice.

"But you survived." She touched his arm as if wanting to remind him she was there. (As if he needed reminding. Every nerve in his body was well aware of her presence). "How?"

"I have no idea." He shook his head. "All I asked for was an honorable death. A death I should have achieved at Dracha's hand had I been deserving. Instead, I awoke near the *Cosanta Baile* with Miranda tending my wounds." And a shame that had nearly driven him to madness.

"How long ago was that?"

"I have lost count. Time passes differently here." He'd learned early on not to dwell on the unending passage of time. Only death at another's hand would release him from this hell and in that, perhaps he had something to gain from confronting Rivalin. Otherwise, like Miranda and the thousands who called The Forgotten Realm home, he'd live for as long as the Goddess dictated. Until then, he was cursed to exist as he was. "Time is its own force here. There's no way to decipher it. We can only move with it."

"Well, when the time comes, ha ha, you can always come back home with me."

Bowen came to a halt, uncertainty hitting him with the force of a fireball. "That won't be possible."

"Don't tell me you love this place? I mean, okay, it's great for camping and a few magical nights under the stars I suppose, but I could really do without the evil soldiers and all the creepy skittering in the bushes…" She halted, turning to look at him. "What?" She circled a finger in front of his nose and narrowed her eyes in a determined expression he was beginning to recognize and dread. "What does that expression on you face mean?"

"I should have been more precise, Clara. I am sorry, but no matter how I might wish it, I can never leave this place." He took a deep breath. "And neither can you."

Clara heard *Cosanta Baile* before she saw it, but she had trouble focusing. Bowen's words echoed in her mind: she would never leave this place.

She'd never see her sisters again. What would she do without them?

The music was unexpected, tinny flute-like notes intermingled with determined strumming and drumming. Laughter and singing danced along the edges of sound, lightening her darkening mood. In the distance, as her eyes adjusted to the perpetual darkness, she saw a line of torches arcing along the top of a stone wall broken only by a wooden drawbridge like gate.

"Sounds like a Ren Faire." She sniffed the air. "Smells like a Ren Faire." She hugged her arms around herself and locked her jaw to stop her teeth from chattering as she inhaled the distant aroma of roasting meat and baking bread. The closer they'd come to their destination, the colder she'd become. It hadn't escaped Bowen's notice. A few hours before he'd dug into that bottomless bag of his and drew out a hooded cloak to drape over her shoulders. "What's the admission price?"

At his blank look, she rolled her eyes. Explaining everything that came out of her mouth was more tiring than the day—or was it night?—long walk. "A Ren Faire is party of sorts. Celebrating a period of history involving knights and bards and lots of mead and ale." Which she could use in abundance right about now.

"I will admit my people excel at revelries, even when there seems to be little to celebrate." Bowen flipped the hood of the cloak up over her hair and knotted her scarf around her neck. "Keep your head covered. Fire-haired women are most uncommon and are associated with the Goddess. You will only bring unwanted attention by showing it off."

"I don't show anything off." Clara mumbled. Truth be told, part of her just wanted to curl up in a corner and wallow while she tried to come to terms with Bowen's bombshell that she was stuck in this realm. Forever. She'd tried muzzling that pathetic part of herself a few miles back. Feeling sorry for herself wasn't going to do anyone any good. "Anything else I should know? Do I bow when I address anyone? Cower at their feet? Call you master?"

"Avoid the eggs?" He caught the edges of her cloak in his hands and tugged gently. She tried not to look up into those eyes that brought her so much comfort; she knew she'd only smile at his teasing. Which is exactly what happened when she surrendered and met his gaze.

How was it he could make her feel better with a mere glance? How was it, so far from everything she knew and relied on, with him, the fear coursing through her abated and she felt a connection stronger than their short association should allow.

"I want to go home, Bowen." The excitement of adventure and fantasy had worn off around the same time she'd lost feeling in her feet.

"I know you do." He brushed his fingertips against her cheek and she was reminded of how gentle he was with her. "But the sooner you come to terms with your fate, the better."

"You mean surrender?" She raised her chin and shook her head, pushing him away. "No. I can't do that. I have a life, Bowen. I have a job I love and a house and sisters who mean more to me than I've ever said." The idea she'd never be able to tell Nellie and Amber how much she loved them, how much she appreciated and needed them, opened a hole inside of her heart; a hole she'd never be able to fill. "I will not stop trying to get back to them. And step one is reclaiming my book."

Her hands instantly warmed, as if she'd slipped on a pair of toasty gloves. Finally, some relief. She flexed her thawing fingers inside her pockets.

"Now is not the time to argue about this," Bowen told her in that infuriatingly patient tone of his.

"How about you take me to this Miranda person. Maybe she doesn't think I should give up so easily."

"There's nothing easy about accepting one's fate." Bowen strode beside her. "Not to mention innocent lives can be affected in the process. I wasted many hours looking for a way out, a way back, only to be proven wrong with each attempt. There is always a price to be paid."

"Yeah, well, I'm willing to pay it. I'm also going to bet on you being wrong again. That book brought me here, it can get me home. I know it." The warmth from her fingers spread through her entire body and she sighed contentedly. She hadn't realized how off she'd been feeling since she'd, well, dropped into this

place. An odd pressure, a power, blossomed inside of her, balancing out the growing heat, controlling it. Guiding it.

"You know nothing—"

"Careful, Jon Snow," she snapped. "And there's another reason I need to get home. No way am I missing that final season of—"

"Bowen!"

The high-pitched cry from down the road had him moving closer and draping an arm over her shoulders as a cadre of children raced toward them. Clara felt the blood drain from her face as they were surrounded by young ones. "Children?" Clara's throat tightened with tears. "What are children doing in a prison realm?" And why had she assumed most of those here were men?

"Life doesn't stop simply because one is banished to another realm. They are the only light this place provides. If anyone asks, you're from Gladahar Province and we are betrothed."

"You have got to be kidding me," Clara muttered as the children surrounded them. Despite their circumstance of being trapped in a realm of darkness, there was a brightness about the children—from their vibrantly scrubbed faces to the pristine condition of their clothes in a rainbow of colors. Funny how she'd expected a prison colony to be mired in grey dullness and despair. Instead, she smiled at the sound of laughter and excitement ringing in her ears.

"The ruse is merely to provide for your—"

"Don't say it." She really didn't want to slug him in front of his fan base who had finally calmed down and stood before him as if being inspected by a general.

"H-hello." A tall, dark-haired boy with bright purple eyes cast a wary glance at Clara before he bowed his head to Bowen. "Welcome back, Bowen."

"Thank you, Joshiah. I've brought my betrothed." Bowen bowed his head in return. "Her name is Clara. We are hoping to sit evening meal with Miranda and her kin if there is room at her table?"

"Aye." Joshiah nodded, but didn't manage to wipe the suspicion from his face. "We can run ahead and tell her you are coming. Will you be teaching again?" His eyes, filled with hope, went wide as saucers.

"If time permits. It will depend." Bowen laid a steady hand on the boy's shoulder. "If there's any chance, I will."

The children cheered and waved at him and a few even gave him quick hugs before racing back down the path and through the gates.

"Thank you," Clara called after the kids as they ran off. "So what makes you such a rock star with them? What do you teach?" It was all she could do not to tell him to stop pushing her as he led her to Miranda's, but it was clear there were certain customs that needed to be followed in this world and guiding women was clearly one of them.

"Rock star?" He shook his head.

"Popular. They like you. Why?"

"When I first arrived, I gave them fighting lessons. I suppose some of them became accustomed to my presence. Fair warning: the blonde little girl with grey eyes?"

"The one in the yellow dress?" Clara had noticed her right away, mainly because of the excitement and adoration shining in those ghostly eyes.

"She's a natural with a staff. I watched her fell two adult males who attempted to rob her father."

Clara gaped. "But she couldn't be more than ten."

"Never underestimate age or size," Bowen told her. "Especially here. Remember, keep your head covered, at least while we are outside of Miranda's presence. We don't want word getting out that a newcomer has arrived. Dracha's men have ears everywhere and they are looking for you. I don't want them coming here."

"Tell me something." Clara stepped in front of him at the foot of the gate. "If there's no escape from this place, what exactly is your plan where I'm concerned? Lock me in some room somewhere and have the townsfolk shove food under the door? Let me out for a walk a few times a week?"

"I have no desire to imprison you, Clara. Only protect—"

"You really need to find another line. You aren't leaving me behind, Bowen. That's something you'd best accept right now." She poked an oddly warm finger into his chest.

And watched in horror as he flew off his feet and went soaring through the air.

"You need to eat, Mistress." The gentle, juvenile voice broke through Clara's cluttered thoughts, scraping against her nerves. She looked at the young woman Miranda had charged with assisting her. Long silver hair wrapped around her head in an intricate braid; the dress she wore was of sturdy, practical woven fabric in hues of blue that reminded Clara of the Pacific Ocean. "You'll do him no good if you make yourself sick."

"I've done him no good already." But Clara accepted the plate of food and set it aside. "Thank you, Veronia. I appreciate your kindness."

Veronia bowed her head in the same way Joshiah had when they'd been greeted on the road. Exhaustion crept over her, threatened to drag her under yet again. Resisting, she turned her attention once more to the man lying prone on the bed in the dwelling Miranda had arranged for them. The large space was kept warm by the fire in the corner hearth. The rudimentary mattress Bowen slept on bowed beneath his weight. Clara rubbed quivering hands over her face. At least she hoped he was sleeping.

Despite Bowen's instructions to stay under the radar, she'd raced through the gate of the town to demand help, only to find herself surrounded by curious—and surprisingly helpful—town folk. Dozens of them. Hundreds. Town folk.

A bubble of laughter rose in the back of Clara's throat. The term seemed so innocuous, so *normal*. And yet nothing had been normal since she'd stepped foot in that bookstore. Something had grabbed hold of her and thrown her into this world. Her stomach growled to the point of nausea and Clara surrendered enough to nibble on a chunk of the pungent cheese on her plate. All she wanted to do was get home. No. No, that was wrong.

Right now, all she wanted was for Bowen to be okay.

She'd stopped trying to decipher the emotions circling inside of her. Whatever was going on, whatever game was being played by sending her here, she couldn't deny that from the moment she laid eyes on the warrior who hadn't once balked at helping her, she'd felt an instant connection. As if she'd found a missing piece of her life.

She'd felt the shock fire through him when she'd poked him in the chest, as if a lightening bolt had struck them both; a bolt that had transformed the mind-fizzling attraction she'd felt for him into something else. Something stronger.

In that moment, it was as if part of him had imprinted on her soul, a tangible connection formed in that moment, and she didn't feel the same without him by her side. He was…hers.

From her curled up space on the floor beside Bowen's bed, she lifted her hand, desperate to touch him, to feel his steady pulse beneath her fingers.

Clara snatched her hand back and shoved it beneath her cloak. The cloak he'd given her. The cloak she refused to remove.

"Never met a woman afraid to touch Bowen before."

Clara snapped her head around as Miranda closed the wooden door behind her. She set a crate overflowing with items on the table at the foot of Bowen's bed and let out a weary sigh. "Not that he paid much heed to women. Always thinking about battles and honor. I see he hasn't outgrown his affection for sleep. Don't know why I thought this would be any different." She jostled a few bottles as she dug around for a leather flask which she handed to Clara. "Drink. Since you aren't going to eat. You need to keep up your strength if you're to be ready when he awakens."

Ready for what? "I'm fine." She accepted the flask because it was the polite thing to do, but set it on the rustic woven mat next to the plate. Miranda grunted, shook her head, and retrieved a rickety wooden chair from where it was wedged under an equally distressed table.

She moved with more grace than her age would suggest. The wrinkles around her eyes, the shimmering silver hair she wore as a long braid down her back, the ever-knowing and all-seeing amber gaze that often left Clara shifting uncomfortably. Like she did now.

"You knew him as a boy?"

"Aye. Him and Keane and Rivalin. The best of friends they were from the moment of birth. Well, perhaps a bit after that." Miranda sat beside her and, since Clara showed no interest in the food Veronia had brought, picked up a cluster of bright yellow bumpy fruit that reminded Clara of mutant grapes. "Have you slept?"

"A little." Finally, she didn't have to lie. The second, smaller bed sat across the room, closer to the fire and had served her well. For the few hours she managed to drift off. But the second she opened her eyes, all she could think of was Bowen. And whether she'd killed him or not. And what she'd do if she had. "What if he doesn't wake up?" She'd have to make her way through this magical world alone. How did she do that when she didn't know what was happening to her? What she was capable of. If Bowen, someone she trusted, someone she cared about, wasn't safe around her…was anyone?

"You do worry a lot for a goddess."

"Please stop calling me that." Clara closed her eyes. "My name is Clara. I'm a librarian from San Diego."

"Sounds regal." Miranda readjusted her dress and strings of talismans and tokens around her neck. "You may as well get used to hearing it, young one. Accepting your lineage will be just as important as accepting your fate if you and Bowen are going to finish his quest. Besides, who you are is hardly a secret. Your arrival has set things in motion that were spoken of centuries before your birth."

"You remind me of someone." Clara rested her elbow on her knee and braced her chin in her hand. "Little green guy. Pointed ears. Lives in a swamp. Name's Yoda." She stifled a yawn. "Ever heard of him?"

"I have not." Miranda inclined her head. The firelight caught against her hair and cast an odd aura around her. "Is he a mentor of yours?"

"In a manner of speaking. Nellie calls him my Friday night boyfriend. I like to binge watch science-fiction—" Tears clogged her throat. She couldn't let herself think about her sisters. It hurt too much. As she blinked them from her eyes, something caught her attention. "What is that?" She pointed at Miranda's neck as recognition sent chills racing down her spine. "That amulet; I've seen it before. What does it mean?"

"It represents the Goddess, Alastrine." Without looking down, Miranda caught the circular token in her hand. The second she touched it, the vine-thick tree it depicted began to glow a vibrant green. "Only her most trusted advisors and priestesses were gifted with them. You say you've seen it before. Where?"

There was no mistaking the intensity in Miranda's voice. Or her gaze. "The old woman in the bookstore. Elya. Except hers glowed this odd blue."

"Elya." The name may as well have been a curse. "I should have known." Miranda gripped the amulet tighter. "She's interfering again."

"Bowen called her a traitor. So she's what? Evil?"

"Misguided." Miranda cringed and stuffed the amulet beneath the thick collar of her dress. "She was seduced by Dracha. Fell in love with him, even as he plotted against us. She was banished from any realm controlled by the Goddess. She must have thought by sending one of Shona's daughters through she could find a way back herself." Miranda seemed lost in thought for a moment. "But you arrived alone, you said. Elya did not come with you. Which means she failed. At least in this attempt. And you are one of three. I wonder—"

"Can you wonder a bit more quietly, please?"

Bowen's gruff voice broke through Clara's exhaustion and had her leaping to her feet. "Oh, wow. Ow." Clara rubbed her hands down each of her legs to get the circulation back. "Bowen, you're okay." She bent over him as he blinked his eyes open. And looked at her. Joy and relief surged through her and make her knees quake. She wasn't alone any more. Even better, Miranda had been right. She hadn't killed him. She wanted to touch him, to feel him breathing under her hands. But she didn't dare. She fisted her hands and clenched them against her chest. And simply smiled at him. "Hey."

The corner of his lip quirked. "You say the oddest things. What does hay have to do with anything?"

Clara couldn't help it. She laughed. Covering her mouth, she found she couldn't stop, until the sound of hysteria had her being pushed into Miranda's abandoned chair.

"Sit, young one. I will tend—"

"Is she all right?" Bowen sat up and threw his legs over the edge of the bed, then bent over and groaned.

"Fine." Clara bent over and tried to take deep breaths. "Just overwhelmed. I'll be fine in a second."

"You two make quite the pair." Miranda tsked and tried to push Bowen back down. When shoving at him did no good, she gave up and searched through her crate of bottles and containers. "More concerned with one another than with yourself. Took your own sweet time readjusting, Bowen. Wasted plenty of it and put this young one at risk."

"I knew you would keep her safe." Bowen croaked. "It's why I brought her here. So you can protect her."

"Don't make me poke you again." Clara's hands trembled at the thought of being left behind. "I'm

not staying here without you." The fog in Clara's mind cleared. He was clinging to the ridiculous notion that she wasn't capable of being a part of what had brought her here in the first place So ridiculous, to be reliant on a man. So…irritating. To feel paralyzed without his presence, without his guidance, and yet now that he was awake, she didn't want to be away from him.

Despite their situation, despite all that had happened, she couldn't prevent the hope from swelling inside of her. She might not know much of what was going on or what fate had in store for them, but she did know she could face it all. As long as Bowen was at her side.

"You did poke me." Bowen rubbed a hand over his chest. "It was so odd. It hurt, but it didn't. Doesn't. And then…" He flexed his hand.

Tiny gold sparks exploded from his fingertips.

Clara gasped. Bowen stared.

And slowly, a smile spread across his full, kissable lips.

"My magic." Awe coated his voice. "It has returned."

"Clara, come here." Bowen sat on his bed, back braced against the wall and watched as Clara paced the room. She'd discarded the cloak that must have been suffocating her and had accepted a change of clothes provided by Veronia and Miranda. To see her in the cinched-waisted dress in the rich blue of a boddingbird's plumage had him appreciating each and every barefooted step she made. He'd dreamed of her. Caught in a fantasy realm he'd begun to believe was real, she'd been with him the entire time, casting that brilliant smile up at him, her red hair shimmering around the face that would remain with him until his final day.

To awaken and find her beside him had sent a wave of affection surging through him until he realized how much danger she was truly in. He couldn't remember being more afraid of failure in his life. Especially now that Miranda was refusing to shelter her.

"Clara, please." He held out his hand.

She stopped, looked at him, looked at his hand and a flash of longing crossed her face. Before she looked away. "I'm fine here." She nibbled, not on any of the food left for her, but on her thumb.

With the effects of Miranda's equalizing potion surging through him, Bowen pushed himself off the bed. The magical charge he'd been bereft without was firing in his blood more and more with each passing moment. Whatever Clara had done, whatever powers she'd possessed had not been stripped from her upon arrival. And now…she'd reignited his.

And given him new life. New purpose. New… promise.

"What are you doing?" As he expected, Clara rushed toward him, hands poised to push him back on the bed. He reached her in two strides, locked his hands around her waist and pulled her against him. She locked her hands behind her back, fear shining in her bottomless green eyes as she inched that stubborn chin of hers up. "Bowen, please. Don't." Tears flooded her eyes as he slipped his hands around and slowly, torturously, slid his fingers through hers.

She caught her lower lip in her teeth and let out a shuddering breath that had her leaning into him.

"I don't want to hurt you again. Whatever's inside of me, I can't control it." Her fingers remained stiff and unbending as he slowly caressed her skin. "I almost killed you."

"No." He brought her in closer and tightened his grasp around her as her fingers began to yield between his. He brushed his lips against her forehead, her soft gasp of surprise and pleasure shooting through him. "You gave me back my magic." He kissed one cheek, then the other, stopping when his mouth was a feather's distance from her lips. "You gave me back that which I thought I'd never have again." He kissed her, not intending for it to be more than a gentle caress, a promise of more. But the moment he felt her mouth beneath his, he couldn't stop. He had to have more of her. As much of her as she would give. But he had to be sure that she understood she had nothing to fear. "You saved me."

"Bowen." She breathed his name against his lips as her fingers clenched around his. "I thought I'd lost you." She gripped his hands and gasped as a spark passed between them. "How can…we barely know each other." She moved against him, tempting him. He went hard and every bit of masculine pride he possessed exploded at the dazed, passion-glazed look in her eyes. "Is this even possible?" She released

one of his hands, brought her fingers to his face and touched his cheek. "Can love happen so fast?"

"Yes." He turned his head and kissed her fingers. "It can. And it has. You are mine, Clara. I believe you have been since the beginning of time."

She stepped back far enough that she no longer touched him. She reached behind her, unlacing the ties of her dress and Bowen watched, awestruck, as the fabric fell from her body. Then she took his hand.

And led him back to his bed.

Warmth brought Clara awake. Warmth that felt like the morning sun. She blinked her eyes, confusion hovering and sat up in bed, clutching the rough wool blanket against her bare breasts. Around the bare everything of her.

As the bed beside her was empty and cool, the warmth had come from the stoked fire in the fireplace. Clara bit her lower lip and tried not to revel in the hours she'd spent in Bowen's arms. Her body ached in that tingly way she'd only read about; as if she could still feel his hands on her body. Every inch of her body. Every inch of his body on her, over her, under her, *inside of* her. Her cheeks warmed as her smile grew. If this truly was all a dream, she didn't think she ever wanted to wake up.

But she was awake.

And as much as she loved…. She pressed a hand against her heart and took a deep breath. As much as she loved him, she needed to get home to her sisters.

She dressed quickly and headed to the women's facilities nearby to clean up as best she could. What she wouldn't give for a long, hot shower or, even better, a long soak in a lavender infused bath, but prison planets didn't come with running water let alone bubbling spa tubs.

She found helpful—and fascinated—women to help her figure how things worked—and even asked one of the mothers if she could braid her hair like hers was done. The woman had looked surprised at first, then something Clara thought of as pride and gratitude crossed her round, freckled face.

By the time Clara emerged, pressed and dressed, she had to remind herself that this world was meant as a form of punishment. But the people she'd met, the dozens of faces that blurred in front of her with every passing step on her way back to the room she shared with Bowen, despite their circumstance, carried their candles and lanterns with seeming unaffectedness, offering smiles of welcome and nods of approval as they went about their daily tasks.

Instead of returning to the hut, she followed the sound of laughter and cheers and the faint clanging of metal upon metal. Much like a market square in the renaissance fairs she'd been known to frequent, a section had been cordoned off for lessons—this one being led by Bowen who stood in front of dozens of youngsters ranging from just walking to late puberty. Boys and girls followed along as Bowen led them in slow movements with swords and knives, none of which looked blunted or dulled for their protection.

Her concern for these children vanished at the abject pleasure she saw shining on their faces. The same pleasure she saw reflected on Bowen's as he corrected and praised in kind.

"He is a good man."

Clara glanced over to find Miranda standing beside her in the crowd, two cups of steaming liquid in her hand. "He thought it best to let you sleep as long as possible given what lies ahead for you both." She aimed a sly smile in Clara's pink-cheeked direction. "Sleep well, did you?"

"Eventually." Clara had never heard Bowen laugh before and the sound lightened her heart. "That tea smells wonderful."

"Clavaris root and honeyberry. Women of childbearing age drink it most mornings unless they're wanting to be with child." Miranda held out one cup. "It also cleanses the system and prevents infection and diseases."

"Well, the pregnancy issue I had covered." The long-term birth control she used was more for cycle regulation than anything, especially given her self-imposed years' long dry spell in the romance department. "But it's not like Bowen carries a bunch of condoms around." Something she had to come to terms with at a rather crucial moment. "I'll happily accept the tea."

"What are cond-oms?" Miranda frowned.

"Oh, um. Yeah." Clara's face went hot as Miranda led her through the crowd to a private spot along the edge of the market. There she found a table prepared with fruit, bread, and cheese, which set her stomach to rumbling. She'd barely sat before she plucked up a thickly buttered piece of bread and nibbled on the edge. "Where I'm from, men use condoms to cover their—" she waved a hand toward her lap as Miranda joined her. "Like a sheath. A thin sheath."

"That sounds most interesting." Miranda's eyes went wide. "Perhaps you can tell me more about these sheaths once you and Bowen have finished your quest."

"Sure, yeah. Happy to." Now she had yet another reason to get back to her world as soon as possible. She sipped the tea and was surprised at how sweet it tasted, with a hint of mint and something spicy. She licked her lips and continued eating. "How long have you been here, Miranda?"

Miranda poured herself a cup of another tea and sat back as the dozens of torches flickered light across the expanse of space in the market. "As I'm sure you noticed, time has a way of moving differently here. Hours, days…I lost track a long time ago. Long enough for my children to have children."

"You have family here?" Clara recalled Bowen saying something about those who were sent here often brought their families—or their families were sent with them as additional punishment.

"I do. My husband, son, and daughter. And now three grandchildren. You've met one of them. Veronia is my eldest grandchild." A sad, wistful smile stretched Miranda's thin lips. "She's a lovely girl." Clara drank more her tea and welcomed the warmth sliding through her system. "You should be proud of her."

"I am. Every day." Tears shimmered in the old woman's eyes as she clasped the dormant amulet around her neck. "But they don't know who I am. And they never will. The punishment," she added as if that would explain everything.

Clara set her cup down with a clank. "I thought the punishment was being sent to this realm?"

"It is only part of what we must endure. The magic that sends us here strips us of that which means the most to us. For Bowen, it was his magic. For me… it was my family. Their memories of me were erased. And when they see me, they see only a shadow of my true self. They know my name, but that is all."

"But you remember." Clara's heart ached for the woman sitting before her. "You remember everything, don't you?"

Miranda nodded. "A blessing. And a curse. I cannot ever tell them, for if I did, they would instantly die. So to protect them, I stay silent. Elya knew what would hurt me the most and she ripped that from me with glee, I'm certain. As I was the one responsible for exposing her betrayal to our Goddess."

Elya again. The old crone had caused more harm than Clara could have ever have imagined. "I'm so sorry."

"Yes, well, my sister and I never got along."

Clara choked on her bread. "Elya is your sister?" Nowhere did Clara see a resemblance, except for the amulets each old woman wore.

"She is. Which makes the punishment all the more bitter. Even knowing what it would cost, I would not change what I did. Her actions cost hundreds of lives and cast our world into chaos that continues to this day. One day she will pay for what she has done."

"In the meantime, you pay for it."

Miranda sighed. "I cannot blame the Goddess for meting out punishment she saw fit to inflict. To do so would be to question all that I have believed since the day I was born."

"Which is why you continue to serve her?" Clara wasn't certain that was devotion or blind loyalty? This Goddess, this Alastrine, was her grandmother! But the more Clara learned about her, the less inclined she was to like her.

"In the ways I can, yes," Miranda said. "I can only hope that before I am done with this world, I will be forgiven and the curse will be lifted. That my family will remember me once more." She kissed her amulet and slipped it under her dress. "Some days that hope is the only thing that gets me through the darkness. A darkness you and Bowen can help end."

Clara stared into the dregs of her tea, that longing to see her sisters again, to stroll down the sun-strewn streets of Edinburgh—or any city for that matter—pulling like an anchor dropping inside of her. At least she thought that's what it was. She rubbed a hand against her chest as she looked back to Bowen as his laughter once again rang up and over the tops of the torches and echoed through the trees. Seconds before his pupils set their sights on him and tackled him to the ground in a giggling bundle of limbs.

Bowen knew the instant Clara emerged from their dwelling. Last night had made them one. Not only in body, but in soul. He could feel her gaze on him, feel the unsteady pounding of her heart as she watched him. It was all he could do to stay focused on the students who had demanded his attention from the second he'd walked out the door; little faces that reminded him so much of himself he couldn't refuse their requests.

Hours later, having dispatched them back to their parents, he found Clara waiting by the door to the hut, arms crossed over her chest, her hair braided in the way of his people. The rich red of her hair shimmered like fire beneath the torches flickering in the breeze. As grateful as he was to her for getting him help, he wished she'd taken the precaution of covering her head. But what was done was done. He could only hope her carelessness wouldn't come back to haunt them.

"You are well?" He touched a hand to her cheek and watched her eyes soften as she looked up at him. The smile that curved her lips had him wishing they had nothing else to do other than disappear into each other's arms and one another's bed.

"I am fine." She wrapped her hand around his wrist, the crackling of magic charging the air between them. "At some point is that going to stop happening?" But she didn't release him. "It's getting a little unnerving. Never quite sure when it's going to spark." She lifted up to press her lips against his. "Especially considering where I prefer to touch you."

"Then it is I who should be worried." He cupped his hand around the back of her neck and kissed her more deeply. "Good morn, Clara."

She nodded, licked her lips and grinned. "Yep. Good morning. Better than a triple shot espresso for sure." She inclined her head, narrowed her eyes. "What's wrong?"

"Nothing." He ducked inside, wishing for the first time their connection wasn't quite so complete. Years ago, he'd been warned of making the soul connection possible for those possessing his form of magic. He'd never quite believed the intensity of it, and likened the warnings to myth and legend. And yet now he stood in her presence, he knew she could feel when he was…off. Anxious. Determined.

Frightened.

But not for himself. What was meant to happen to him had been set in place long before either of them had been born.

What terrified him now was what would happen to Clara when he was gone?

"Something is bothering you. Please don't lie to me, Bowen." She followed him inside and watched him as he began to pack what few belongings they had. "There are some things from my world I'd prefer to leave there." She wedged herself in front of him, pushed his hands to his sides. "We aren't going to accomplish anything together if we keep secrets. Whatever it is, you can tell me." She cupped his face in her hands.

The words escaped before he could think to lie. Again. "I want us to be bound."

"Bound." Clara's green eyes dulled as she deciphered his meaning. "Bound as in *married*? Betrothed like with rings and—"

"Miranda could perform a handfasting ceremony before we leave. It would be—" How did he put this so she'd understand "It would be another way to protect you as we proceed with our quest. There are dangers out there, situations that can be avoided if we were bound."

"Oh! So being married will save me from being eaten by one of those water creatures that killed Keane?" Oh, the romance of this world. "Yeah, thanks for the offer, but I'm not feeling like getting married today. Wow." She shifted away. "You sleep with a guy one night and bam! He's trying to put a ring on your finger."

"I do not take this idea lightly," Bowen insisted. "But it would make what I need to do far easier if—"

"And now the guilt trip. Just goes to show, doesn't matter what realm you end up in, you men are all alike. Who says I want to get married?" Clara demanded. "No offense, but right now, all I want is to get that book and get home. To my family. To my life. I thought you understood that?"

Bowen shook his head. "And if that's not possible, you will remain in this world, unprotected."

"Why? You going somewhere without me?" She planted her hands on her hips and glared at him as he resumed packing. "Aha! I knew it! You're still looking to ditch me."

"No." He should have known not to give in to the desire of normal men. He hadn't been normal since he'd been chosen as one of Alastrine's wardens. Nothing about his life had been normal. Not before he'd been banished to the Forgotten Realm and certainly not since Clara's arrival. But he had a chance to right his wrongs and given their connection, bonding with her would only strengthen her magic once he was gone. Magic he knew Miranda and possibly others, could help her learn to control. "I promised to protect you and bonding with you is simply another layer of that protection. You are more than welcome to refuse." He wasn't hurt. Exactly. He's clearly misjudged how strong their connection was. Now he'd have to find another way to make certain she was kept safe. "I won't ask again."

"Passive aggressiveness does not suit you, dude. Do you love me, Bowen?"

"I-what?" He shook his head. What was wrong with the woman? "Last night was—"

"Sex," Clara cut him off. "Last night was really great sex and if I remember, only one of us mentioned the "L" word. And it wasn't the one of us who needs a shave." She came dangerously close to poking him in the chest again. "Do you love me?"

"Yes." He didn't know when it had happened. Or why. Or how, but it had. The sight of her filled him with happiness and hope; emotions he'd given up any claim to years before. He longed to see her smile, to hear her laugh, or listen to those ridiculous names she called him. But with love came something else he had no idea how to deal with. "Yes, I love you."

Fear descended on him; fear that hadn't come with him to the Forgotten Realm. Or onto the battlefield. Or when Dracha had attempted to follow them to where they'd hidden Shona. Or even as he'd watched his friends die.

No, Bowen was afraid because now, for the first time since he arrived in this place he had something to lose.

"I need your help, Miranda." Bowen waited until after mid-morning meal before approaching the old woman. Clara had made friends with some of the women and was currently obtaining supplies for their journey north. A journey that, with Clara's rejection of him, just became more complicated.

"Nothing with you is ever simple, Bowen." Miranda stepped back and let him into her dwelling. Similar to the hut he and Clara had been sharing, it was strewn with reminders and tokens of memories she was unable to share with anyone who truly mattered to her.

Since his arrival many cycles ago, Bowen had longed to return Miranda's family to her. Now that his magic had been returned, he had an advantage; an advantage made stronger by Clara's presence. He still had no doubt he wouldn't live to see the results of his quest, but he did have more hope of succeeding than he had only days ago.

"Clara will not agree to bond with me."

"Ah." Miranda gave him a slow nod. "I cannot say I am surprised. She is inordinately independent."

"Bonding with her would have strengthened her magic. Would have given her protection should something happen to me. Since she will not agree, I need another solution. I need more to join my quest. I need help." If she wouldn't bond with him, perhaps there was another…he pushed that thought out of his head before the bubbling jealousy could take hold.

"And you want to know who to trust." Miranda took a long, deep breath.

"I have kept myself alone for too long. I don't know who—"

"*Taobh Amiuigh.*"

Bowen straightened. "The Outsiders. I thought Dracha and his soldiers killed the last of them six cycles ago?"

"He tried. There were survivors. They've grown in numbers since, but now keep to the eastern shores near the sea." She hesitated, clasping her fingers around her amulet. "They are not who they were," Miranda continued. "They have become more brutal, more distrusting. They will not be easy to convince that you can succeed where they have failed. Not even with your magic or Clara's."

"Sounds promising. Do you think they would protect Clara?"

"If it were in their interest to do so, yes. If it would earn them your loyalty, they could be persuaded."

"Declaring my loyalty to another is part of what put me here in the first place." The idea didn't sit well with him. "I will not make that mistake again."

"We all must make concessions for the greater good. If you wish to protect Clara, if you wish to stop Dracha and regain your honor, then you must do what it is you fear the most." Her eyes glistened with determination. "You must be willing to lose it all."

"Backhanded, ulterior motive proposal. That's just great." Clara tugged her cloak tight at her throat as she stomped through the insect strewn, shadowy, root infested never ending forest that seemed to whine against the darkness. Darkness abated significantly along their way now that Bowen could snap his fingers and become an instant flashlight. Not to mention the forest parted in front of him, clearing their way before recovering itself once they'd passed. "Nothing a girl loves more than having a knight in shining armor trying to ride to her rescue with a great big stick up his—"

"Clara." Bowen sighed her name and not in the way that made her thighs quiver. He stopped walking and just stood there. "Stop. Please."

"I don't need rescuing!"

He looked over his shoulder and arched that obnoxiously silent brow of his.

"If memory serves," Clara continued, "I'm the one who rescued you, Bluto, so don't you dare—"

"If you don't wish to be bonded why do you keep on about it?" He looked genuinely confused as he faced her. "I asked. You said no. I will find another way to keep you safe. That's all that needs saying. Can we please—?"

"I don't want to be anyone's obligation." Clara grabbed his arm when he turned to move on. "I don't want to be proposed to because it's the right thing to do or because it's the honorable thing to do. That's just—insulting."

"How is it insulting to want to keep you safe?"

"Because I'm perfectly capable of keeping myself safe. Especially if you're around."

He flinched as if she'd struck him.

And the pieces fell into place. "Oh, wow. Wow, wow, wow." Her stomach flipped and she pressed the heels of her hands into her eyes until she saw stars. "I am such an idiot. Of course. This isn't just about keeping me safe, it's about making sure I'm protected once you're gone." Anger and fear twined themselves into a knot in her chest. "You're not expecting to come out of this alive, are you?"

"Clara—"

"No!" She stepped back and snapped at him, anger overtaking the fear pounding inside of her. "No, you don't get to keep something like this to yourself. We are a team! We have been since that frakin' book left me here. We are in this together! We get the book and we get out together."

"No, Clara." He shook his head as he moved closer. She stood her ground, determined not to show any more weakness. Determined not to let the tears clogging her throat show in her eyes. "It's not possible for me to leave. Not when my people are still suffering. I will do all I can to get you home, if it's possible. But I cannot go with you. I will not leave them behind while I am free. But this isn't only about you. This is about Rivalin and the promise I made to my friend. I cannot allow him to live this life of servitude. Not when it's back in my power to save him. I cannot walk away." His hands locked around her waist and pulled her into his arms. "No matter how much I might want to. I love you, Clara. Don't ask me to choose between you and my sworn duty to Rivalin."

"To what? Kill him?" She croaked.

If I must. His magic has always been more powerful than mine. I don't know what I'll be facing when I face him. Killing him may be the only way to free him." He pressed his forehead against hers. "I would want him to do the same for me."

"Why didn't you tell me?" She whispered and touched her fingers to his face. The face she saw whenever she closed her eyes. The face she'd remember every day for the rest of her life. "Why didn't you tell me all this before I—" Before she what? Before she slept with him? Before she fell in love with him?

But then she never would have known the pleasure—and wonder—of either.

"I'm sorry." He kissed her, softly. "I didn't think it would matter so much."

"What? You dying? Well it does." She tried to laugh, but couldn't manage. "At some point were you going to fill me in on all this or are we just winging this whole kill Dracha and Rivalin thing?"

"I was planning on telling you if my next steps don't pan out. First and foremost I will find a way to protect you from Dracha." He kissed her again, and swallowed the expletives she was about to shoot his way. "On this there will be no argument. I am taking you to The Outsiders and will strike a deal with them to take you in. They are the only group strong enough and they will help you learn to use your magic. And hopefully, one day, help you get home. End of discussion."

Clara smirked. That's what he thought. She had ways of getting under his…skin. It might take a few nights, but somehow she'd convince him there was another way for him to achieve his goals, save his friend's soul, and walk away: alive.

"How long is it to find these Outsiders?" Clara asked as Bowen opened his palm and reignited the guiding flame.

"Miranda said to go east toward the sea. That they would find us."

"Oh, great. So we could be set upon by a ruthless band of outlaws at any time? Marvelous."

A horrendous crash erupted behind them. Followed by an inhuman roar that split the air.

Clara covered her ears as Bowen swung around, opening his other hand for light. In the distance behind them, neon purple flames exploded up from the trees and set them cracking and splitting.

Wild animals she'd only heard in the past, but never seen, skittered toward them. Grey and white blobs with long ears and pointed noses; horse sized deer-like creatures with horns sharper than razor blades crashed through the shrubs and trees, grazing the trunks and leaving gashes and chunks torn out.

"What is that?" Clara demanded of Bowen as he grabbed her hand and started running.

"Wargari fire demon. They're usually hibernating this time of the cycle. Guess someone woke one up."

"You mean like a dragon?" Fire demon? Was he freaking kidding?

Clara's dress kept catching in the thickets and vines as she raced beside him. Around them, the darkness receded as the forest was set alight in purple and blue flames. She tried not to look behind her, but couldn't help it.

Her hand slipped from Bowen's and she faltered to a stop, frozen, transfixed by the sight crashing toward her. Trees were swept aside as a path opened up, closer, closer....

Odd. She moved closer to the fire. The forest was burning and yet...not.

"Clara!" Bowen grabbed hold of her, but she couldn't move. Couldn't blink. She wanted to do as he ordered, but there was something inside of her being drawn back...to the flames.

Back to the beast.

She heard Bowen cursing—at least she thought they were curses—and then he began rustling through the debris on the ground near her as if digging a hole. Shouts exploded from the direction they'd been headed. The forest began filling with thick smoke that whipped into small funnel clouds and spun around them. The trees and leaves and shrubs and branches caught on fire and yet... nothing seemed to be burning. Flames danced over the surface of everything around them yet nothing turned to ash. She felt no heat. Felt nothing other than warm air spinning around her.

"Clara!" Bowen stepped in front of her, blocking her view as he stared down at her, gripped her arms so tight she knew she'd have bruises. "Clara!"

The heat suddenly exploded around her and she coughed. Smoke sailed into her lungs. She looked around, her eyes watering against the flames and she realized she'd waited too long. Fire encroached from every side, every angle. They were trapped.

Bowen ripped off her cloak and pushed her onto the ground, face down. He dropped down on top of her, whispered a few words she didn't recognize, then covered them both with the cloak. Nose pressed into the ground, she could barely breathe. All she could smell was fetid soil. Tiny rocks dug into her skin as the fire disappeared beneath the darkness of the cloak. Bowen's weight pushed her deeper into the soil as the world raged around them.

Wind and funnels of fire and heat spun and tried to catch them, but Bowen gripped the ground on either side of her and held on, as if he could tether himself to the earth.

Ground water began seeping up under her, soaking her from the bottom up as the dirt turned to mud in her mouth. Was that what Bowen had been digging for? She gagged, choking and wondered if the fire was a better way to die than drowning in mud.

Thunder boomed through the forest. No, not thunder. Footsteps. The dragon creature was coming closer, its screams slicing through her, threatening to rip her skull in two. She screamed, wanting to clasp her head in her hands, but she couldn't move, not with Bowen holding her firm.

The world went silent.

No sound from the fire. No roars. No scream. No...pain.

"I've got you," Bowen whispered in her ear as he brushed a hand over the back of her head. "I've got— ugh!" Bowen collapsed on top of her, his head falling heavily into the crook of her shoulder.

Clara gasped, tried to move, to look over her shoulder as the silent world continued to spin.

The cloak was ripped off them. Clara blinked up at a hooded figure who possessed eyes as purple as the fire. He couched down in front of her as the fire raged around them. The man paid it no notice. Not as he gripped her chin in his hand and forced her face up.

She cried out, wanting to get help for Bowen, not able to talk because of the smoke coating her throat.

The man ripped off his hood, exposed the same brilliant yellow hair she recognized from Dracha's soldiers. He gripped the back of Bowen's hair and hauled his head up, took one look at Bowen's face and yelled something.

Clara didn't know what. Sound was returning to her ears, but she felt as if she were under water. Bowen's weight was pulled off her and she could breathe again, but not much better as the heat from the fire continued to glow around them.

The hooded figure's hands came at her and she tried to push up, to scramble away, kicking and moving while searching frantically for where they'd taken Bowen. In the distance, she saw the fire-creature lurch away from them and back into the darkness.

"Enough!" The hooded man shouted loud enough to break through her deafness. She'd be damned if she'd do what he said. Bowen needed her. She *had* to find a way to fight. Maybe this magic she possessed....

She gripped her hands into the ground, felt the dirt squish between her fingers as something built inside of her. Power coursed through her, up through her toes, into her torso, down her arms and she wrenched her hands up in front of her, aiming at their attackers.

When she screamed, the power released in a bolt wide enough to catch all his men off guard and send them soaring through the air.

The same way Bowen had done days ago.

She was on her feet in seconds. About the same time it took the hooded figure to do the same. He came closer, stalking her as she backed away and felt the flames at her back. The man or the fire.

She looked behind her.

Then back at him.

And found him right in front of her.

"I said, enough." He tapped a finger on her forehead.

Clara fell into darkness.

"Is it possible to have a migraine and a hangover at one time?" Clara groaned as she rolled over onto....

She yelped and sat up, scrambling back in panic before she realized she'd been unconscious beside Bowen.

"The next time I tell you to run, you run." He turned his head toward her and held out his hand. "Come here."

She collapsed into his arms, relief and uncertainty coursing through her as she breathed in the scent of him intermingled with sulfur and ash. She shivered. "I swear I'll never barbeque again. Where are we?" She croaked. She could barely talk. Her throat hurt. Her chest ached and she smelled like...she cringed. She didn't want to think what she smelled like.

She lifted her hand, flexed her fingers and marveled at the blue sparks flying out of her fingertips. Bowen gripped her hand, folded her fingers between his and the fear swirling inside of her settled.

"How do you like your magic?" Bowen pressed his lips to her forehead.

"I don't. You can have it. Bowen, where are—"

The heavy wooden door burst open and the man who had tapped her unconscious stood in the doorway. "You've been summoned."

"Of course we have." Clara sighed and sat up as Bowen pushed himself to his feet. "If it's by some little creep named Goffrey—"

"Clara, not now." Bowen guided her in front of him into the stone hallway. Torches lighted their way as they followed their escort down hallways and curving staircases.

She stopped to peer out of an arched window, but she found the same darkness that had been in place since her arrival in this realm. Her dress was ripped beyond repair and her hair had lost any cohesion of the braid.

"Is this the keep?" She whispered to Bowen who took her hand when she reached for his. "Is this Dracha—"

"You will wait in here." Their captor, still wearing the same black uniform he'd worn in the forest, pushed open double wooden doors that opened to a wide, welcoming hall. "You will not leave."

"No problem," Clara said when Bowen looked as if he might pounce. "We have a lot to talk about while we wait." She grabbed Bowen's arm and dragged him inside. They both stopped short when they saw the table filled with plates of food and jugs of drink. "But we can always eat first. I don't even know what half this stuff is and I don't care." She went for the pastries first, if only because they didn't smell like meat.

Bowen walked over to one of the large open windows and it was then Clara realized the odd sound she was hearing was the sea. Waves crashed upon rocks in the distance and brought her an odd sense of calm.

"So I've been thinking." She wiped her mouth and picked up a pastry for Bowen. She joined him at the window and held it in front of his lips. "Given how close we both just came to dying, I think I might have overreacted earlier today. This handfasting thing you mentioned? I think I might be up for it after all." It hadn't taken her more than a few seconds of suffocating in that fire to realize she didn't want to die without having given this marriage thing—at least with Bowen—a shot. Especially if it would put his mind at ease.

Bowen looked down at her, awed confusion shining on his face as he smiled. "There really is no one else in this world like you, Clara MacQueen." He pressed his lips against hers. "Let's see if we're still alive in the morn and we'll discuss it then."

She grinned. "Sounds like a plan. Any idea where we are? Or who summoned us?"

"You're the only place Dracha won't look for you." A loud voice boomed from the other side of the room.

Clara and Bowen spun around as a tall figure appeared out of the shadows. He was tall, as tall as Bowen, but with lighter, shorter hair. Fit. Toned, with an angular face and a jaw as firm and tight as granite. The cane he carried was topped with a shimmering circle of gold displaying an intricate Celtic knot, glowing in the same way Miranda's amulet had.

But it was his eyes that left Clara gasping.

Eyes as pure as the first snow of winter.

"It's not possible," Bowen whispered as he drew Clara harder into his side. "I saw you die."

"Nah! You saw me get those swimming lessons you always threatened me with." The man walked forward, his footfalls echoing in the stone hall. "It took me a while to recover. It's good to see you again, brother. So to speak." The grin that spread across the man's face seemed genuine.

Clara stared between the two men. "Bowen? Who—"

"Keane." Bowen dropped a hand on the other man's shoulders and, after a moment, released Clara so he could embrace his friend. "Goddess above, it is you." He slapped him hard on the back. "What happened? You have to tell me everything."

"Let's sit and eat while we discuss all that," Keane said. "And you must be Clara. Miranda sent word Bowen would be bringing along a very special companion." He didn't act as if he were blind, finding her hand effortlessly and lifting it to his lips. That same grin danced across his lips and teased hers into a smile. "It's a pleasure."

"Some things never change." Bowen tugged his friend away none too gently just as the ground beneath them shook. "What—"

Bowen and Keane stumbled as Clara stared out the window across the room. A streak of light shot across the sky as a boom broke across the darkness.

She gripped the frame, staring out into the distance as her heart pounded in her chest.

Bowen came up behind her, his hands coming to rest on her shoulders as she trembled.

"Any idea what that was?" Keane asked.

Clara nodded and swallowed hard, blinking happy, terrified tears from her eyes. "I think one of my sisters just arrived."

...to be continued in Issue 8

Copyright © 2018 by Anna J. Stewart.

LEZLI ROBYN

TINA SMITH

EDITOR'S CLOSING

by Lezli Robyn

As we close out our first issue as co-editors, Tina Smith and I would love to send our thanks first and foremost to Denise Little, who started this magazine and without whom we would not have this remarkable market to offer writers and readers delicious bite-sized selections of romance.

Tina and I also hope you fell in love with our authors and their stories as much as we did, because we are delighted to tell you that we will be welcoming them back for future issues. Next month we will have the second part in Anna J. Stewart's paranormal serialization coming your way, more smart and sexy contemporaries from L. Penelope and Petronella Glover, a return from our regular columnist Julie Pitzel, and more. We also have not one but two interviews in issue eight! One with the powerhouse Marie Force and another with the amazing Jamie Beck. And we're delighted to announce we will be showcasing fiction from international bestselling authors, Brenda Novak and Juliet Marillier!

We look forward to having you between the sheets and under the covers with us again as we embark on a bright future for short romance fiction. We literally, could not have put this all together without you, our readers, and we look forward to delighting and scintillating you for many more issues to come.